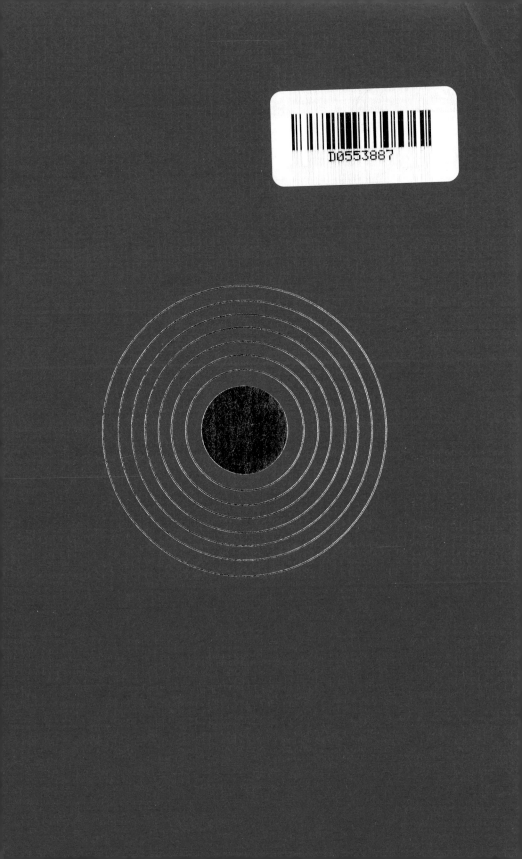

MONKOLOGY

Also by Gary Phillips

Violent Spring (1994)
Perdition, U.S.A. (1996)
Bad Night is Falling (1998)
Only the Wicked (2000)
High Hand (2001)
Shooter's Point (2002)
The Perpetrators (2002)
Bangers (2003)

MONKOLOGY

THE IVAN MONK STORIES

GARY PHILLIPS

DENNIS MCMILLAN PUBLICATIONS

2004

"Dead Man's Shadow," *Spooks, Spies, and Private Eyes*
(Doubleday, 1995); "Boom, Boom," *New Mystery,* Vol. VI,
#1, Summer 1998; "Stone Cold Killah," *Blue Lightning*
(Slow Dancer Press, 1998);"'53 Buick," *Murder on Route 66*
(Berkley Prime Crime, 1999); *The Desecrator,* (A.S.A.P. Press, 1999);
"The Sleeping Detective,"*The Shamus Game* (Signet/NAL, 2000);
"Lowball," *Griots Beneath the Baobab: Tales from Los Angeles*
(International Black Writers and Artists, 2002); "Wild Thang,"
After Hours (Plume, 2002); "The Raiders," *Flesh & Blood III*
(Mysterious Press, 2003); "Bring Me the Head of Osama bin
Laden," *Show Business is Murder* (Berkley, 2004); "Through the Fog,
Softly," "To Live, Only to Die," and "The King Alfred
Plan" appear for the first time in the present volume.

Photo credits: Pages 161 & 162–The Southern
California Library for Social Studies and Research
Pages 163, 166-170, 172, 176, 177–Slobodan Dimitrov
Pages 164, 165, 171, 173, 174, 178–Mary Ann Heimann
Page 175–Service Employees International Union, Local 1877

FIRST EDITION
Published August 2004

Dustjacket, interior artwork, and
book design by Michael Kellner.

ISBN 0-939767-49-X

Dennis McMillan Publications
4460 N. Hacienda del Sol (Guest House)
Tucson, AZ 85718 Telephone: (520)-529-6636
email: dennismcmillan@aol.com
website: http://www.dennismcmillan.com

CONTENTS

To my pops, Dikes, a poor boy from Texas whose stories and deeds thrilled me when I was a kid, and have forever fired my imagination.

Ruminations
at 1 A.M.

That you're thumbing through these collected short stories of Ivan Monk is a personal and professional blast for me. I first created my private eye character more than a decade ago in an unpublished novel entitled *The Body on the Beach.* Thankfully, you'll never see that effort. But I knew then, even as that first manuscript failed to land me an agent or a publishing contract, that Monk, Jill Kodama, Dexter Grant, Marasco Seguin, and the other people who populate Monk's world would reappear.

Sure enough, "To Live, Only to Die" was the next—and first—short story I wrote about Monk. Originally, Gary Lovisi's fanzine, *Hardboiled,* accepted the tale. The modest payment, enough to buy a couple of donuts and a cup of coffee, would be issued post-publication. For a variety of reasons, "To Live" never saw print until this particular volume, *Monkology.*

Then came the civil unrest—or riots, depending on your socio-political lens—of April 1992 in my fair city. Those events became the impetus for the next Monk novel, *Violent Spring.* The plot unfolds in the year-and-a-half after the upheaval as politicians, community leaders, and the self-appointed of the City's ethnic and racial *fellaheen* jockey for power and position. *Violent Spring* was initially published under the West Coast Crime banner and was optioned by HBO. Its fate as a "property" going through development hell is a tale of the blues for another day and venue.

Anyway, somewhere in the midst of the second Monk novel, *Perdition, U.S.A.,* being picked up for mass market by Berkley Prime Crime, my then a-few-doors-down neighbor Paula Woods (who has gone on to have her own series about policewoman Charlotte Justice) kindly asked me to contribute a short story to her *Spooks, Spies, and Private Eyes: Black Mystery, Crime, and Suspense Fiction of the 20th Century* anthology. "Dead Man's Shadow" was the result. It is a mystery with a touch of the odd, a la the "Twilight Zone." The story acknowledges the influence Rod Serling's work had (and has) on me. Further, I discovered I liked to experiment with the short story's structure and content–blending genres or fooling with sequencing and the like. You'll see evidence of that in another story herein called " '53 Buick," first published in *Murder on Route 66,* edited by Carolyn Wheat.

As to where the hell these stories come from, well, when you're a writer, you're a thief. Not in the plagiaristic sense, but in the sense of the hustler who's always on the lookout for the next score. I'm a sucker for pop culture so I freely admit I'm always grafting on some new brain stimulant: images that leak into my brain from music videos, video games my son plays, teenage phrases my daughter says to her friends as they ubiquitously yak on their cell phones, hyper comic book art, and so on.

Most of the stories in this collection came about because, as with Paula's *Spooks, Spies, and Private Eyes,* I was asked to contribute to this or that anthology. These anthologies usually have a unifying theme, and that's what tweaks my imagination: can I construct an Ivan Monk story that fits those parameters? Or better yet, stretches those parameters? The Shamus-nominated "The Sleeping Detective," first published in *The Shamus*

Game, edited by El Rando, Bob Randisi, and "Bring Me the Head of Osama bin Laden," from *Show Business Is Murder,* edited by Stuart Kaminsky, are two where I consciously used a more stylistic approach in tone and/or form.

There are also two new stories here, "Through the Fog, Softly," the first time Monk's dad has been in his own story, and an extended short (or is that novelette?) "The King Alfred Plan," written expressly for this collection. These were done at the behest of the present publisher because it was decided we needed to have a Lucky 13.

I should mention that the "King Alfred Plan" exists in urban lore as supposedly a real plan—or at least it is according to the purported secret document that I read back in the day while doing anti-police abuse organizing—by The Man in the '60s to round up all black folk and send us to concentration camps. That this myth has purchase—it was originally something invented by writer John A. Williams in his novel *The Man Who Cried I Am* and involved the "Final Solution" applied to African Americans—is evidenced nowadays in a time of detainees denied legal assistance of any kind for years at Guantanamo Bay, the Abu Gharib prison mess, and all sorts of nasty anti-Constitutional measures enacted or pending under versions of the Patriot Act . . . well, you can judge this story, and the others in this volume, as you please.

I remain, as always, your guide to the strange and the profane.

Gary Phillips
Los Angeles
June 2004

MONKOLOGY

Through the Fog, Softly

Milky gray and silent, the fog hung over the tops of their foxholes. The stuff lingered about their clothes with a sticky dryness like cloudy cigarette smoke in a crowded back alley dive. Billie Holiday mourned "Don't Explain" and Hester started to wail.

"Oh God," he said, gripping his helmet tightly as if to block the lyrics from his skull.

"Cry to hear folks chatter," Lady Day sang in her ancient voice of suffering.

"Christ." Hester arched his back and jammed his boots further into the mud of his hole.

"And I know you cheat, right or wrong, don't matter. . . ."

"Please," Hester begged. "Please tell me it's all right. God."

"Can't you give him some more? Can't you give him something to stop his goddamn yelping?" O'Keefe repeatedly stabbed his knife to the hilt in the wall of the foxhole. "Just to quiet his nerves."

"His or yours?"

"What the hell difference does it make, Goodman? Can't somebody do something?"

The music stopped.

"Everybody pipe down," Sergeant Monk groused. "Don't let those bastards get you jumpy."

"I'm not." Greenlee peered into the vaporous muck, his

1

mouth slack and eyes wide. "Their tricks won't work on my mind."

"That's 'cause you ain't got no brains, hambone," Goodman joked.

"All right, you two, this is not the time for Lum and Abner." Monk shifted his position, his fingers working circulation into his cramped left leg. "We gotta stay sharp."

"That's our problem, sarge," Younger answered. "We've been on pins and needles. If this keeps up, we're gonna go off like Fourth of July skyrockets."

Monk responded. "We can't. We don't have much of a choice, private."

The fog had rolled in unexpectedly after a brief, heavy rain. Regrouping after a furious engagement with enemy forces, the men of D Company had made good time, despite the wounded Hester. Doses of powdered morphine and fatigue had kept him alert, and Monk hoped to make it back to base before midnight.

That was before the fog bank, which seemed to sprout from the very ground. The squad was surrounded by thick mist and the men moved cautiously, relying on their hearing and any remaining senses that would prove useful in getting them home.

As they felt their way in an easterly direction, the shooting had started, driving the squad to crawl over and, as much as possible, into the soaked ground for cover. Lastly came the music, the jazz tunes filtering to them with an eerie clarity.

"Ansara," Monk called out, "how's Hester holding up?"

"He's not breathing so good. The bleeding has stopped, but he's weak and feverish."

"At least he shut up," O'Keefe quietly rejoiced.

Monk considered one bad option after another. By his watch,

they'd been hunkered down nearly an hour, and except for the music, there hadn't been any more action.

"What do you want to do, sarge?" Younger said.

Josiah Monk rose from his foxhole, his finger on his grease gun's trigger. He wound his way through the curtain of gray. His destination was an arthritic clump of intertwined stumps that looked as if they'd been knotted together and then sheered off by the swipe of a titan's sickle in some prehistoric era.

The sergeant went to a knee near Greenlee and Younger, the radioman. Corporal O'Keefe had his M-1 perched on one of the stumps, aimed into the fog.

"Anything on the Angry?" Monk asked.

"No, still no signal and no response," Younger replied. He was tapping the telegraph key rhythmically on the AN/GRC-9 radio set. The dropping temperature and their time in the field were depleting the battery. Using the Morse code function required less juice than voice transmission.

"It's like we've dropped off the map," Younger commented, giving his finger a rest.

"Reds must be jamming our equipment," the corporal said, licking his bottom lip.

Monk and Younger knew the mountains of Korea were natural radio barriers to begin with, and the lack of relays to boost the signal was another factor in the limited send and receive.

Greenlee couldn't resist. "The commies cause B.O. too?"

"Go on, funny man, keep joking," O'Keefe muttered between gritted teeth. "But see if you can make with the Fred Allen when Joe Gook, who's just out there on the edge of this pea soup, gets his buddies together and they drop on us like ripe grapefruit."

"Take it easy, corporal. We've got a long night ahead of us," Monk said.

3

"I'm good. I'm fine."

"We need each other, right?"

"I said I'm good."

Monk took a moment, then moved off to the next hastily dug shallow foxhole. He put the back of his hand to Hester's forehead. "How you feeling, soldier?"

"Yeah, yeah," he said, bobbing his head slowly.

Monk squared eyes with Ansara. "What about you?"

"How you mean?"

"Up to some scouting?"

"Because I'm the Indian?" He tightened his lips around his Chesterfield.

"I might need company when I go out there."

The private tapped the side of his helmet with a knuckle. "Okay, chief."

Monk grinned. "That's colored jive talk, man." He called out. "Goodman, come on in." Both men frowned when he didn't answer. Monk called out again.

"Maybe he fell asleep."

"And maybe O'Keefe isn't always wrong." He climbed out. "If I holler, you start laying down fire in my direction."

"I could hit you."

"If I yell, I'm already in trouble." Monk belly-crawled forward, creating wide rivulets in the muddy ground. Goodman was posted behind what remained of an overturned cart used by peasants for hauling.

The cart's bulk became more distinct as he neared it. Monk stopped, squinting into the haze. "Goodman," he repeated several times. The lack of response left him no choice. He ran and slid the rest of the way there. Goodman was gone.

"Great." The sergeant duck-walked some paces from the cart, trying to scan the hidden terrain, but he might as well have been staring into molasses. He called the men together around the deformed tree stumps.

"Son of a bitch, I knew it, I knew it," O'Keefe stomped around, jerking his rifle violently.

"We need to be calm, corporal," Monk advised. "We're in a jam and we can't get all unglued." The music started again. It was a Glenn Miller number.

"They told us about this," Greenlee said, pointing into the mist. "They said the Chinese would break us down, play on our minds to make us go ape and start crying like babies."

"Brainwashing, that's what I heard a headshrinker call it," Ansara added. "That's what those chinks are doing to us."

Monk wished he were back at that hole-in-the-wall joint in Watts where he'd met that fine-as-wine librarian with the crooked front tooth the day after he'd received his letter from Selective Service. He wished he was sitting in his mother's kitchen eating her mustard potato salad with the paprika sprinkled over it, her collard greens and the silver dollar-sized hunks of ham shank, on a plate with her smothered steak, topped off with a can or two of Pabst.

But he announced, "I've got to look for Goodman."

Younger said, "He's already on his way to one of their camps where they're gonna work him over good, sarge. I was in a class in basic and one of the white coats showed us this movie about how the Red Chinese do it."

Younger continued, the session vivid in his head. "There was a GI, stripped to his BVDs and shivering, tied to a chair, and the reds kept shouting and hitting him. They slapped him and laughed, and even made fun of baseball." Recalling this, even though it was a production of the War Department's film office, made Younger shiver.

"If the enemy was able to snatch him, then why not go after

the rest of us? Why not open up on us?" Monk reasoned aloud.

"They can't see any more in this shit than we can," Greenlee answered.

Monk compressed his lips. "Fine. But something about this doesn't seem right." Miller swung on his trombone solo. "It don't make no sense to send a couple of soldiers to snag one of ours, then just turn around and go back."

"It does if they want to scare us," Younger said. He looked over at Hester, who was sweating and shaking. The music stopped again.

Noting this, Monk told Ansara, "You stay here and try to keep him warm or comfortable or, you know." Absently he tightened the oiler knob in the base of his machine gun's grip. "This fog can't last forever. If I don't make it back in half an hour, you have to decide what to do, O'Keefe."

The corporal wiped the back of his hand across his lower face. "Of course, sure."

Monk checked his watch and his compass, then pointed. "Best guess is the reds have to be in that bunch of pear trees we spotted before this damned fog fell on us."

Greenlee zeroed Monk. "You just gonna waltz in there and take Goodman back?"

"At least I'm going to get a look-see."

"I'll go with you," Younger offered.

Monk considered this. It seemed the four healthy ones should stay together. It would take two of them to get Hester back if he got weaker, and the other two to watch out for them. He was worried about O'Keefe being so agitated. Would he be doing his men any favor by leaving him in charge? That alone was a reason to leave the levelheaded Ansara behind.

"Okay, Younger, you're with me and everyone else stays together. The password is . . . Sugar Ray Robinson. Got it?"

"You betchum, Red Rider," Ansara cracked.

"You hear anything and it's not me or Younger yelling out, you shoot till you can't shoot any more."

O'Keefe declared, "Don't worry about that."

"Right," Monk winced and he and Younger set off.

They went slowly, picking their way forward. "You know this could be what the gooks wanted us to do."

"Split up, you mean," Monk observed. "I wondered about that, but we have to do something. We can't let them knock us off one by one."

"So you do think the slants have Goodman?"

"How many guns opened up on us?"

"What? I wasn't counting, sarge, I was trying not to get a bullet through my naturally conked head."

Monk laughed appreciatively. "I'm with you on that. Now, don't write home to mama about this, but I recollect there was only a few bursts I heard."

"Meaning we were worried about a couple of squares instead of a patrol hidden out here?"

The sergeant lifted a shoulder. "Like I said, don't write home yet about it. I could be wrong, and it doesn't answer what happened to Goodman."

"Yeah." They trudged on, then Younger said, "Kind'a funny us two colored boys out here looking for an ofay."

"If it was the reverse, you figure two whites wouldn't go looking for a black man?"

"I can't see O'Keefe doing it, can you? Or that goldbricker Wayne Ogden."

Monk decided not to answer that.

Younger was reflective, then commented, "You know what goes on in this man's Army, sarge. I got a cousin in Second

Battalion and the fights in the barracks is putting more of us in the hospital than them damned Chinese 88s."

"I know, man. But what can we do except do the best we can?"

"All that 'be a credit to our race' business? Like we gotta be twice as good to get some respect?"

"It ain't right, but that's the way the dice roll."

"Amen, brother." They both chuckled and kept easing forward.

Younger waved an arm before him. "Is this shit ever gonna let up?"

"Shhh." Monk held up a hand, simultaneously crouching down, his finger on the grease gun's trigger.

Younger mimicked his sergeant's actions. He squinted into the listless muck. "What is that?"

About fifteen yards ahead of them, to their left, a form loomed.

"Could just be a big rock. It's not moving," Monk whispered.

"And there could be some cat with a rifle hunkered down on the other side of whatever it is."

"If he is, he can't see any better than we can."

"I hope you're right," Younger said as the two proceeded toward the form, their weapons primed in shooting positions. They got closer, then stopped.

"How'd the hell did it get here?" Younger exclaimed.

Lying on its side on the ground was a tiger, a full grown male. One of the beast's eyes was missing from its socket and the tongue lolled out of a gaping mouth.

"Be careful," Younger advised as Monk poked the creature with the barrel of his gun.

"I'm pretty sure he's dead," Monk surmised. He bent over the tiger, aiming his machine gun, waiting for that mighty head to suddenly rear up and those hydraulic jaws to gobble him up to the elbows. His shaking fingers touched the head. The fur was soft, the skin beneath warm.

"How come there's no blood?" Younger was also standing near the tiger, his M-1 gingerly poking its rib cage.

Down on a knee, Monk probed the carcass. "Damned if I know. Looks like that eye has been missing for some time. Way before this kitty bought the farm. Which must have been recently, considering the body isn't cold." He straightened up, checking the time. "We better huff."

"Okay." Younger looked back at the dead tiger, the fog once again shrouding the animal's carcass as they neared the edge of the grove of pear trees.

"We stay tight on each other, keep each other in eye sight."

"Roger that." Younger said.

They marched into the stand. The trees were between 25 to 30 feet tall with their leaves fully fanned out in wide ovals. Red-brown pears like bloated teardrops dripped from their branches and littered the ground.

"Could be hiding in these damned trees," Younger said, looking upward.

"No," Monk corrected. "Pear tree branches get brittle as the tree gets older. The weight of the fruit makes 'em snap all the time. No way even a smaller NK or Chinese regular could be up in one of these."

Younger remarked, "For a fella that worked on jalopies before the war, you know a lot."

Monk smiled awkwardly. "Don't have much book-learnin', but I don't know, things like that stick in my head when I hear about 'em. I guess I find facts about this world of ours fascinating."

Slowly they moved through the grove, each tree trunk that materialized before them a potential attacker ready to deal death. It was colder now and the puffs of their condensed breaths became indistinguishable from the goop they moved through. Their boots pulped over-ripe pears lying about, the meat of the fruit caking on the leather.

Monk sniffed the air. "You smell that?"

Younger frowned. "No, what?"

"Neck bone, baby."

"Huh?"

Monk wagged a finger. "Day in and day out of C-rations has given me a real appreciation of Korean cooking. Got me a down home taste for *gamjatang*. It's a kind of stew with potatoes, spices, and neck bone."

"And you smell that?"

Monk was already moving off in a specific direction. "Yeah, and garlic too."

"Sure hope your nose don't get us killed."

Monk snorted and stalked on. Younger breathed close on him. There was a scraping sound and the radioman hit the ground, squeezing off several shots from his rifle.

The sergeant cranked his machine gun. Each man crouched and waited but there wasn't any return fire.

"Where are they? Where are they?" Younger blurted.

"Keep it cool, man." Monk strained to hear and there was another scrape, then snorting and something bounded out of the fog.

Both men let loose and their bullets severed the tendons in a fleeing deer's hind legs. The creature rammed against a tree, striking bark off and slumping to the ground. Its front legs bucked fiercely as it lay mewing in agony.

"Shit," Monk swore. The creature's wide eyes looked at him in unblinking fear.

Wordlessly, Monk unholstered his .45 and he simply and efficiently took the creature out of its misery. After that, the two discovered the source of the cooking food. It was a section of ground almost at the perimeter of the grove. A hibachi was propped on one side by a small pile of rocks, with a large pot on its grill, its contents steaming over the thing's ashen coals.

Three bowls and wooden spoons were scattered around as well. There was an SKS Soviet-manufactured rifle broken in two and a Japanese 8mm Nambu side arm lying on the ground. The reds used a lot of surplus armament. A hand and a portion of a wrist were attached to the gun. The man that hand belonged to, or any other soldier, was not in evidence.

"What the hell?" Younger wondered. "Did the tiger snack on the NKs and die 'cause it ate too much?"

"We have to sweep the area."

His voice quavering, Younger said, "You sure?"

"We need to know about Goodman."

"You're too good for this man's Army, sarge."

Monk went to the right in a widening arc and Younger to the left of the smoldering stew. This took them beyond the pear trees and into an open area that was muddier than where they'd been.

"Keep talking so we don't get lost from one another."

"Brother, you ain't got to tell me twice." Younger, his ears pricked and an anvil in his stomach, lurched forward, his feet sinking down, then sucking free of the muck. As far as he could tell there were only the fog and an empty night. "Anything?" he called out.

"No. But there's got to be bodies. Something happened back there."

"I just don't want that something happening to us." On he went, over and into and out of the mud again and again. "Hey, can I ask you a question?"

Monk's voice came back through the pall. "What?"

11

"How come they call you Joe?"

"How you mean?" he said.

"Well, your name is Josiah, right?"

"Yeah."

"So how come your nick name isn't Jed? That's what they call gents back where I come from with your name, Jed."

He didn't answer right away. Younger could only hear the sound of his boots sucking in and out of the mud.

"Do I look like a Jed?" Monk eventually asked.

"I guess not."

Two more minutes elapsed, then Monk said, "Looks like we threw craps, Younger. And this damned fog doesn't seem to have any end." His voice echoed back to him. "Younger. Kevin, you there?"

"Fuck," he stamped his foot and started to retrace his steps. He yelled out again, and again got no response. First Goodman and now Younger. What the hell would they say about him back at base camp? See? That's what we get for putting negroes in charge, they'd snicker. Coons can't find their own noses in the dark, and this one wound up losing two of his men. You know how they are, those cracker officers would cackle over their bourbon and popcorn in their hut. Once he saw that dead tiger, if there was a dead tiger, he got all mealy-mouthed, blubbering about needing goober dust, they'd go on.

Oh, they'd have a goddamn good time at Monk's expense. "Fuck 'em," he seethed. He wasn't going back empty-handed. He just couldn't. Creeping through the gray, heading toward the food and the torn away hand, he stumbled over a prone form he'd missed before.

Monk went down, the machine gun sliding away. Crawling on all fours, reaching for the weapon, he came right up on the body of a North Korean soldier. He was on his back, his eyes vacant and not a mark on him—save for his missing right hand. Yet no blood had seeped from that wound.

The sergeant ripped open the man's shirt and felt the torso. There were no discernible bullet holes or stab wounds. Examining the stump, he could see it had been a clean cut, and the dangling veins and capillaries had been sealed by some method. There was very little blood on the sleeve.

Standing over the body he gave it one last look, then resumed his trek. Ahead he could make out the trees again and two human silhouettes just outside of the first row. He steadied his weapon. "What's the password?"

"Sugar Ray Robinson," came the terse reply.

"Younger, where you been?"

"Get over here, sarge."

Monk approached. The radioman stood in front of a naked Goodman. His hands were rigid at his sides and he stared into the silvery maw of the fog. He seemed oblivious to the cold.

"What did those bastards do to you, Goodman?" Monk stared hard at him. There were several elliptical incisions in Goodman's neck, jaw, and cheeks.

"Don't," the missing man started. "Don't," and he put his hands to his face and started to cry. "Oh God, they had that poor Oriental flayed open like a steer." He fell to his side and pulled himself into a tight ball, shuddering.

"They must have tortured him," Younger pronounced.

"I got the feeling," Monk began, bending down with the other man to get Goodman off the ground, "that he ain't talking about the Chinese."

Younger turned his head in the direction the frightened soldier had looked and something frozen wrapped itself around his spine as he imagined what lay in the pall. "Let's get the fuck out of here, Joe."

"Damn straight."

The two half-walked, half-carried the weakened Goodman back to the rest of the squad.

"You made it." Ansara displayed a tight smile upon seeing Monk. Without asking about his nakedness, he helped them with the now shivering Goodman.

Greenlee ran up. "What the hell happened to him, you guys?"

"Can't say. Younger found him wandering out of the fog." Monk looked over at O'Keefe. He was squatting next to the tree stumps, his rifle held upright between his knees as he rocked back and forth.

"How long has he been like that?"

"Since Hester died, sarge," Ansara said.

Monk could now see Hester was laid out on his back, his arms folded over his chest. "Got his tags? Any other personal items he had on him?"

"Yeah," Greenlee nodded. "There was a letter from his mom."

Monk began undoing Hester's belt. "I'll make sure she gets one from me."

"What are you doing?" O'Keefe stopped rocking.

"He's gone on, corporal, and I've got a man who needs 'em."

"Stop that."

"Stow it, mister." Monk continued to undress the corpse.

O'Keefe was on his feet. "That's not Christian."

"Goodman needs clothes. I know it ain't right, but it's necessary. Now don't interfere. That's an order."

O'Keefe's knife came out in a dull flash, the tip creasing the sergeant's breast bone. "You black devil. Niggers don't have any souls. But let me tell you, snowball, if you don't get your unclean hands off that white man, I'm going to cut them off."

Ansara steadied his rifle. "Put it down or I drill you."

"Shut up, Cochise, you're next." He jabbed the blade, and Monk, who was moving backward, was sliced across his left breast. But he'd reached out and grabbed the corporal's wrist, pulling him forward. As the body of Hester was between the two, O'Keefe stumbled over it as Monk had over the dead NK soldier earlier.

"I'll split you open." O'Keefe slashed with his blade even as he fell forward. Monk hopped to the side, his six-two, two thirty frame agilely up on the balls of his feet. A straight right caught his opponent flush and spun him to the ground. Monk got his .45 free.

"Put the knife down, O'Keefe."

"Nigger I'll—"

Ansara cocked his M-1. "You heard him."

The corporal reacted to Ansara, and Monk stepped in close and backhanded him with the muzzle of the automatic. O'Keefe reeled and the sergeant clubbed him with the gun butt, stunning him.

"Put it down or I drill you here."

Hate in his eyes, with blood welling underneath the skin of his face, O'Keefe dropped the blade. "They'll give me a medal."

"Tie him up," Monk said, kicking the knife away. "And keep him under guard." He glanced at Greenlee. "I mean you, while Ansara keeps his rifle on him."

Greenlee started to say something but didn't. He did as ordered.

Monk got Hester's clothes on Goodman. He was taller, but skinnier than the dead man. "You'll have to hold the pants up. Understand?"

Goodman shook his head slightly.

"Let's move out, men. This goddamn fog is finally lifting."

15

The squad started to make their way back to the base at Chinju. Ansara kept pace with O'Keefe, his rifle at the ready as they walked. The corporal's hands were tied behind his back. Greenlee stayed close to Goodman, who had put his hands together and was mumbling a prayer.

About seventy yards on, a thin whine pierced the air. Younger and O'Keefe happened to be the first ones to look around.

"Did you see that, sarge?" Younger asked, his mouth agape.

"Some kind of reflection of lights. I couldn't tell."

As the whine receded, there were also the echoing notes of a fading trumpet.

"It was a sign from God, you black heathen."

"One more squawk out of you, O'Keefe, so help me," Monk promised. Inwardly he was glad he'd be able to replace this cracker with the tough Corporal Nehemiah Flowers, who went by the nickname he'd earned in the ring, 'Tiger.' Was it some kind of a sign that they'd seen the big dead cat back there? He shook himself, and didn't want to know what it meant. "What did you see?" he asked.

Younger swallowed hard and looked at Goodman. "They had you *on* that thing, didn't they?"

Goodman only looked at the ground.

Younger adjusted his helmet. "I didn't see nothin'; not a damned thing. No sir, I didn't see no Buck Rogers flying saucer," he muttered and hurriedly marched on.

Sergeant Josiah Monk and the rest of his squad followed.

Dead Man's Shadow

The corpse hung head first below the parapet of the factory by a rope. Buried in the middle of its forehead was a short-handled ax. Dried blood, the color of old copper, trailed from the fatal wound into the salt and pepper hair of the deceased man.

"That's how he was found. That's how they found my father."

Ivan Monk looked up from the photo at the woman sitting across from him. She was younger than he was, in her early thirties. His potential client wore form-fitting jeans, snakeskin boots, and a loose black T-shirt. Her hair was done in a combination of dreads and plaits prevalent among black women her age. A sort of homage to the motherland by way of Alice Walker and Angela Davis.

"What have the police produced?" he asked evenly, unsure of the emotional territory he might be treading.

"In the three weeks since the murder, not a goddamn thing." She glowered at him unblinkingly.

"This is a particularly gruesome and brazen method of murder. Killing a man at his place of employment, then putting him on display." He paused, unsure of how to proceed.

"What are you suggesting, Mr. Monk?"

"Who might have had it in for him this bad?"

Belinda Bolden snorted and shifted her body in the Eastlake

chair in Monk's office. "Now you sound like Tierney, that lazy slab of beef who's supposed to be finding my dad's killer."

"The cop in charge."

"From the Foothill Division." Bolden leaned forward. "My dad worked at Velson Aircraft Manufacturing for thirty years. He started out there when the Machinists Union was barely letting blacks into the skilled trades. And that was because people like him organized protests with the help of the NAACP.

"Dad didn't take a whole lot of shit from anyone, but he was a fair and honest man. So yeah, you figure it out. A black man who stood up for his rights was bound to upset some white boys. You must know what that's like, brother."

Monk smiled and his eyes drifted back to the photo. "Had your father been getting death threats?"

"No. But there are all those bikers hanging out over in Chatsworth, and white trash heavy-metalheads cruising Ventura Boulevard just spoiling for an excuse to mess with black folks. Don't you think those are logical places to start? There has been an increase in hate crimes in the Valley."

"But the police don't think that's an angle?"

A side of her mouth lifted in contempt. "They don't, but at least they don't trip like the clowns down at the Spur bar."

"What?"

Irritation pinched her face. "There's a story been going around out there since I was a kid. And now with dad's murder, it's gotten to be the hot topic again."

Belinda Bolden didn't seemed inclined to talk further on the subject, but Monk hated incompleteness. "So what's the story?"

"All right, just to get this over with. Back in the '40s, around the close of the war, some strange killings happened out there in Pacoima."

"Like this?" Monk pointed at the picture.

"Wait, I'm getting there. Velson was booming in those days. And because there was a shortage of white men to fill the shifts, women and minorities got the work despite the feelings of the companies and the unions.

"Pacoima was more benign in its racism. Unlike other parts of Los Angeles, they didn't have restrictive housing covenants. My dad's people settled there when he was a kid. It was my grandmother who'd worked at Velson during the war."

"And these killings?"

"It all started in December of '44. The black and brown workers at Velson, including some hipster whites, had a club they hung out at called the Kongo Room.

"On this particular Saturday night, four drunk white Marines marched into the club and demanded a halt to this fraternization between the races. Naturally a fight erupted. Henry Swankford, a big raw-boned-so-black-he-was-blue-black man off the Delta laid out two of the jarheads with his bare hands. The third one he killed with a blow to the temple."

"I can imagine what happened next," Monk said sympathetically.

"Despite eyewitness testimony that the third Marine had pulled a knife on Swankford, he was convicted by an all-white jury of second-degree murder."

"Swankford goes to prison," Monk finished.

"Folsom, May of '45. A couple of days after Hitler committed suicide," she noted sarcastically. "The fourth marine said on the stand he'd seen no knife in his buddy's hand. He was lying of course. My grandmother was there that night and had testified to the truth."

"And the killings?"

"Swankford escaped in '46. Less than a week later, the

Marine who'd lied was found murdered in his apartment out in Indio."

"An ax buried in his forehead," Monk visualized.

Bolden said, "In the fall of '48, one of the other surviving Marines was discovered the same way in a cab he drove over on Chandler in Burbank." The woman stared at Monk, then went on. "At each site they also found a red parrot feather."

Intrigued, Monk asked, "Which symbolizes. . . ?"

"A sacrifice to Eshu, also known as Elegba," Bolden explained. "An orisha, a deity of the Santeria religion. Some folks consider him to be the devil, but most certainly he is the god of tricks."

Santeria was a practice whose roots wound back to the Yoruba people of Africa and transmogrified with Catholicism in Cuba during the slave trade. In the modern world, it had followers from the South Bronx to South Central. What little Monk knew about it he'd learned from a documentary on PBS.

Bolden continued. "The rumor among those who used to frequent the Kongo Room was that Henry Swankford had made a deal with Elegba to exact revenge on the four leathernecks."

"Were Swankford's prints found on the handles of the axes?"

"I don't know. My grandmother would know the details." She stopped short, scrutinizing him. "I'm going to pay you to find out who killed my father, Mr. Monk. Not run around digging up ghost stories."

"Okay, but what happened to the last Marine?"

"I don't know, and I don't care. I only told you this so you'd know what you'd be hearing out there and not get sidetracked. There was no parrot feather found near my dad."

"It's not impossible to believe that some copycat killer

chanced upon the old articles about the murders and decided to try it out. But I don't believe in goblins either, Ms. Bolden."

She rose, offering her hand as she'd done when she'd entered his office. But this time, as Monk stood to shake it, she put some effort behind the grip. "I think I'm glad I asked around and got to you."

• • •

The restored '64 Ford Galaxie 500 purred along the 210 Freeway like a well-oiled sewing machine. Its midnight blue shell gleamed like alien skin under the unforgiving afternoon sun.

He approached Pacoima in the east end of the San Fernando Valley. As he did, Monk passed through Lakeview Terrace, a section of L.A. County made infamous by the videotaped beating of black motorist Rodney King by members of the LAPD's Foothill Division. Consciously, he checked his speed and headed into the town whose name meant "rushing waters" in an American Indian tongue.

Using the directions provided by his client, he arrived at Velson Aircraft Manufacturing at the end of a row of red brick businesses on a deadend street called Aerodrone. It was a long three-story affair. Over the large entrance, in arched Parisian lettering, the hand-painted sign spelled out the company name. P-51 Mustangs, wind lines streaking behind them, circled around the first and last letters.

Monk parked and entered the facility. Men and women were busy at drill presses, short block stands, and the many other accouterments of airplane engine assembly. He took a flight of metal stairs to the offices on the second floor, and gave his name to a flat-chested receptionist. After a few moments, Karl Velson, one of the owners, ushered Monk into his office.

"Have a seat," Velson said, angling back behind his desk.

21

"When Oliver's daughter called to tell me you were coming out, I made you a copy of his company file." Velson's hair was a thick, trimmed mane topping a pleasant face. The image suggested he took his children to the park and honored his wedding anniversaries. The eyes behind the thin lenses of his glasses were observant.

"I appreciate that, Mr. Velson." Monk looked at him across a desk littered with papers, parts, and a steel model of a Cessna.

From somewhere in the swamp before him, Velson produced the file and shoved it at Monk. "All I can tell you is that everyone here at the shop was shocked at Oliver's brutal death." Idly, he moved some of the papers around.

Monk said, "Mr. Bolden's body, according to what the daughter was told, was spotted hanging from the roof around 6:00 A.M. I take it there's no guard at night."

"Nor in the day. We're not Hughes or Lockheed, Mr. Monk. We ain't cranking out stuff for the Stealth Bomber. Velson hasn't manufactured those kinds of parts since pop ran the operation. Now we do finished blocks for Cessnas, Pipers, and other commuter aircraft."

"And Bolden was here the night of his death on company business?"

"Yes, he had keys to the place. I'm sure Belinda's told you he was the shop foreman and union rep. There were some new specs on an engine contract, which would, ah will, necessitate some shift changes. Oliver needed to go over them to plot out how we'd swing it with our existing personnel."

Monk remarked, "Isn't that something that you and he would have gone over together?"

A perturbed expression flitted across the pleasant man's face. "My brother was supposed to have done that. In fact, it was the second meeting he'd blown."

"So what happened to him both times?"

The door to the office suddenly swung open, and in stepped a man with unkempt hair, older and heavier than the other Velson. That they were brothers was easy to detect given the resemblance of features. But this one's face had a harder, cynical set to it. The eyes were wary and his color florid. Monk sized him up as a man who took his lunch over the rocks.

The older brother appraised Monk too but said nothing. He started toward a door to the right.

Chidingly, Karl Velson addressed his sibling. "Why don't you tell Mr. Monk here where you were the night Oliver was murdered, Otto."

Otto Velson halted in mid-stride, turned on his heels, and stomped over to Monk. He glared down at him with a snarl parting his lips. "I already told that partner of yours, Tierney, why I didn't show that night."

Karl Velson answered for Monk. "This man isn't a police officer. Mr. Monk's a private eye Belinda Bolden hired to find out who killed her father."

There was a deeper reddening working up from Otto Velson's neck. Grimacing, he swiveled his large head at his brother. "What my dear brother is riding me about is I was down at the Spur unwinding when I should have been here with Oliver. But that doesn't mean that I could have prevented his death."

The head moved in Monk's direction. "It could have been me, too, you know?"

"Tell him how else you unwind." A cruel note manipulated the younger Velson's voice.

"Fuck off." Otto Velson disappeared into his office and slammed the door.

The other brother looked at the door, then Monk. "There's a hagged-out bleached number who works the Spur. My brother is one of her steady, if not exactly favorite, customers. He was doing the horizontal bop with her that night."

"What's her name?" Monk inquired.

Karl Velson's mouth made an ugly line. "She goes by the original title of Lola." Something in Monk's manner made him rear back as if struck by lightning. "Wait a minute, I know what you're trying to do. My brother may be a drunk, but he's no murderer. He had no reason to kill Oliver."

Neutrally, Monk said, "Just being thorough." With that he took hold of the file and rose. "Thanks for your time."

"Sure," Velson responded, a note of hesitation in his voice. "If there's anything else, you let me know."

Monk was almost to the door, stopped, debated with himself, then turned around. "What do you know about this Henry Swankford business?"

What could have been a laugh escaped from the younger Velson. "I think I believe that Oliver was killed by some zonked out crack-head looking for cash. Hell, man, the Valley is filled every night with runaways, Manson groupies, and God knows what else. This area is a lot different than when I was a kid. The ax in Oliver's head was from our fire box."

"Was the petty cash taken?"

"Yes, about $700."

"Yet," Monk pointed out, "according to what Belinda was told, there were no prints on the ax handle. It's been my experience that drug addicts aren't what you'd call advanced planners."

Velson did a thing with part of his face that committed him to nothing.

Monk said goodbye again and drove over to Gloria Bolden's house. She was the mother of the deceased man and the grandmother of his client. He parked under a billowing pepper tree and got out into the oppressively still, hot air.

The house was a ubiquitous modest 1950s era tract number with an attached garage. Its saving individual feature was an overhanging porch bordered by low hedges. The neat lawn was a mixture of fading green splotched with yellow stains like giant liver spots. A Royal palm commandeered the right side of the grass, which was divided by a flagstone walkway.

At the front door, no one answered his repeated knocking. He left a brief note on the back of one of his business cards, and went away.

In nearby Arleta Monk found a public library. And despite the most recent round of county budget cuts, it was open. But the newspaper clippings they had on microfiche only went back to 1953. The librarian, a brunette in her fifties with the shoulders of a swimmer, directed him to the San Fernando Valley Historical Society for older information.

The Society was contained in a mock Tudor two-story on a quiet residential street in Van Nuys. There he went through bound clippings concerning the trial of Henry Swankford, his escape, and the subsequent murders of the two Marines. All the pieces were written by the same man, a Frank Ameson. Another article, also by Ameson, was an interview at an undisclosed location with the last Marine, who was scared witless.

"Excuse me," Monk said to the elderly gent who had helped him. "You wouldn't happen to know whatever became of Frank Ameson?"

The old man had an affliction of palsy that caused his left hand to shake slightly as he talked. "I should know, young man. Frank and me worked on the *Valley Herald* damn near thirty-five years. Frank's been dead at least another twelve. Smoked like they wouldn't make 'em no more." He shook his head in remorse.

"Do you know if he kept notes about the Swankford case?"

The older man cocked a grey brow. "You ain't one of those tabloid journalists, are you?" He spat out the question.

Monk showed him his license. This produced a chuckle from the other man.

"Yeah, you got that look. Frank's notes went the way of the dime phone call when the paper folded. Who knows? I don't have most of mine either." He seemed to be winding down but then got his second wind. " 'Course now, I keep my ear to the ground, Ivan Monk. Got some working reporter friends on the *Daily News* and *L.A. Times* who tell me what's going on in these parts."

The old boy was getting geared up for a long one. He injected, "Thanks for your time, Mr. . . . ."

"Garrity, Homer Garrity."

Monk shook his hand warmly and started off.

"Let me know if you solve the Henry Swankford murders," Garrity cracked.

Monk drove about aimlessly, absorbed in arranging the pieces in his mind. Eventually he came across a Carrow's and got a bite to eat. Afterward, he traveled back into Pacoima. He found the Spur as the evening began to chase away the light.

The interior was a comfortable enclave of people socializing, teasing, drinking, and playing pool. Working stiffs savoring the unreality alcohol and the smell of the opposite sex afforded. But closing time always rolled around and brought you back to the grinding reality of your small life.

It was a bar like a thousand others he'd been in over the thousand years he'd been running after lost hopes. Getting kicked in the ribs for his efforts while trying to decipher human misery, and looking down the long drop to oblivion. Waiting for his turn to make the leap.

He found a perch on a stool. The bartender, a stout Chicano

with greying temples and slitted eyes, sauntered over to him. "What it be, Sportin' Life?" He wiped the bar clean with a soggy cloth.

"Miller."

The bartender left and returned with the beer. "Buck and a quarter, bro'."

Monk laid a ten on the counter. "I'll run a tab. Is Lola here tonight?"

Blank-faced, the bartender replied. "She'll be back in about fifteen." He picked up the note and moved off.

Eighteen minutes later, a dyed-blonde in a slit skirt and low heels entered. Her hair bounced past her shoulders and was done in a perm that needed refreshing. Even in the dim light, Monk guessed her age to be late forties, but she was slim, athletic of build.

Lola carried a purse big enough to haul around a couple of phone books. She made her way to the bar where she leaned across at a gesture from the barman. They talked, and he pointed at Monk. She came over. Lola liked garish eyeshadow but no lipstick.

"Hey, baby." Her breath smelled of mints and gin and something else. She hefted the purse onto the bar with a dull thud and sat next to Monk. "You're new around here, big boy." Lola sized him up and down. "With a build like yours, I bet you work construction."

Monk put a twenty on the bar between them and signaled for the bartender. "Another beer for me, and. . . ."

"The usual, Enrique." She eyed Monk as Enrique filled their orders. "If you add another thirty to that Jackson, you can put your balls on my chin."

Enrique delivered the drinks and drifted off once more.

Monk smiled. "Some other time when I'm not on the clock myself."

27

Lola cocked her head when he displayed his license. She held up an index finger, and with the other hand dug out a pair of half-glasses from her voluminous purse. She put them on and said, "Show me that again, honey."

She slowly read the green-colored, Bureau-of-Consumer Affairs-issued license to snoop, silently mouthing the words as she went along. When she finished, she picked up the twenty and buried it in the bag. Lola crossed her legs and sipped her drink.

"What time were you with Otto Velson on the 23rd of last month?" Monk had some of his beer, anticipating her response.

"Jesus, this is about the murder."

Monk said nothing.

Nervously, she plucked at a corner of her full bottom lip. "Well, I was with Otto from about seven to ten."

"He get some kind of special rate?" Monk wondered if the time of death had been pinned down for Bolden.

She batted her eyes. "My regulars always do, Ivan. They don't go away unsatisfied." Her smile revealed a rotted bicuspid. "'Course in Otto's case, you gotta allow for the fact he passes out a lot. Hell, I even let him stay the night sometimes."

"When he left you did he go home?" Monk gulped more brew.

"Hey, man, what are you getting at?" She laughed loudly, nervously. "Otto kill somebody? Shit." Lola sampled more of her gin.

"Otto into kinky stuff?"

"Otto ain't much on variation or technique, if you know what I'm saying. 'Sides, why you want to know, sweetie?" She winked broadly.

He let that go. "Tierney talk to you already?"

"Sure," she mumbled over another mouthful of booze. She put the empty glass on the bar. "Thanks for the drink and the twenty, handsome. If you get back to these parts, look me up." She inclined her body and whispered to him. "I'll put some ice on your dick, we'll snort some crank, and I'll wear your big ass out."

She got off the stool and glided further into the bar's cloud of promise, the lure of easy, hot sex coming off her in palpable waves.

Presently, Lola left with a rotund, sweating man lapping at her heels. Monk followed them out and watched the duo walk off the lot, swallowed by the lonely streets. He went back inside to sit, think, and drink.

Time passed. Otto Velson wandered in and sat at a booth. He hadn't noticed Monk. Velson ordered a sandwich and two drinks while he looked around for Lola.

Presently, Velson got up and headed out the front door. Monk came up behind him in the parking lot. "I'd like to have a word with you, Mr. Velson."

He swung unfocused eyes onto Monk. Recognition sharpened them. "You're that private guy."

Before he could continue, Lola appeared again.

"Where you been?" Velson demanded. Jealousy crowded his slurred words.

"Guess," she said contemptuously. She sparked at noticing Monk. "Come on, linebacker. I bet ya Otto'd pay to watch you and me go at it."

Velson's face got even more purple under the blue spot-lights lining the eaves of the Spur's roof. He lurched at Lola who side-stepped him effortlessly. The drunk man stumbled onto the ground.

Monk made to help him and a siren went off. A squad car

coasted close, its lights pulsing. Two uniforms emerged, guns drawn. A cool anxiety chilled Monk's heart.

"This man bothering you, miss?" One of the cops asked Lola, advancing on Monk, 9mm first.

"Men been bothering me all my life." She laughed at her own joke.

Monk's hands went up.

Velson righted himself, fuming. "Arrest this cocksucker."

The other cop politely said, "He attack you, sir?"

"Yeah," Velson lied.

"He's full of shit," Lola offered.

The first cop stepped close and could now smell the liquor seeping from Velson. He glared at Monk, then Lola. "Maybe we'd all better sit down and sort this out."

The other cop took a glance at his partner.

"Okay, slick, looks like you know the routine," the first cop said to Monk. He motioned for him to lean against the wall.

He complied and was patted down.

"Clean. Let me see some ID."

Monk produced his wallet and handed it over to the one who'd searched him. The cop got a sour look upon reading it. He walked back to his partner, and the two conferred quietly. Lola stood apart from Velson, who was sweating like he was in a contest. The first cop returned and stood close to Monk.

"You better come down to the station with us, Monk." He said it real quiet, real intense.

"What for?

"We'd like you to come down to the station with us," the cop emphasized.

"Am I under arrest?" Monk straightened up from the wall.

"We'd appreciate your cooperation."

A beat, then, "All right," Monk conceded.

Lola smiled crookedly at Velson. "My gravy train."

Monk got in the cruiser unhandcuffed. As the car pulled away, Lola blew him a kiss.

• • •

Detective Sergeant Hugh Francis Tierney was a tall, boxy built white man rummaging in his early fifties. His face was jowled and topped by a bad haircut. He possessed a loud checked sport coat that was draped over a chair. The cop walked with a slight limp and talked as if his vocal chords were tied in a knot.

"Tell me once more," he demanded.

Monk fixed his gaze on the acoustic tile lining the interrogation room and sighed. For the ninth time he told the cop how he came to be at the Spur.

When he was finished, the large cop asked, "Why do you think Otto Velson killed Oliver Bolden?"

"I didn't say that. I said I think it's interesting his alibi is so weak."

Tierney sat across from Monk, placing his elbows on the table. His fingers were like bloated sausages splayed across the scarred surface. "What I think is you're a second-string peeper and sometimes bounty hunter who's milking a grieving daughter for whatever you can get."

"That's what makes America great, sarge. There's room for all kinds of opinions."

Gritting his teeth, Tierney squeezed out an, "Uh-huh."

Just to annoy him further, Monk asked, "Do you think the rumors are true? An old ghost is stalking the Valley?"

Tierney grinned wickedly. "Sure, Monk. I believe Henry Swankford is the cause of all this like I believe private eyes serve a useful function."

They stared at one another for a few minutes. Then, "Get out of here, knob shaker. Go home if you got one."

31

Monk walked out. A man in overalls with a police ID badge clipped to his breast pocket entered the room he'd just left.

Monk heard what the man said as he continued walking. "I hate to tell you this, sarge, but your car's still not ready."

The bulky cop finally let his anger out in a string of invectives at the mechanic, the city budget, and General Motors' cars in particular.

By the time Monk trudged back to his car and got to his apartment in Mar Vista, it was past four in the morning. He stripped down to his boxers and sank into bed. In a dream, Lola chased him with an ax, a red feather clutched between her teeth.

After ten he was up, showered, shaved, and got breakfast from Khan's Golden Chariot Coffee Shop on the next block. A little past one he finally got out to North Hollywood and Oliver Bolden's house.

The place was a freshly painted stucco Valley wonder done in somber beiges. Monk let himself in with the key Belinda Bolden had given him. Inside it was quiet as a sanctuary. The lights still worked; the Boldens hadn't closed the place out yet.

Sometime later, after pouring over the paltry yet personal material accumulated in a person's life, Monk found nothing to help him decipher Oliver Bolden's death. Just the detritus of photos, papers—including the funeral program for his wife's service, and the handwritten scraps that marked one's passage on the stone called Earth. He picked up the phone and called Gloria Bolden.

"Hello," an older female voice answered on the first ring.

"Mrs. Bolden?"

"Yes, who's this?"

"My name is Ivan Monk, your granddaughter—"

"It's Mr. Monk," Gloria Bolden announced to someone out

of range of the handset. Back into it, she said, "Where are you now?" Her voice had taken on an urgency.

"I'm in the Valley." He wasn't going to tell her he was digging through her son's belongings.

Mrs. Bolden said, "Can you come over right away? Something's come up."

"I'm there."

Twenty minutes later Belinda Bolden opened the door before he was halfway up the walk.

"Harriet Stubbens has been murdered," she announced.

"Who?" Monk said, gaining the porch.

"She called herself Lola."

"Shit. Ah, excuse me, Mrs. Bolden." The grandmother, a refined woman with silver hair and a straight frame, stood just inside the door.

"I've used a lot worse, Mr. Monk. Come on in."

Belinda talked excitedly as Monk entered. "About nine this morning, they found Lola dead behind the Spur. An ax buried in her forehead."

"Otto Velson's been arrested for her murder," Gloria Bolden added.

Monk sat down. "How do you two know all this?"

Mrs. Bolden stood next to the mantel over a bricked-up fireplace. "Pacoima's a small town, Mr. Monk. Something like this gets around quick." She wrung her hands, then went on. "You better see this too." Mrs. Bolden took a legal-sized envelope off of the mantel and brought it over to him. The older woman's unblemished hand extracted a red feather. "This came in the mail two days after Oliver's murder."

Illogically, the feather made Monk queasy. "Did you show this to Tierney?"

She gazed at Monk steadily. "No, I didn't. It shook me up

so bad, I was scared to tell him about it. And too scared to throw it out."

"Did you know about this?" he asked Belinda.

"Not until today. Mama told me about it when I got here this morning. After she heard about Lola, she called me and I came over. We'd been calling around trying to find you."

Monk put his hands on his knees to steady himself. Reality seemed to be slipping away beneath him. Like those times when he was in the merchant marines and plowing through rough seas, land nowhere in sight. "Why would Otto Velson kill your son, Mrs. Bolden?"

"I don't know," there was a quaver in her voice. "I do know that Henry Swankford was the kind of man who didn't take a slight from black nor white."

"What are you saying, Mama?"

Gloria Bolden sat on the thick arm of the couch heavily. "Your grandfather fought in the war. The European theater. I worked at Velson with the other girls making intercoolers for B-29s. Oliver was just a big-headed boy then. Dreaming of flying secret missions with Spy Smasher on the radio."

Monk noticed the barely concealed boredom on Belinda Bolden's face. Evidently, she'd heard this tale many times before.

Mrs. Bolden paused, the past seeming to overwhelm the present. "Henry Swankford also worked at Velson. He wasn't one to enlist and fight some cracker's war, no sir. 'No white man's Army wants this nigger with a rifle and the right to kill other peckerwoods,' he used to say. Henry was a big-fisted vital man who could drink a quart of raw whiskey and still work a double shift. He had an eye for the ladies, too."

The way she said it got Belinda's interest.

"One night all of us were at the Kongo Room, carrying on and all, you know how it gets." She looked at the floor.

Belinda Bolden sat upright, enthralled by this new chapter of the story.

Mrs. Bolden continued. "One thing led to another and me and Henry went back to his place over the garage and talked about the money he was going to make." She stole a glance at her granddaughter, then continued.

"Maybe it was the liquor I'd drunk . . . but before I knew it we were. . . ."

"Making love," Belinda incredulously finished.

Gloria Bolden waved a hand, failing to give it a light air.

"What money?" Monk prompted.

"Henry had some fool notion of getting enough money for us to run away with Oliver in tow. Later I told him that night we spent together was a mistake. And it was a bigger mistake if he thought he could get away with robbing the plant. He was furious that I wouldn't go away with him."

"Didn't he worry you might tell Velson what he planned to do?" Monk said.

"Henry was wild, but crafty. He knew if I told, all us colored folks would be under suspicion. Shoot, they'd've strung him up and them white folks would've rounded up the rest of us for being saboteurs.

"See, his vice was women, Mr. Monk. Money was just a means for him to get from here to there."

"So what happened?" Belinda Bolden cut in.

"Those four Marines is what happened. Henry was still set to rob the factory that Sunday night. He'd kept goading me the week before about it, about how he was going to have all that money and how I'd be sorry if I didn't go with him."

Monk passed a hand over his face. "So now a mad killer on Geritol has come back to exact revenge on your son because you dumped him more than fifty years ago?"

No one responded.

Monk got up and began to pace aimlessly. "Then why kill Lola?" He held up a finger. "Ah, maybe she's the daughter of the missing Marine." He stopped, feeling disoriented. "Look, I'm not about to go around chasing some dead man's shadow. There's an answer to be found in this world, and I'll find it."

Monk started for the door, eager for forward motion. As he passed by Belinda Bolden she rose and approached her grandmother. He left them to wrestle with the onus of old sins.

He spent futile time at the Foothill Division trying to see Otto Velson. He did manage another run-in with Tierney, which ended in another insult.

From Karl Velson he learned his brother had awakened in Lola's apartment with a crippling hangover. Beside him in the bed lay Lola, head cloven by a short-handled ax, a beet-red feather stuffed in her mouth. Otto threw up on the corpse, but even with the shakes managed to call his brother.

Karl, sure of his brother's innocence, called the company attorney, who in turn remanded Otto to Tierney voluntarily. Unfortunately, the older Velson's fingerprints were on the axe handle. And Tierney was working on the theory that Otto, in a drunken state of pent-up fury, killed Bolden. Some years ago there had been a strike, and Tierney was advancing the idea there was still bad blood between the two. The younger brother said that was bullshit, but the cop was working hard to prove it.

For the moment, Otto Velson was being held as a material witness, with the prospect of being charged with murder looming quite near. As for why he killed Lola, apparently everyone in town knew the late Ms. Stubbens treated Otto like a door mat.

Monk wound by the Historical Society and asked Homer Garrity to check with his newspaper friends on a couple of things. Eventually, he swung by Lola's apartment. A black and white was parked in front, a cop getting out. Monk watched for a few moments from down the block, then drove off in the opposite direction.

He spent the next day criss-crossing the Valley on several errands, and took a trip to Long Beach that night.

• • •

The door eased open. A figure entered, the beam of a flashlight pierced the dark like a leak of phosphorescent radiation.

"Turn the lights on, asshole."

The switch was flipped. "Monk."

A lone ceiling fixture illuminated the interior of Lola's Spartan apartment. Tierney shut the door. Monk had his .45 aimed at the cop's spreading gut. "Drop the light, then take out your piece, carefully," a thrust of the automatic underscored his words. "Put your gun on the floor and kick it away," he ordered.

"A police officer never gives up his weapon."

Monk sneered, "Honest ones don't."

Tierney blanched, but did as he was told. From the flapped pocket of his tasteless coat, Tierney removed a white envelope. Protruding from its torn flap was a red feather. "You had one of Lola's ho friends leave this with the desk sergeant." He shook the envelope accusingly at Monk.

"That's the one you sent Mrs. Bolden, but I added the note. My office administrator wrote 'I know the truth' so it would be in a feminine hand. I figured that would send you scurrying around."

Tierney's jowls got rigid as concrete. "You're talking out of your head." His ham of a fist crumpled the envelope and shoved it back into his jacket pocket.

Monk's gun remained unwavering. "Three and a half years

ago there was a bust in Palmdale of a big methamphetamine lab. Bikers, some of their chicks, enough loose cash to choke a horse, and, oh yes, a couple of trunk-fulls of crank and crystal ice."

Tierney passed a dry tongue over parched lips. He glanced at the door, then back to Monk. "I had nothing to do with that."

"True. But Lola was one of the women arrested. Only she was calling herself Monique that week. She goes down on one of the vice cops back at the station house and, surprise, only gets slapped with a misdemeanor."

Tierney remained motionless.

Monk went on, "Now this vice cop only wanted a blow job. But you," Monk pointed with the .45, "wanted a different kind of piece. You and this vice cop were drinking buddies and he told you about the vivacious Harriet Stubbens."

Tierney surveyed the room, his shoulders sagging. "I didn't want to wind up in a place like this when I retired."

"Save it for *Hard Copy;* you ain't nothing but a greedy motherfuckah trying to muscle his way to the trough. You got a hold of Lola, who, for a cut, provided you with leads to other amphetamine labs." Homer Garrity, at Monk's request, had checked with his crime beat contact at the *Times*. Among other things, the reporter told Homer about Lola's past and the crowd she used to hang with.

"How'd you put it together, Monk?" Tierney's voice was toneless.

"I kept thinking about the first killing. If Otto'd done it and not left his fingerprints in a mad drunken stupor, let alone been together enough to tie a man up and suspend him from the roof, then why would he be so sloppy with Lola's murder?"

Tierney seemed unnaturally calm. "That still wouldn't put you onto me."

"Lola told me the night Oliver Bolden was killed Otto'd left her around ten."

"So?" Tierney challenged.

"That was the second time Otto had stood Bolden up. Needless to say he was upset. When I talked with Karl after Otto had turned himself in, he told me he'd gotten an irate call from Oliver at ten-thirty that night. He'd said two things: it was Karl's duty to look for Otto since he'd done it the first time, and he'd stay at the shop and try to get some work done on the scheduling. After that, he hung up with a slam of the receiver." Tierney's large body stiffened.

"So Karl went out looking for his brother. It didn't take an advanced degree for him to guess that Otto was probably with Lola. Only it took him a while to find out where she lived. But he saw Otto's car out front at 11:30 when he arrived. He'd checked his watch. Karl left in disgust, deciding to confront his brother the following day, once he was sober."

Tierney stared straight ahead.

"You told Lola to lie about the time Otto had left her to make a tighter frame around him. You knew Otto was supposed to be working with Oliver Bolden because Lola told you. And given his increasing blackouts, there were a lot of hours Otto couldn't account for. He was the ideal fall guy for you."

"That lie made you curious to know more about Lola," Tierney said bitterly.

Monk nodded. Garrity's reporter contact had written about several unsolved robberies of meth labs and their caches in the Valley and Long Beach over the last two years. And the reporter had told Garrity that he'd heard Tierney and his drinking pal, who was one of the officers investigating these robberies, had an unexplained falling out. Maybe the vice cop suspected Tierney, or was mad he hadn't been cut in on the action.

"Lola's comment about 'gravy train' referred to you, not Otto," Monk added. "Seeing the patrol car, she figured you were keeping closer tabs on her."

Tierney rasped, "Bitch was getting sloppy with her talk. Goin' on about how her end of things wasn't sufficient all of a sudden. Hell, I was taking all the risks, doing the scores and dong the deals with out of town buyers." The big cop did a motion with his upper body but stopped when Monk rose.

"You saw me the other afternoon, didn't you?" Tierney asked.

"In the black and white, yeah. Your build and limp are hard to miss."

"I was getting nervous about you, Monk. Maybe Lola wasn't as scared and stupid as I'd hoped, and she'd left something behind to implicate me."

"Even though you'd already searched her place the night you killed her, and put Otto's hands, who was passed out, on the ax handle." Monk moved toward Tierney. "But I guess you were kinda rushed then. Let's go."

"I was thinking you might be her new partner," Tierney said, oddly in a jovial mood. "She was so goddamn friendly with you, the uniforms told me." Without the slightest warning the big cop produced a short-handled ax from beneath his coat and took a vicious swipe at Monk's head.

Ducking and twisting his body, Monk's shot missed Tierney and struck the overhead light. Blackness eclipsed the room. Each man fought to get his breathing under control so as not to give away his position to the other.

Monk circled to his left, anticipating Tierney, who'd think he'd naturally go to the right. Close to his ear he felt the whisper of the ax as he flattened his body, lashing out low with an arm. His hand latched onto the plainclothesman's leg, and he yanked it. Tierney tumbled and Monk swarmed onto him, praying he wouldn't have to find out what it felt like to have an ax buried in his skull.

The cop rolled and Monk's body went off-balance. A disturbance parted the air, and tears of fire went off behind his eyes. A wet pain engulfed Monk's side where the ax had sliced into shirt and flesh. Blindly, he blasted off two more rounds to drive Tierney back.

The cop pounded across the threadbare rug. Monk was sweating and he knew shock was setting in. He scuttled across the floor as Tierney got the front door open.

The beefy man was briefly outlined in the doorway, but Monk couldn't get up, he was too weak. Feebly, he reached out for the fleeing man.

Tierney brought the ax down at Monk's hand, who pulled back quickly, letting off a shot in reflex. The slug bore into Tierney's calve, upsetting his balance.

There was no landing outside the door, no purchase for the cop to fall on. Tierney yelled and did a whirly gig down the stairs. Monk couldn't see anything as he elbow-crawled to the edge of the top step. A scream came from the darkness below, and Monk involuntarily gasped for breath.

"Tierney," he called out but there was no answer. Monk involuntarily gasped for air. In a few moments, fibers from the carpet were swirling around in his slack mouth.

• • •

Monk concluded Hugh Francis Tierney had killed Oliver Bolden because the shop forman had encountered the cop outside of Lola's apartment. That was the first time Otto and Bolden were supposed to have done the scheduling. Tierney probably went to see Lola to set up another score, or to make sure she wasn't geting any independent ideas. Otto confirmed he wasn't with her then, he was so out of it he'd been sleeping it off elsewhere.

Bolden must have asked Tierney, probably assuming he was a john, had he seen Otto. As Tierney began to implement his plan to rid himself of Lola, he realized he had to kill Bolden also. Otherwise he'd be around and would remember where he'd seen Tierney once Lola was dead.

The big cop got real clever and decided to put the Swankford legend to use. Just in case the set-up against Otto failed, the authorities would be looking for some crazed killer imitating the past.

Tierney'd been found dead at the bottom of Lola's apartment, the ax embedded in the center of his forehead. The police department's bio-mechanical criminalist and two investigating detectives couldn't agree as to how Tierney had managed to kill himself. For one there was the angle, and two the amount of force it took for the ax to penetrate the bone.

And nobody had a sound theory to explain the parrot feather leaving the envelope and Tierney's flapped pocket, and jumping into the corpse's mouth.

The cops wanted to believe Monk had done it, but the paramedics swore he was unconscious when they'd arrived. The PI had been leaking blood, and there was none on the stairs.

Subsequently, Lola's garage apartment was rented to a history student taking classes at Cal State Northridge. He was doing a paper on local Valley history and thought staying in the last pad Henry Swankford had lived in before going to prison was way beyond cool.

Boom, Boom

S andi Rollins was mad. Angry because she had to be up and out the door ten past eight on a Saturday morning, and pissed she had to catch the bus. Or try to, given what passed for mass transit in Los Angeles. Especially in South Central where she made her way along Avalon Boulevard near the park at 52nd Street.

The master cylinder and brakes of her '89 Hyundai wouldn't be redone until Tuesday. Except she had to be at her job at the Newberry's in the University Shopping Village by 9:30. A half an hour before it opened, so as to straighten up the items on the shelves and what not.

As she walked toward the bus stop a block past the park, Rollins watched three older men playing dominoes on one of the outdoor benches. "Fit'een," one of the men exclaimed, slapping down a tile with gusto.

"Don't stop writin' yet, scorekeeper," the second one added, positioning a tile of his own. "You can read twenty, can't you?"

The man charged with tallying the points, an individual displaying the excitement of cardboard, dutifully recorded their scores. He drawled laconically, "Forget both y'all country asses, an' give me twenty-five." With that, he downed a tile and the three laughed.

The young woman reached the next block and was just in front of the Del Rey Fish Palace, "You Buy, We Fry," prominently displayed in their window, when its glass unexpectedly blew apart. Instinctively, the woman got her arms up over her face even as a funnel of wind knocked her to the ground. She felt like she'd been punched in the stomach and something was wrong with her ears. A wetness spread across her lips but she couldn't taste what it was.

Groggily, she watched the men from the domino game gather around her, moving animatedly. One of them propped her up as the other two pulled boards and pieces of black and orange plastic off her legs. Their mouths were moving but she couldn't hear anything. There was a vicious tightening going on in her head, and she was terrified she'd lost her hearing.

". . . girl, are you all right, I said." The words floated to her as if coming through interminable layers of gauze. The acerbic scorekeeper was talking to her, genuine concern contorting his leathered features.

She started crying, she was so happy she could hear.

The man shook his head in sympathy. "Poor darlin' has gone into shock."

"I seen the same thing happen in '51 at Taejon," the one who'd scored fifteen stated emphatically. "The reds blew up a supply Quonset and grown men sat around ballin' like three-year-olds they was so scared."

The third player, who was staring at the maw left of the place next to the Del Rey, looked scornfully at the one who'd just spoken. "Negro, the only thing you saw in Korea was the bottom of them pots your ass was scrubbin' in the mess hall."

This brought a rejoinder from his partner and they went on at each other as people came out on the avenue to see the latest destruction wrought in their neighborhood. But even the jaded residents of 51st and Avalon, too used to some luckless teenager sprawled out from a drive-by or a drug deal gone sour, were stunned at the sight of what had happened to Omar's Check Cashing No. 7.

Three days later, on the night of a windy Tuesday, Omar's Check Cashing No. 13 in a strip mall on Washington Boulevard went up like Argentina's inflation rate, its recognizable black and orange sign pirouetting through the night. Flame whooshed into the air and hot sparks blew onto the roof of the auto parts store next door. The establishment went up in a swirling column of red and yellow before the fire company arrived.

It was the third Omar's Check Cashing business to be blown up in about a month's time. It was the first one to include a fatality. A homeless man had been sleeping in the recessed area in back of the parts store, next to the check cashing outfit.

"Tina, this came for you yesterday." Helen Stanton, the L.A. City Councilwoman's chief aide, handed her a single sheet of white paper. "Unfortunately, we opened it before realizing what it was."

Tina Chalmers, a handsome woman in a Donna Karen navy blue suit, took the paper. "A love letter from one of my constituents?" she joked.

Stanton performed a non-committal inclination of her head.

The letter contained one paragraph near the top, neatly typewritten. "The leeches who attach themselves to the body of the black population must be removed. Sometimes this can be accomplished with merely plucking them off, and sometimes radical surgery is called for. As economics is the basis for any people's empowerment, we must pose the question: Why does South Central have so few banks and so many check cashing places which charge exorbitant percentages and provide no financial services? The answer is plain, the solution is simple."

"Signed the 'Disciples of Determination.'" Chalmers looked at her aide. "Did you keep the envelope?"

"Yes," Stanton responded. "It has a Los Angeles postmark and came in the regular mail. Janice opened it in the course of looking at all your mail that comes to the field office here. She realized it might be important and gave it to me.

"I knew you'd be coming over this morning after getting back into town last night, so I thought it best you see it before we turned it over to the police."

Chalmers nodded and looked at the letter again as if it would reveal the identity of its author. "Make a copy for us, then let's get the chief on the horn." She looked up. "This is going to be a mother, and it *would* have to happen right before the primaries, with Cross yapping at the heels of my pumps."

Stanton could only shake her head in sympathy.

"You know why Foreman can take Tyson? I'm going to tell you why."

Ivan Monk was trying to tune out retired postman Willie Brant's explanation as he and Elrod, his giant shop manager, affixed replacement glass in the donut case.

"See, Foreman has got what they call ring savvy. Oh, I know Tyson has *some* experience, but Foreman was heavyweight champ 'fore that boy knew he liked pussy. You can't buy that kind of knowledge."

Brant continued with his odd analysis and Monk and Elrod gently got the plate into place, pressing it against the still moist sealant.

The bell over the front door to Continental Donuts jingled and Brant exclaimed, "Shit."

Monk turned his attention from screwing one of the metal moldings in place to secure the glass and saw three people standing in the shop with their gloved hands in the air. The trio, two men and a woman, had paisley handkerchiefs tied around the lower parts of their faces and their eyes were hidden by sunglasses. Identical black watchcaps were pulled low on their heads.

Elrod, six foot eight inches, 325 give-or-take pounds of potential pain, was surreptitiously reaching for the Remington automatic shotgun in its rig below the counter.

Monk touched his arm for him to stop. "Haven't you got this robbery thing backwards?" he asked the three.

"We're the Disciples of Determination," one of them said. The youthfulness in his voice couldn't be masked.

"Damn," Brant exclaimed again.

"You a new rap group?" Monk came from around the counter.

The Disciples put their hands down but remained standing with their backs to the front windows. "No, brother," the woman answered sharply, "we're the ones who blew up the two Omar's Check Cashing stores."

"Three of 'em got blasted," Elrod amended.

"That's what we're here about," the first one went on. "Somebody's been copying our action. We didn't kill anybody. We didn't do the one on Tuesday night."

"Tell the police that." Monk said.

"Quit bein' smart," the woman admonished him. "If you check, you'll see the first two were designed to explode in a certain way, thus minimalizing the chance of fire. The one the other night was an amateur's job."

"What you want with Monk?" Brant interjected.

"We want to hire him to find the copycat," the woman said evenly. "Not only is he a killer, he's messing up our agenda."

"Which is?" Monk inquired.

"To see to it the ones who profit from our community

understand business won't continue as usual," the woman emphasized.

"This is a new day, and our message is coming on strong," one of the others added.

"I'll give you this for free. Turn your would-be revolutionary butts in before you wind up getting killed yourself," Monk scolded them.

The one who'd been silent reached underneath his shirt, and Elrod produced the shotgun. "It's cool, big man." He handed Monk a lunch bag folded into a rectangle held together by rubber bands.

"Why don't we just arrest you now?" Monk warned.

" 'Cause then you wouldn't be a hero and be able to tell the cops where the next bomb is." The young woman one-upped him, placing a hand on her hip.

"It's set. If you clamp us, it's on. If we leave, we call you later and let you know in time." From the way the handkerchief lifted, Monk could tell the woman was smiling.

"Why you got to drag *me* into this mess?" Monk pleaded.

"Why *not* you, brother? You s'pposed to be the people's detective. You the one that owns a *donut* shop." The three laughed mirthlessly and started out.

"If you try to follow us, we'll blow it by remote, dig?" the woman added.

"I got it," Monk replied.

As they'd promised, one of the Disciples called within the next forty minutes and told Monk where the bomb was. The LAPD's bomb squad took the device from the trashcan inside of a check cashing place at the southwest corner of Slauson and Figueroa. It was not one of Omar's.

"Christ," Andrei Brazinov said in his native Estonian, hitting the side of the television set with one of his Tony Lama boots. His inner line buzzed and he picked up the handset. "Yeah," he growled in accented English, then listened without interrupting, which was unusual. "Show him in."

Monk entered the ornate office of the man who was Omar.

"Black man," Brazinov beamed, extending his hand. They did an elaborate soul handshake complete with knocking the flats of their fists together. "Pop a squat and lay it on me." He was easing his angular frame back down, then stopped midway. "You want to whet your whistle?" His multi-ringed hand swept to the right side of the swank office, indicating a built-in marble finished bar.

"No, I'm all right."

"Cool." Brazinov settled into his high-backed swivel, the San Gabriel mountains in bold relief behind him through the large tinted window. "So you know something about these bombings of my facilities?" He played with one of his rings while he talked.

"Have you received any kind of blackmail demands from some people calling themselves the Disciples of Determination?" Monk noted a clock placed in the belly of a nude woman's cut-out photograph on the check-cashing king's wall.

Brazinov remained still, thinking. "No. They the ones supposed to be fucking up my places?"

He tried to make it sound like an idle query, but Monk was sure he could hear the eager retribution roiling behind it. "They've admitted doing two of the three to me."

"You the one who tipped the cops about the fourth. It was just on the TV." He pointed at the set he'd turned off as Monk entered. "You know them?" More of the friendliness wore away.

"I don't."

"Then why they come to you?" he demanded.

49

"To prove their relative innocence," Monk said, crossing his legs.

"So they hired you? Or did Toliver?"

"Who's that?" Monk asked.

A quick jerk of his head toward the TV. "Pamela Toliver. She owns six places to my fifteen, uh twelve. That was one of hers where they find the bomb." His dark eyes narrowed into cat slits. "You want me to pay you?"

"I just want information."

"Maybe it's funny how the bomb that gets found is in her place, not one of mine."

"I've been thinking on—"

"What you come up with, private guy?" Brazinov interrupted, naturally falling into his impatient manner.

"Don't know yet. Let me ask you something frank—"

"Okay," he said, looking at the nude woman and her belly-clock as if for guidance. "Go ahead."

In a off-handed tone Monk said, "There's rumors about how you made your money a few years back. About how you and some fellow emigres were hooked into the loose-knit Russian Mafia and sold untaxed gasoline and telemarketing scams along the eastern seaboar—"

"Never been convicted," Brazinov said by rote, cutting him short.

"My point being, you must have given it some thought—"

"What thought?" he said agitatedly.

"That somebody you might have stiffed in the old days has returned for a little payback."

Brazinov leveled a finger at Monk's nose. "You say these Disciples come to see you."

"Could be a put up, you know—a front for the real player." Brazinov processed the data. "Blacks working for the

Azerbaijans," he murmured, then leaned forward in his seat. "Could be, could be," he mumbled, settling back.

"Or you're behind it yourself," Monk s. 1 gravely.

Brazinov blinked at Monk like a newborn. "My brother, how could you say that? I employ people in the community. I put money out there when all your Caucasian bankers redline and deny black and brown folks loans.

"I got responsibilities I don't run from. I don't need the insurance money that bad." He shook two fingers placed together emphatically.

"You loan money," Monk commented.

Brazinov stopped short from answering. "Look, see this." He produced an ad slick which offered $25,000 for the capture of the bombers. "That's going to run in the *Sentinel, Watts Times,* and in Spanish in *La Opinion* this week." He moved the stat under Monk. "You could be a high roller if you catch these bums."

"Could be." He got up, leaving the slick on the table.

Brazinov gave him a cagey look. "So how you making money on this deal?"

"The truth is my payment," Monk shot back.

"A man in a cold room tell me that once too, Monk." Brazinov got up and came around the desk, clapping him on the back. "But in this country, officials like Tina Chalmers work for us, right?"

Monk showed surprise. "You know Tina?"

"'Course. Several of my places are in her district. The last one that went boom, in fact. She's having a candidate's forum tonight. Some of my employees are going to ask her what she's doing about this. Put her on the spot, you know." As he showed Monk out, the woman with the clock embedded in her belly continued to smile enigmatically.

The candidate's forum at Manual Arts High School on Vermont at Martin Luther King, Jr. Boulevard had a good turnout in the auditorium. Chalmers' main opponent was Nathan Cross, a corporate lawyer and a Department of Water and Power commissioner. There was also another woman named Jean Fordham, a community activist from the southeast end of her district, but nobody considered her a real comer.

Monk was in the audience, waiting for the debate to be over so he could get to Chalmers and ask her some questions. They'd known each other since going to Jefferson High as teenagers growing up in South Central. Had been boy friend and girl friend in those days when Monk was a starter on the varsity football team and dreamed of being the next Deacon Jones.

"In closing, I just want to remind the good people of my district that I was recently back in Washington working to ensure that the Enterprise Zone monies for our district were in place." Chalmers paused like a pro, "Of course I'm happy to say the money will be coming through by the first of summer."

Applause went up, but over that was an explosion which had everyone craning their necks heavenward.

Monk was moving out onto the street with the first wave, and could see a group of people starting to converge on an area a bit west of Vermont on King. He ran over and knew instantly, since he'd passed it on the way over, that it was a check cashing place which had gone up. This one had been an Eazy Money store, owned by Brazinov's competitor, Pamela Toliver.

One of the news crews who'd come late to the forum was now filming what was left of the store. Nate Cross strolled up. He was a good looking black man with greying temples, a little older than Monk. Sharp in a cobalt blue double-breasted suit, he carried his jacket over his shoulder.

"This is why we need new leadership in our community," he said into the minicam. "This kind of lawlessness can not be tolerated."

"Opportunistic cocksucker," Chalmers whispered to Monk, moving close to him. She smiled slyly. "Since you don't live in my district, I take it you're here for something else?"

"How about your office tomorrow," Monk said, scanning the crowd for anything.

"I'll be at my field office 'round 8:30."

"Got it. Second round begins, champ." He patted the small of her back, and she moved off to joust further with her opponent, her aide trailing behind her.

"You see the kind of work we do," the voice on the other end of the line said without arrogance.

"You stake out the places, don't you?" Monk demanded. "That's how you know when it's clear to blow, and how you knew I was there tonight."

"Correct."

"What the hell happened on Avalon? You almost killed someone there."

"I know," the voice said heavily. "It was probably a glitch caused by cable signals, an interference that caused a delay in the detonation. We've re-tuned our equipment."

"I'm happy for you." Monk was sitting in his trusty wing-backed chair in the study, the portable phone in his hand. He'd had the incoming calls to his office and Continental Donuts forwarded. He'd figured the Disciples might make contact.

The study was in the Silverlake house of his girlfriend,

Superior Court Judge Jill Kodama. He still wasn't used to calling it his home since moving in with her.

"Okay, fine, you know what you're doing. But you do realize there's too many uncontrollables you can't always account for? A kid suddenly dashes by, or the gas main goes up, or something else you three can't plan for." Like maybe you really did kill the homeless man and are trying to obfuscate the crime, Monk speculated to himself.

The voice didn't say anything for a while until, "We got to talk about this."

Monk didn't know if he meant among themselves or with him, but he said angrily, "We have to meet again and I mean soon. That thousand you laid on me don't buy blind obedience."

The line disconnected and Monk reprimanded himself for not having Caller ID.

At Tina Chalmers' field office the next day on Manchester, Monk related to her his interest in the bombings.

"Ivan, you've got to bring these maniacs in," the council-woman demanded. "You could be found culpable if you're not careful. And this could have repercussions for Jill."

"I know. That's why I haven't mentioned anything to her."

Chalmers' eyebrows went up. "Negro, you think you all the time ahead of everybody, but you can get your you-know-what caught in the wringer just like us poor mortals."

Monk chuckled without much conviction. He was standing in Chalmers' inner office, with the door open to a larger area which contained couches and chairs for her constituents. Several of her staff went about their duties, coming in and out of the office as they spoke. "Can you get me a copy of the tape from the news crew that was there last night? I believe it was Channel 9."

Chalmers pursed her lips. "I thought you said your Disciples were wearing masks."

"I did. Would you get me a copy, please?"

"On the condition that I'm made aware of your progress, Mr. Monk."

He bowed and spread his arms wide. "Of course."

"Now get out, I've got a race to win," she retorted.

"I figured you for a lock," Monk said earnestly.

"That goddamn Cross has come up seven points since the middle of last month."

Monk said goodbye and went to his office in Culver City. It was a building sitting where Washington, Culver, and Main came together, and was a smaller version of the famous Flatiron Building in New York's Tribeca. He put in a call to Brazinov and finished off some notes from a previous case. The phone rang and he picked it up.

"People can go boom too, Monk," the accented voice said, then hung up.

"I got to get that damned Caller ID," Monk mumbled, trying to make light of the threat. Less than a minute after hanging up, the instrument jangled again.

"What up?" the voice said on the other end.

"Who's this?"

"Mr. B, you called, right?"

He recognized the owner, Brazinov. It was different than the previous caller, but that didn't mean he wasn't working with mister check cashing. "I got a favor to ask."

"Favors don't do jack but take money out my pocket and time off my schedule," the convert capitalist shot back.

Monk said, "Can you ask your pal Pamela for copies of her surveillance tapes from last Tuesday, going back to Saturday morning from her store on Slauson and Fig?"

"Ah," was all the former Soviet citizen said.

"Yes or no?"

"Clues, huh?"

"When," Monk prodded.

"Tomorrow if not tonight, home fries."

Sometime after a lunch of rigatoni in pesto sauce, Monk got a call from Tina's aide. She said they were having a copy of the tape sent to him by messenger from the TV station. He got it and played it on the VCR in the conference room. Part of the shared office expenses he split with the architect-rehab firm of Ross and Hendricks.

Monk watched it twice, making a few notes. There were a few pans of the crowd before the camera operator concentrated on Cross when he arrived, then Chalmers. A knock on the door interrupted his study.

"Yo," Monk answered.

Delilah Carnes, the invaluable administrator he shared with the architects, put her head in. "Nate Cross is here to see you."

Monk shut the machine off and came out into the hall. Cross, crisp in a brown houndstooth coat and tan slacks, extended a manicured hand. "Mr. Monk, I'll be quick."

"All right," Monk said, returning his firm handshake.

"Have you developed anything on these bombing incidents?"

"How do you know I've been looking into that?"

That got a Cheshire grin. "One must be thorough if one is to be a leader in the 21st Century."

"One supposes." Monk started for his office. "What's your interest in this, Mr. Cross?"

"Nate," he said, pressing close to him. "As the next councilman to represent the area, of course I'd have a desire in seeing these troubles cleared up. I can't have my part of the city becoming downtown Dublin."

"Belfast," Monk corrected.

"Exactly."

They'd reached the doorway of Monk's office, and the PI made a point of not entering. "Have you been to see the cops?"

"Naturally."

"What did they have to say?"

He did an open-handed back and forth movement with his palm. "I give, you give, okay?"

"What I can," Monk conceded.

"The only thing I got was from one of the detectives who allowed that the bombs didn't seem to be too sophisticated. He said it was sad that there was enough literature around which could show someone how to make them." Cross leaned against the wall, putting his hands in his pockets. "Now what do you have?"

"I think there's more than one bomber."

His shoulders went up. "That it?"

"For now, yes." At least as much as he was going to give him.

He lingered, but Monk didn't move. Finally, he made to leave. "See you soon, my man."

"Yes, sir."

"Usually you're pretty expansive about your work," Kodama remarked to him over dinner at the kitchen table that evening.

Monk chewed his food and took a swallow of some carbonated water. "Tough case."

"It's about these bombings," she said, lifting a fork of spinach to her lips.

"Does *everybody* know my business?"

"It's kind'a obvious when we talk about everything else *but* what everybody else is talking about in town."

"This one time, let's not bring the office home, okay?"

57

"What do you know, Ivan?" That judicial tone invaded her voice.

"How big your ears get when you're curious." Monk was keenly aware that to go on might reflect badly on Kodama's career if his dealings with the Disciples went bad. It still might, even he *didn't* say anything.

Kodama made a clicking sound in her mouth. "Be that way."

"I will."

She stuck her tongue out and put a cherry tomato on it.

Later, Monk left a message on Tina Chalmers' machine at her home and one at her office. Upstairs in their bedroom, Monk read an article in *Emerge* while Kodama made notes on a legal pad in longhand for an upcoming trial.

Around eleven-thirty, someone rang the doorbell twice; then silence. Kodama went to the window and looked out. "There's a car pulling away."

Monk was already in his robe and at the bedroom door, his automatic in hand. "Be back."

"Like hell," Kodama added, putting her robe on, too.

No use arguing. The two went downstairs, Kodama behind him, touching him on the shoulder. They stopped at the bottom, waiting. "You got the gun, go ahead," Kodama joked shakily.

Monk started, until she grabbed his arm. "Maybe we ought to call the bomb squad," she advised.

"Maybe," he allowed. "But would bombers ring the bell?" If it was the Disciples, they would. They'd want to see him open the door if it was one of their radio-controlled devices. As Monk got closer to the door, that possibility made him skip several heartbeats. "Get back in the den, Jill."

"So you think it's a bomb," she said, not moving.

"I'm serious." He looked at her hard.

She looked back hard. "Come on, it's not as if your .45 can block the blast."

Monk agreed, but wasn't about to let go of his loaded security blanket.

Kodama went to the door and snatched it open without hesitation. A small plastic bag which had been propped against the door fell inside. She and Monk stared at the package, reading the big pink post-it on the thing.

"You see, I deliver, ha, ha. 'B'," Kodama read out loud.

Nervous, Monk said, "It is a bomb."

Kodama kicked the bag and video tapes spilled out.

"Damn, it's the stuff I asked him for."

"Well, I've had enough palpitations." She shut the door and started upstairs. "Those the X-rated ones with Evangeline and Candy Samples you been salivating to get?"

"Yes," Monk said picking the package up. "It's part of the series with the special introductions by Clarence Thomas."

"That's nice. Let's go to bed."

Monk walked upstairs with the tapes, concerned that someone like Andrei Brazinov knew where he lived.

He rose early, made coffee, showered and nuzzled Kodama goodbye. He was down at his donut shop before eight. He parked on the lot he shared with the Alton Brothers Auto repair shop. It was actually owned by Curtis Armstrong, as the Altons were long-deceased, but Curtis was too cheap to get a new sign.

The thrifty Mr. Armstrong was already working in the bay of his garage. "Monk, I was hoping you or Elrod would be here soon to open up," he said in a pleasant tone not often associated with his normal personality. Armstong and the only other mechanic who worked for him, Lonnie, had a motor raised by a hoist and suspended by chains over the engine cavity of a 1967 Comet Cyclone.

"Give us a hand getting this rebuilt into position will you?" Armstong asked.

Monk sighed but helped out. Forty minutes later, he was rounding the fender of his restored '64 Galaxie when something drained the color from his vision. Blinded, he got socked in the head and knocked to the ground. He was having a difficult time orienting up from down, and he had the impression he was crawling across the sky. Suddenly he forgot how he was accomplishing such a feat, and he fell down a shaft lined in moist crushed velvet.

"Ivan, what the hell's wrong with you?"

"Hi, mom."

His mother, sister, Kodama and Tina Chalmers were gathered around him.

"I wish I had me four fine womin' comin' to see 'bout *me,*" someone cackled.

Monk looked over at the man in the next bed with tubes and monitors hooked to him. He smiled weakly.

"The bombers blew up your donut shop," his sister Odessa said. "The good news is nobody was inside when it went."

"Actually, it was mostly the front section. The room with your files held up all right because of the steel door you had on it," Kodama added.

"Swell, I guess. How long have I been unconscious?" He tried to shift in the bed, but found it painful.

"Five hours," Chalmers folded her arms. "You better turn those Disciples of yours in. I think this was their way of saying you're fired."

"Those the ones mentioned on the radio?" his mother, Nona, asked.

"Yes," Chalmers said. "These so-called freedom fighters released a communiqué to the press stating they did the bombings to dramatize the conditions in the inner city. And they came to see Ivan."

All eyes bored into him. "Hey," Monk rationalized, "they said they didn't do the one where the homeless man was killed. And it's not like I know where to find them anyway."

"Jesus, Ivan," his sister said, shaking her head.

"And whether I believed them or not, by keeping my hand in I figured I could catch the ones responsible."

"Except you the one that got caught, bub." Kodama sat on the bed next to him.

"You left me a message last night about Cross," Chalmers said.

"Yeah," Monk said as a pain worked its way along his side, "he came to see me."

Chalmers looked intently at him. "Really?"

Fighting an urge to scratch his arm where the IV was sunk into it, Monk went on. "What I wanted to ask you was, wasn't there something about Cross and some shady products sold over the phone he'd invested in awhile back in Florida?"

Chalmers sneered. "I guess I should listen to you and Helen. She said I should have brought that persistent rumor up in the campaign. Maybe if it gets into a run-off, I won't be so proud," she said, laughing nervously.

Monk was considering if Brazinov and Cross had had dealings in the past.

Later, as the afternoon waned, the older gent in the next bed took a nap after telling Monk in detail about his theories of big-legged women and ju-ju spells. Monk was zoning out watching Jenny Jones on the common TV, and trying to figure out if he could make a few million by doing a private eye's tell-all show. When the door creaked, he had a momentary panic while he reflexively groped for a gun that wasn't there.

"Lookie, lookie, here comes cookie," Police Lieutenant Marasco Seguin effused as he came into the room.

"Thanks for stopping by, now get out," Monk kidded.

"What the docs say?" his friend asked, studying him.

"I managed a slight concussion but nothing too serious," Monk said.

Seguin took off his Pour Homme suit coat, hanging it in the closet. "The bomb at your place was like the other ones that have been used. Kitchen table stuff, but still potentially powerful. This thing was on the roof, and not inside your shop when it exploded." Seguin scraped a metal chair close to the bed and sat down. "According to the bomb squad, the goddamn thing was some homemade plastique using something called Hexamine. Tablets of which one can buy legally."

"Ah, the price of the free market," Monk quipped. "Does this method match the other bombings?"

Seguin searched his memory. "The first two they said were done with some kind of an ammonium nitrate compound as the active ingredient. You know like the stuff that blew up the federal building in Oklahoma City."

"Killing all those kids," Monk recalled bitterly.

Seguin shook his head in assent.

"And the last two before they blew up my shop?"

"The third was another nitrate number, and the fourth they're not sure yet, but are inclined to think it was also a bargain basement plastique."

Monk put his head back on the pillow, disappointed and confused. Was it the Disciples? Were they nothing but shake down scammers and incidental murderers? Was it Brazinov, and was he actually behind the Disciples?

Sometime after Seguin had gone, a tall heavyset black woman in an expensive outfit came into his room. She wore a large brimmed cartwheel hat with a flower in the band, a necklace of fake pearls the size of oysters, and a chartreuse eyepatch.

"You must be Pamela Toliver," Monk concluded.

"Is that goddamn foreigner behind this shit?" She stood glaring down at him with her one hawk's eye.

"I'm not sure."

"But somebody tried to blow you into the next life."

"Brazinov has put up reward money," he countered.

She made a flatulent sound with her mouth. "When you get out of here, come see me. I'll pay you to find out." She leaned close and Monk could smell beer on her breath. "I don't trust that Ruskie."

With that bit of Nixonian nationalism, she departed after tossing her business card on his blanket. The next morning Monk was released and he went home to view the tapes Brazinov had sent over. He also re-studied the tape from the station on a monitor he'd asked Delilah to deliver.

After that he went to work out at the Tiger's Den, a fighter's gym, weight facility, and sauna on West 48th Street. It was owned and run by ex-middleweight Tiger Flowers, who among other occupations had served in Korea with Monk's now dead father. Sweating through his fourth set of curls, a kind of epiphany came over him.

"You just see Jesus, son?" Flowers said in a voice the quality of ground pumice. He was passing by and had noticed the expression on Monk's face.

"I finally got a good idea, Tiger."

"Figured out who tried to blow you up?"

"Maybe, see—"

"Good." And he was off; such was the extent of the ex-boxer's interest in details.

• • •

The back door to the office wasn't locked, and Monk and Tina Chalmers went inside. He got a shot of the lovers kissing, and breaking apart after the flash went off.

"In all my years in the business, this is the first time I've actually taken compromising photos," Monk said, pleased with himself.

Nathan Cross moved toward him, bunching a fist. "I'll sue the fuck out of both of you morons, not to mention winning the election with a huge majority next Tuesday."

Chalmers could only smolder at Helen Stanton.

Cross stammered, "So we're seeing each other, so what? There's nothing you can do about it now."

Monk lobbed, "There *is* something we can do about murder, asshole."

Stanton seemed to get a shade or two lighter.

Cross started to shout. "Hug my left nut, Monk. You must have gotten your already fucked-up brains turned to mashed potatoes in the explosion." The four of them were the only ones in his campaign headquarters, and his voice echoed in the room.

"Helen used to be a chemistry teacher once upon a time," Monk said casually. "It's in her resume, on file at City Hall."

"You don't know what you're talking about," Stanton said.

"I know you were the only one besides Tina who knew I'd be at the donut shop around eight that morning."

"Pardon." There was a little quaver in her voice. "There's quite a few people in the office, Monk."

Chalmers answered, "The message on my machine at home is where he said he'd be at the donut shop. At the office, he just said he was looking for me. As my chief aid, you're the only one I told my call-in code to so you could retrieve messages from my home phone."

Cross hit Monk in the stomach, grabbing for the camera. The thing skidded across the floor as Monk grabbed Cross, sending the two of them back against a desk. The candidate's legs bent back against the lip, and he was in position for Monk to jam a knee into his upper thigh. Then he hit him once, full on the jaw. That quieted things down.

"You ain't got shit, neither one of you," Stanton screamed. She turned to Chalmers. "I'm tired of being the one answering all the bullshit little letters that come in, and taking the flack from angry constituents." She moved real close. "I want something for myself, not just table scraps when the lights are out."

"You're not running for council, Helen, Cross is," Chalmers pointed out in a sarcastic tone.

"Bitch," Stanton retorted, "a council seat is the least of our ambitions."

"Helen," Cross warned, sitting up.

Stanton and Chalmers glowered at one another, close to blows. Monk broke the tension. "So I've been following you around for the last two days after you left Tina's office, Helen." He'd used his sister's car, not his Ford, which she knew. "Caught you and our married man here going over to the Mustang Lodge on Western to knock boots."

"That doesn't implicate her in the bombings," Cross said, already trying to distance himself from her.

"Motherfucka," Stanton snarled at him.

"Well kids, we'll leave you two to sweat that. Right now, we got a campaign to turn around." Monk hefted the camera and left with Chalmers.

"You're letting them go?" she asked as they drove away.

"I haven't got enough to take to the cops, but I've got one more card to play."

"I guess I shouldn't know about it, huh?"

Monk could only grin.

The late edition of next day's *L.A. Times* ran the revealing photos on the front page of the Metro section. By then, Stanton and Cross' dalliances had been the subject of several local radio talk shows. There was even a rumor about their involvement in the bombings. Though that was yet to be proven.

But by the time the tearful wife of Nathan Cross was being interviewed on "Good Morning L.A.," the momentum in his campaign had hit a wall.

Cross, laying low to avoid the press, was staying at a residential hotel in Lynwood. He was angry at short circuiting his campaign, and pissed to get up one morning to find the hood of his car loose. He cursed, assuming someone had stolen his battery. When he lifted the hood, the sight of the pipe bomb strapped to the firewall damn near made him wet himself.

He gratefully told the cops that the two bombings they'd done had been Helen's idea. After the Disciples had blown up the Omar's that Saturday, Stanton saw this as a way to boost his campaign into the win column.

If a bomb went off in Chalmers' district, she'd be under pressure to do something about it going into the election. But as the challenger, all he had to do was say some tough words, but the burden to deliver would all be on Chalmers. That would be good for ten to fifteen points, Helen figured, he said.

Oh, the letter from the Disciples? That was real, officer. It turns out they'd sent a copy to each council member whose district included an urban area. That was convenient, wouldn't you say?

And whose idea was it to dust Monk?

Cross looked contrite. Why, officers, that was that ruthless

Helen again, sirs. She couldn't have him studying tapes, possibly identifying the Disciples, or maybe even convince those rascals to turn themselves in. Not yet at least.

The cops didn't mention to him the bomb he found inside his car was a fake.

• • •

Monk picked up the handset. "We'll send you the rest of the money we owe you," the voice said.

"Keep it, and listen to me." He went on to describe the woman who he'd seen in Toliver's surveillance tapes and who the TV camera man that night had shot in his pan of the crowd. Both times the same woman, the one with the attitude her mask couldn't hide.

There was shallow breathing on the other end like a slough running dry.

"Now I'm all for the redistribution of wealth, but not like this," he said emphatically. "And when the revolution comes, you'll probably have to knock my tired ol' ass out of the way. Fine. But until that wondrous time, no more boom, boom, all right?

"Or maybe I just get an attack of good citizenship and send my local FBI office a certain still from a certain video."

The line clicked off, and Monk got busy arguing with his insurance company about repairs to his donut shop.

Stone Cold Killah

A punk ass named Murray/
Drives his Benz in a hurry/
He got skillz in rippin' an' runnin'/
An' make you think he ain't up to nothin'/
But he's jammin' and scammin' the brothers bank/
And somebody oughta yank this stealin' gank/
With a .44 an' put him on tha' floor/

N ow look, either she shoots the video the way they want,
or my clients get a new director." Reed Hanson down-
shifted into third and came to a stop at a light on Ventura. He
switched his cell phone to his other side to better scope out
the two honeys alongside him in the lavender Mustang. He
was trying to make eye contact, but the one with the pert
breasts at the wheel wouldn't look over. The light turned green
and Hanson engaged the just rebuilt clutch of his BMW
convertible Z3 roadster.

"Uh-huh," he said in a cursory fashion. Hanson had only
been half-listening for the last few seconds. He was late for
his meeting at Too Fly Records, and wanted to be shut of this
ball buster on the other end of the phone like yesterday.

"Listen, Shelly, Ten Deep are straight-up gangsta rappers.
Their last CD outsold Stone Temple Pilots and U2 two-to-
one. If they want a scene of women in minis tied up and
they're dripping chocolate syrup over their bodies, what's

the damn fuss?" He got into the left turn lane for Coldwater. "No, they're not going to be holding guns, okay, yes, yes, there will be some nines and money on a table nearby. But I don't see that as sexist, it's sexy, it's their image."

Hanson was turning left, one hand on the wheel, when a late model Volvo station wagon suddenly roared up on his right side. The vehicle was illegally turning left from the middle lane, cutting him off. The papers inside his attache case, lying flat with the clasp undone on the passenger's seat, tumbled out as he hit the brakes.

"Fuck!" Hanson dropped the phone and grabbed the steering wheel with both hands. "Asshole," he screamed. He shoved his foot down on the accelerator, completing his turn.

"Reed?" he could hear over on the cell phone.

"Hold on," Hanson yelled, intent on giving this Valley soccer mom who'd cut him off some vociferous driving tips. Bitch probably forgot her nail appointment. There was a Greenpeace sticker on the bumper, and that just made Hanson madder. Goddamn self-righteous peacenik probably thinking about the next whale to save when she should be concentrating on driving. Women.

He pulled next to the Volvo on the driver's side, his finger thrust at the window as it slid down. Hanson's jaw was working and then it stopped. He gaped in recognition.

The first shot issuing from the Volvo entered his mouth and destroyed $3,000 worth of bridge work. The second round pierced his right eye and penetrated his brain. Hanson's car crashed into the bus bench in front of the building housing Too Fly Records. The bench back, with an advertisement of his client Ten Deep's upcoming album, rammed through the windshield, shattering his jaw.

Over the cell phone, Shelly's voice repeatedly asked him what was happening.

•••

MC Molotov moved about the office, alternately picking up and fooling with items such as a gargoyle statuette on the bookcase, a stylish letter opener on the desk, or looking out the window. Taking up more than one cushion on the couch was a stout individual in over-sized jeans and scuffed Skeecher boots. Just inside the office door stood a regularly proportioned man in a Fila workout suit complete with Grant Hill signature tennis shoes. His right forearm was enclosed in a cast, and his immobile face was like something made of plastic.

"Naw, man, I ain't got clue one as to what's going on." Molotov had folded the *Vibe* that was on his manager's coffee table, and was hitting the magazine against his open palm. "I *do* know 5-O's been sweating me like a fat girl in a three-way."

The man on the couch snickered. He had his arms folded, and stared straight ahead.

"The split you and Hanson had was very public, very nasty." Monk looked over at Molotov's current manager and lawyer, T. Ray Pierce, for a reaction.

Pierce lifted a corner of his mouth, then let it drop. "An unfortunate occurrence; more miscommunication than anything." Behind him and his banker's chair was a large hand-colored shot of the Nat King Cole Trio. Nat was displaying that radiant smile of his as he worked the piano keys.

Monk put his eyes back on the young man *Billboard* had voted the number-one rap CD and cassette seller last year. He was lanky and moved fluidly, like he was waiting for a break on the basketball court. He wore a charcoal grey shark-skin suit and a dark blue shirt buttoned to the collar. His hair was cornrowed, with the sides of his head shaved clean.

The gangsta rapper's real name was Randy Irvin. He was

twenty-six, and he'd made more last year from record sales and ancillary endeavors than Monk's dad ever saw as a mechanic in his entire life. He sat down again.

"I don't give a *fuck* about *that*, man." Molotov tossed the magazine onto Pierce's immaculate desk.

Monk expected Couch-man to signify, but he maintained the Buddha thing. "And the rumor is that both shootings have been inspired by songs on your new *Stone Cold Killah* CD."

"Yeah, ain't *that* the shits? First Harold, now this." Molotov shook his head. "The sick thing is, sales ain't slacked off. Fact, they been bustin'."

"Hell, yes," Extra-large said from the amen corner.

Molotov got up again ready to continue, but Pierce cut him off, holding up his hand like a traffic cop. "Let me say something, Randy. As you must know, Ivan, the two who have been killed were at one time involved with my client."

"Tried to punk him," Wide-load emphasized. His cell phone rang and he answered it. He talked in low tones, then handed the instrument to Molotov.

Monk addressed Pierce. "Harold Bell was the producer of Molotov's first two albums, and there was a falling out over profits." The rapper was pacing once more as he talked on the phone in the rear of the room. "And Hanson was his manager before you."

"You've done your homework since we talked yesterday." Pierce stared evenly at his client.

He took the hint. "Later, I got business." Molotov clicked off. "That's old news, brah." He plopped into a chair, underhanding the phone back to Triple-x-large. "So what'd'ya think, my man Hawk?"

"You and your crew got alibis for the two shootings?"

Molotov barked. "That a harsh question to a man 'bout to pay your freight."

"We haven't agreed to anything yet," Monk said casually.

Strained silence filled the room until Pierce spoke. "There is an ongoing investigation, and none of these gentlemen are considered suspects."

"Meaning their alibis are provided by members of the entourage, or what?"

Molotov looked at Pierce but pointed at Monk. "This fool sound like the law dogs that questioned us. We need somebody on *our* side. Shit."

It was Monk's turn to get up. "I came here because you *called* me, and you know Parren," referring to his lawyer and friend Parren Teague. "You want me to look into these killings for damage control purposes, that's fine. Now just 'cause we're all black don't mean I do it on the half-step. If you want somebody to provide cover, that's not me."

"Let's all relax, okay?" Pierce said soothingly.

Monk and Molotov had a stare-off.

"Ivan, come on," Pierce implored. "I'll give you the transcripts of the interrogations the police had with Randy, Marcus"–he indicated the man on the couch–"and Lionel"– nodding toward the man in the cast. "They're not involved. Why in the world would I seek your assistance if they were?"

Monk had a few notions about that, but let it slide. "I still want to talk to you gentlemen myself." He sat down. "It's not as if rappers and their bodyguards haven't been involved in retaliations before."

"You just playin' into the sterotype." Molotov sounded disappointed, like a five-year-old denied ice cream.

Monk grinned. "Some would argue you the ones that perpetuate–or is that perpetrate–such an image."

"If we could focus," Pierce interjected. "Randy and I have been discussing this matter with some sense of urgency, as you might imagine. The rumors about the song-inspired killing started hours after Bell's death."

"He was shot coming out of a night spot in Beverly Hills," Monk recounted. "Witnesses say a heavy-duty SUV pulled up, bang, bang, then whipped away."

"Yes," Pierce confirmed. "And because there is a cut on the album called "Who's Ringin' the Bell," an admitted satiric look at certain situations in the record business, the rumors flew fast and furious."

"Yeah, they be trippin," Molotov contributed. "Like when Tupac was gunned down, people go on about like he faked his death and shit."

"Chillin' out eating nanchos with Elvis," Marcus added, chuckling.

Monk crossed his legs. "And there've been no notes to the newspapers, no call-ins to radio shows from this supposed crazed fan?"

"Fan?" Molotov's voice went up two notches.

Monk explained. "There're plenty of examples where some sick bastard will be inspired, if that's the right word, by a poem or book, or more than likely these days claim they were imitating a scene out of a movie. Or like Hinkley, the man who tried to assassinate Reagan. He said he did it to impress Jody Foster."

"For that matter, many murderous acts have been committed by those saying they were given such power by passages in the Bible or talking chihuahuas." Pierce emphasized his words with a jab of his index finger in the air. "Huge parts of the world are either the Torah adherents versus the Qur'An thumpers, or both versus the Bible shakers, and each side claims theirs is the only true interpretation."

"Ain't that a blip, they always be jammin' *us* up for inciting violence when this thing is always about that scandalous behavior them politicians do." Molotov twisted around to look at the man by the door, who acknowledged his words with a lift of his eyebrows.

Monk resumed. "Usually, there's some attempt to communicate. Nobody's sent you *anything?*"

Molotov glanced at Pierce, then said, "I get all kinds of wack stuff, man. Honeys sending me their soiled panties with a love note clipped to 'em an' shit." He started laughing and the man on the couch joined in.

Monk tried not to, but he also snickered.

"Actually, there was supposed to have been a call to a hip-hop DJ in the Bay Area from the killer," Pierce contributed. "But the LAPD is taking the tack that these murders are not the work of a psycho, but yet another feud among rappers."

"Who else among your crew ran with a set?" Monk abruptly turned and asked Molotov.

The rapper sunk in the chair, disgusted.

"He's just being thorough," Pierce said, but his frozen mouth told Monk he was also annoyed by the question.

"The cops are talking to your homies," the PI said, "and I don't want to be blind-sided with information I should have."

"I'll get you the list I gave the police." The receptionist buzzed Pierce on the phone's intercom, reminding him that Molotov had to get to a photo shoot.

"I assume your client was not the only one who had a beef with these two."

"Exactly." Pierce adjusted the sleeve on his Jack Taylor jacket. "Those possibles, in my opinion, are likely suspects. Does this mean you're in?"

Monk also got up. "I want a list of those people, too." Together, the three moved toward the door. "I'd also like a lyric sheet from the album, and if there's any other song intended as a knock against a particular individual, I want to know that as well."

The man in the Fila opened the door. They filed out and into the elevator heading down to the basement parking structure. Monk told Pierce he'd get one of his contracts over to his office later in the day. He then watched the four drive out of the underground lot in a dark green and chrome Suburban, Marcus at the wheel.

Pierce had the lists messengered rather than faxed to Monk after three that afternoon. The first thing he noticed while reading the lyric sheet was that the killings seemed to be following the order of the songs. Side A's first track, "Who's Ringin' the Bell," compared producers to leeches and expressed the view that their only function was to interfere with an artist's vision and rip them off. The song clearly contained autobiographical elements of Molotov's time with the late Harold Bell.

The second track, called "Those Big Titties," was exactly about that. And the four minute cut managed to not have anyone killed in the story line, only the ravishing of several ho's and bitches who wanted it and couldn't get enough. The third number was called "Down on tha' Floor," and railed against corruption in many forms–from cutthroat record company presidents and crooked managers to abusive cops. Hanson's death was linked to this song.

The fourth cut was the title song, "Stone Cold Killah." This jam was meant to portray what it was like in the mind of a serial killer who now hunted other serial killers. "Lovely," Monk murmured to himself, sitting at his desk and smoking a Partagas cigar. Pierce had also sent over the CD, and Monk inserted it into the portable player he kept atop his empty file cabinet. He punched in the number and listened.

Here it is tonight/
Inside the wall my dog howls and calls your name/
You used to be the one, now I got your game/
The plans you made and the times you charged/
Caused all a rage and pain, but there was no gain/
To understand the hurt, you must see the real/
Look in the suites and their no-good deals/
Tonight's the night, for the steel night thrillah/
Tonight's the night for the Stone Cold Killah/

And so it went. Monk could only imagine the tune, currently the hottest rap single in the country, covered by the likes of Tony Bennett and Erikah Badu.

He forced himself to listen to the rest of the album, and as he'd suspected, he could divide the tracks into two categories. The first was the payback variety, and the second the other gangsta rap staple, sexual prowess. All of it shot through with enough testosterone to poison a rhino. Still, he had to admit the arrangements were bumping, and the lyrics, narrowly focused as they were, worked in the context of what Molotov was putting across.

"Westsiiiiide," Superior Court Judge Jill Kodama hollered, throwing up her hands in a W, her index and little finger out at angles, her two middle fingers crossed one over the other.

"Why don't you do that in court today, smart ass?" Monk moved past her in the kitchen to the refrigerator. He got the eggs and turkey sausage from the shelf.

"Aw-rite, aw-rite, big M, you ain't got to step to me like that. I thought we was pardners," she retorted in hip hopese.

Monk started breakfast. "Do something useful and toast the English muffins."

Kodama placed her agnes b. pale tweed jacket onto the pile

of newspapers and magazines crowding the kitchen table.

Kodama came up behind Monk at the stove and put her arms around his waist, biting his back through his shirt. "How late were you up last night?"

He bussed links around the skillet. "Too damn late." He kissed her and she walked over to the breadbox. "I worked out all sorts of connections among all the possible victims and suspects, and developed various theories as to who the killer might be. Plus I've listened to that damn album so much I know the words better than the Pledge of Allegiance."

"That's frightening." She stuck three slices of blueberry English muffins in the four-slot toaster. "The rapping detective," she mused, sitting down to read the front section of the morning's *Times*.

After making room at the table for their plates, the couple ate breakfast. Afterward, Kodama left for the Criminal Courts building downtown, and Monk drove to his office in Culver City to catch up on some paperwork, then over to the Boulevard Café in the Crenshaw District to interview Marcus, the guardian of couches.

"I love grits," the large man pronounced over a mouthful of the hominy. He dabbed his slice of biscuit in some gravy and slathered grape jelly on top of that.

"Any ideas on who's doing these killings, Marcus?" Monk drank coffee.

"I think it's them Rolling Daltons, man." Marcus polished off his biscuit. "See, I got a couple of play-cousins who still run with a set, and they be tellin' me the Fo'-Trey Gangster Lords clique been havin' it in fo' Bell since he cheated a few of their boys out of a record deal."

"If that's—" Monk began but was interrupted when Marcus' cell phone buzzed on the table and he answered it.

77

"Yeah, uh-huh," the massive man said. He forked in more grits yellowed by runny eggs. "Look, Ricky, I tole you befo', you got a business thang, ya gotta run it past T. Ray—*he* handles the cash flow, understand?" He listened and ate. "Naw, fool," he said and laughed uproariously. "You can't get him to read your sorry-ass plan trying to get him sprung with none of them stank ho's *you* run around with." He laughed again. Monk had more coffee and waited.

"Yeah, son, T. Ray got some fine hammers he hangs with. I seen him with an actress from that show with the buck-toothed kid . . . yeah, yeah, that's the one." He looked at Monk and gulped down orange juice. "That's what I'm sayin'. Lately he's been hooked up with this big-booty lawyer from his old firm—Tricia, Celia, something like that. He brought her to Assaultz's album-drop party last week." Once again he paused to listen and eat. He said a few more words, then hung up.

Monk finished the discussion with Marcus. Molotov was doing some re-mixes and would be available late in the afternoon. Monk was scheduled to talk with Lionel, he of the workout gear, tomorrow. Saying adios to the big man, he drove to the Valley to Too Fly Records for his next appointment.

The day was clear and the smog was minimal as he guided his restored 1964 Ford Galaxie 500 over the hill on the 405 Freeway. Along the way he reviewed his more prominent ideas about the murders.

If it was a crazed fan, and if the triggering of the murders was following the songs in order, then the "Stone Cold Killah" cut would seem to give him carte blanche to randomly target anybody in the city. Unless, he hoped, the person would adhere to some strict, twisted logic of his own and continue to go after those he judged as having dis'd his idol MC Molotov.

There was one other song on the album, "The Pulpit,"

derived from an actual incident. The song related a tour Molotov and his band had taken through the Midwest, and a run-in he'd had with a Christian Right leader named Erhard Dinoble on a radio talk show in Green Bay, Wisconsin. But Dinoble's safety seemed less in question, given that the extremist reverend always traveled with a cadre of the committed who'd willingly jump on the sword for him. Included in the material Pierce had sent him were newspaper accounts of Dinoble doing the talk show circuit decrying the murders as the evil that rap breeds.

The Ford descended into the bowl of the San Fernando Valley, where the movement to secede from Los Angeles the City was ongoing, and the temperature, possibly reflecting the local political climate, was ten degrees hotter than the rest of town.

The competing scenario he liked was that Molotov had ordered the hits simply to exact revenge, the nutty fan a good cover. Monk was aware that Molotov's background included links to the Scalp Hunters street gang, and such contract jobs were not unheard of in this end of the record business.

"Damn, homes, I was one of the first ones to come outside and see Reed all sprawled-out like," Candy Jack Lee said, rubbing her temples. She was the vice-president of A&R for Too Fly Records, and the woman Reed Hanson had an appointment to see. She'd started out as a reporter for a hip-hop music mag.

Here was an Asian woman who'd earned her props in a business noted for its misogyny and racial insensitivity. "It was like wild, ya know? As soon as I saw his body, I knew it was the Killah's work."

"That's what people are calling this guy?" Monk sat across from her in the record label's conference room. On the walls were various blow-ups from albums featuring the company's biggest acts.

For an answer she shoved a copy of this morning's *Billboard* magazine, the music industry's trade publication, toward him. The cover article was about Hanson and Bell being gunned down, and the growing belief that a deranged fan was the murderer. Lee and several others were quoted in the story entitled "The Stone Cold Killah's Reign of Terror." A sidebar mentioned that the CD had already gone back for additional pressings.

"Can I get a copy of this?" Monk continued perusing the article.

"Oh yeah, I'll see to it before you leave."

"And witnesses said they saw a Volvo station wagon cut Hanson off?" He put the article aside.

"Yes, that's what the cops asked me—did I know someone who drives that kind of car." She pointed west. "I told them every other house over here in Sherman Oaks has one in the driveway."

"What did you do when you saw Hanson?"

"I just stood there, stunned, ya know? A couple of dudes in a pick-up came and pulled the door open on Reed's car. I don't think they knew he'd been shot." The pained expression of her face indicated she was reliving her shock. Then she frowned.

"What?" he asked gently.

"I remember when the door opened, some papers fell out. They had been on his lap, I guess. Like I was out-of-body, I could see myself picking them up to put them in order for Reed." She swallowed hard. "There was this one sheet, an auditor's report, reminding me I had to get one done for *my* department." She shook herself. "Funny, huh?"

"I know," Monk said sympathetically.

Lee also reconstructed the conversation she'd had with an LAPD detective named Frazier assigned to the case. The cop had been very interested to hear that Bell had filed suit against Molotov for breach of contract.

"Goes to motive," Monk observed.

"That's what he said."

She also provided Monk with the names and contact information she'd given the cop of others in the business she felt might have it in for Hanson and/or Bell.

"But that ain't it, man," Lee stressed. "You be in this wack business long enough and you see some shit. It ain't too hard to imagine some fool snappin' and going straight off, know what I'm sayin'?"

Monk set his pen down on his steno pad. He leaned forward on the table, interlacing his fingers. "Then who do you think the Killah will go after next?"

Lee looked up at him like a bad girl caught in the act. "Now the cop didn't ask me that. Fact, he didn't want to hear no parts of the psycho/fan drama. He was def on this being a gang-related situation." She was bursting to tell him.

"Candy. . . ." Monk prompted.

She chuckled, looking past him, then at him. "This is just speculation, right?"

"Just you an me, homegirl, unless this room is bugged."

She wagged a finger at him. "Okay, I'm this guy, man or woman, and I'd say a woman is a strong possibility, by the way."

"Someone desperately in love with Molotov and wanting to prove it," Monk ventured.

"Yeah. Aw-rite, I'm the killah. I've capped two for my love, obsession, whatever, for my man. Now, who else should be on my list?" She held up a black-nailed index finger. "There's Lysa Daine, she's an R&B singer on the Jupiter label. She and Molotov had a real swerve on 'bout a year ago. She dumped him in a very loud way, know what I'm saying?"

"Indubitably."

"Uh-huh," she smiled, and it was dazzling. "Second on my list, but maybe first, would be Greg Illson."

"Who's that?"

"Peep this," she said conspiratorially, "not too many know this but he's the dude Molotov settled out of court with over a song writing dispute a few months ago. Or more accurately, a series of songs. Pierce did his job on that one, and for the most part squashed any mention of the hassle in the press."

"But you know about it."

"It's in my interest to know."

"And something an obsessed fan could learn," Monk concluded.

"I called Lisa's people and told them what I was thinking. Illson was paid to go away and he did; ain't nobody seen the boy around since he cashed his check. You should also know Daine and Illson were friends."

Lee gave him a photocopy of the *Billboard* article, and her list, and Monk thanked her for her time. He got back to his office, hungry.

Delilah Carnes, the office administrator he shared with the rehab-architecture firm of Ross and Hendricks, had made a few calls at his behest. "Your upstanding Reverend Dinoble will indeed be coming to town on Friday." She crossed her shapely legs, scratching a kneecap. "He plans to hold a press conference denouncing the devil's own music, gangsta rap."

"Did you find out where?" Monk was getting an anxious feeling.

"At the Silver Pavilion."

"Christ," Monk declared.

"Precisely," Delilah said.

Monk managed to get a few minutes with Lysa Daine in the afternoon. She was guest-starring on a popular sitcom about a struggling career woman, and was taping over at CBS studios on Beverly Boulevard.

"I realize this is an awful thing to say, but I hadn't thought much about the two killings until Candy Jack called me." Daine was sitting in a canvas chair, the make-up artist dusting her smooth cheek with a fine hair brush. Two bodyguards packed into Zegna suits also occupied the small room. "Well," she reconsidered, "people were saying how unusual it was that the two were white. Usually we do ourselves the most damage." The pretty woman cocked an eyebrow at Monk.

"When you and Molotov were dating, did you ever hear about this business with your friend Greg Illson?"

The bronze-skinned young woman shifted in her seat, her wide flecked eyes moving about. "Something," she said laconically.

Monk held off with a follow-up until the make-up woman was done and Daine also asked her guards to step outside and close the door.

"I'm not out to hurt Randy," she began. "I didn't want to get into this in front of the others because everybody and their mama sells a story to the tabloids."

"Good point," Monk agreed. "But I've been on this job less that 24 hours, and already it seems like I'm moving too slow. I can't shake the impression more killings are in the offing."

She rocked back as if he'd slapped her. "You think Greg is the one?"

"Should I?" he wondered.

Daine, who was all limbs and busty, grinned sardonically. "The thing is, I introduced those two. Me and Greg went to high school together. He was always writing poems, short stories, the whole bit. Randy is strong at arranging, but weak on lyrics." A contrite look settled on her face. "At first it was like they were going to be a modern day Gamble and Huff."

"Randy set out to screw Illson right away?"

"No, it wasn't like that. See, this is when Randy was hooked up with Bell. It was really Bell and all his bullshit that created the bad blood between Greg and Randy." She stared beyond the moment, imaging what might have been. "I had Greg talk with my lawyer right off, but when you're eager to break in, you get got." She made futile gestures in the air. "I put a couple of Greg's songs on my latest album. He only did the gangsta rap stuff as a way to get his foot in. He's gifted like a Billy Strayhorn."

"You know your music history," Monk commented appreciatively.

As if it were an afterthought, she said, "I graduated from Berkeley School of Music in Boston." There was a knock and "Two minutes" the voice on the other side announced.

"Where are Illson's royalties sent?"

"To, to ASCAP, of course," she stammered. "They must hold them or send the payments on, but I don't know where."

Monk processed that and asked, "Who wrote 'Stone Cold Killah'?" The credits on the CD were vague.

"Greg did. It was his way of making a comment about the music scene. It was his take on the producers, managers, and so on who he saw as ruthless as a serial killer." She was standing now. "How'd you figure that out?"

"Thinking about the lyrics and what you've told me about Illson, hindsight suggests that *that* number had a more subtle, ironic quality that the rest of the songs on the album."

"Like I said, Randy is good at the music part."

They walked toward the door. "That why you two split up—for artistic reasons?" He opened the door for her.

"The oldest reason there is. He couldn't keep his hands off all those hoochies throwing their treats in his face out on tour."

Monk remarked sympathetically. "It would take a mighty strong man not to."

"Dog." She lightly slapped his arm and went off to do her scene.

Monk drove to Continental Donuts on Vernon Avenue at the edge of the Crenshaw District. He owned the shop with its giant plaster donut anchored to the roof, but saw little in the way of profit after expenses and overhead. Yet it was his, and it was a neighborhood fixture.

"Well, well, if it ain't the darker-than-amber Peter Gunn," Bill Landrew commented when he entered the shop. Landrew was a probation officer and was playing chess in one of the '40s-era red leather booths with another man Monk tried to place but couldn't.

"Gentlemen." Monk waved at them and Elrod, the ex-con, six-eight iron-titan shop manager. He went along the ell of the shop's hallway and unlocked the security door to the room he kept his files in along with other tools of his profession. For though he had a computer at his Culver City office, here was the computer he did most of his background work on routinely. The cloistered enclave made such intrusive pursuits natural.

He called the American Society of Composers, Authors, and Publishers on Sunset. He was informed by the registry desk that any inquiries about Greg Illson were to be directed to Beatrice Klanski at Latham Grand, an entertainment law firm. He called and left a message for the attorney.

Monk also searched through several news links for information on Bell, his client, Candy Jack Lee, and anybody else connected to the case. He downloaded several articles and left. On his way back to Culver City he stopped for gas.

He'd been playing a Zoot Sims tape and exited to the deafening beat of a kid pulling up in a lowered Chevy Blazer with smoked windows. The rear hatch was open to allow everyone in the vicinity to enjoy the rich bass of a Mack 10 number blasting from the speakers embedded in the cargo compartment.

The youngster got out, leaving the vehicle's juice going. He was bopping his head as he squeegeed his windows clean. Monk had paid for his pump and was walking back to his Galaxie when the DJ on the rap station came on after the window-rattling song.

"And check this," the DJ snickered. "Molotov's gonna throw down with a free concert at the Denver Lanes Roller Rink in Burbank, less than a mile from the Silver Pavilion in Glendale where that tight-ass preacher Dinoble will be spewin' and spoutin'." Under this, "Stone Cold Killah" had been queued up. "Is Molotov the man or what?"

Monk sighed and called Pierce when he got back to his office. He didn't waste time arguing the pros and cons of this concert escalating tensions.

"That's right, John Shaft. It must be those Christian right punks who're doin' these killings." Monk was on the speaker phone and could tell the rapper was pacing about his manager's office. "I'm'a show 'em what time it is."

"What led to this breakthrough," he said sarcastically.

"Ain't it obvious?" Molotov replied incredulously. "T. Ray found out the dude had been trying to pull together a Country and Western and gospel fest."

"That's pretty damning," Monk laughed.

"You tell him, T. Ray," Molotov ordered. Monk imagined that Fila and couch man were there too.

"Hanson pulled out of putting the concert together when

he discovered several of the acts were tied to Dinoble," Pierce said in his soothing tone.

Confused, Monk said, "I'm not exactly following this."

"Dinoble knew of the split between Randy and Hanson, and sought to exploit that. He has connections out here and was using them to pull Hanson in until he got on to it."

"But how does that get us to some family-values-lovin' Bible thumper running amok?"

"My friend tells me Hanson agreed to be interviewed for a piece in *Esquire,* blowing the cover on Dinoble trying to manipulate elements of the music scene for his agenda."

"And we know the reverend called Hanson up and threatened him personally," Molotov broke in. "So tadow, how you like me now?"

"You ever talk to Greg Illson these days?"

"You've seen Lysa." The wistfulness in Molotov's voice came across the handset.

"Is he your suspect?" Pierce demanded.

"How come you didn't tell me about him before?"

"It's complicated, Monk." Pierce adopted his lawyer tone. "And he's been more than fairly compensated for any misunderstanding."

"He's not listed as the author of 'Stone Cold Killah.' Maybe he thinks a credit is worth more than money."

"Naw, man," Molotov broke in, "I ain't heard from Greg; he's supposed to have left town. We wasn't tight, but we was coming up with good lyrics, man. But you know, like, I listened to the wrong people and let that get in the way of doin' right. But look here, Greg ain't no roughneck, Monk, he's an artist." Molotov said it reverentially.

"That don't mean he didn't put down his pen and pick up the gun."

"Rather than paraphrase dead revolutionaries, Ivan, why

don't you make some effort to find him?" Pierce commented, eager to deflect any further criticism the PI might have for his client.

"So who might he call, Randy—who might Illson still talk to from time to time?"

"Him and Lysa, man. She was kind'a his big sister, ya know, from back in the day."

Monk told the two he'd call back later. He then called around and left several messages for Lysa Daine, to no avail. He was restless. He wanted to be in motion, but he wasn't sure which direction to take. He got an idea and called Candy Jack Lee.

"Who represents Lysa Daine—I mean, in legal affairs?"

"Johnnie Clarke of Latham Grand," she said. "Their firm reps quite a few people in the music business."

"Thanks."

That night, after driving all over town and talking with several people connected to the case—including Harold Bell's secretary—and not hearing back from Daine, he lay next to Kodama in bed as she watched the "Politically Incorrect" TV show.

"I think you've been working too hard, baby." She rubbed her hand on his bare stomach.

Monk gently stopped her fingers as she reached past the elastic of his boxers. "I need the analytical part of your brain right now, my dear."

"Fine," Kodama said in mock petulance, withdrawing her hand. "What up?"

Monk clicked the set off with the remote. Bic metal-point in hand, he ticked off items on his yellow legal pad. "According to what I've found out, Dinoble has been rumored to be connected to some rough play before. It seems he doesn't take criticism or inspection well, and some of his flock have been known to forcibly try to change the mind of a reporter or two."

"Bit of a jump to wanton murder." Kodama rested her head on his shoulder.

"Really no more fanciful than a disturbed fan carrying out their love of Molotov." Monk looked up from his pad. "Maybe the rev ordered the hits as a way to further tarnish gangsta rap, and to build his crusade out here in the West."

"Plausible," she conceded.

"Then there's Illson, the dis'd song writer. Daine lied, or at least misled me. She and Illson share the same firm."

"That still doesn't mean she's heard from him."

"Doesn't mean she hasn't. Several of the witnesses outside the club in Beverly Hills said they saw two people in the sports utility truck."

"So they're in cahoots to bring Molotov down."

Disgruntled, Monk grabbed the stack of papers he'd generated about the case from the nightstand. "Or maybe they want to bring him up. The album sales have already gone double platinum."

"Then it's some devilish master plan by Molotov to eliminate his enemies, increase sales, and make it seem like he fell out with his girlfriend."

"I think that's too complicated for him." Monk scanned his lists and printouts. He paused at one.

Kodama watched the slow smile develop on his face. "What is it?"

"Maybe the real motive and the real killer."

"You go, boy." Kodama reached her hand inside his boxers and he didn't object.

• • •

The crowd in the roller rink pumped the air with their fists. More people came in after going through metal detectors and hand searches. On stage MC Molotov stepped out from behind a battery of bodyguards and grabbed the mic. His band Most Wanted struck up the music, and Molotov began rapping his number called "The Pulpit":

> You standin' like you was right-e-ous/
> But really you be treach-er-ous/
> 'Cause the snake in the garden from the start/
> Done sunk his fangs in you heart/

Outside the rink, a sizeable number of Christian rightists demonstrated across the street. Members of the LAPD, some on horseback, were on vigil in the street.

A little more than a mile away, the Reverend Erhard Titus Dinoble prepared to address the gathered in the magnificent Silver Pavilion. The edifice was a modern paean of burnished steel and cut glass whose flat planed spires pierced the evening sky and glinted from the halogen lights illuminating the parking lot. The Pavilion was the showpiece of the Christian Coalition of Southern California, the church and public hall used for all their important events.

The Revolutionary Communist Party, the stalwart soldiers of all things ultra radical, had a cadre of their members marching and chanting in front of the event.

The Pavilion's crowd also had to pass through metal detectors, and encounter random pat-downs if you had that heathen look in your eyes.

"The world body can no longer tolerate this vile tumor of gangsta rap. This abomination of sexual excess, the endorsing of wholesale marijuana consumption, and calling for the death of brave and courageous law enforcement officers must cease." Dinoble, a tall gangly-constructed man with a hollow log of a voice, raised his arms and the place exploded in applause.

It was the perfect time to get off his shot.

Monk, sweating and shouting, tackled him and the two tumbled out on stage through a prop made to look like a graffitied wall. The music stopped and bodies and hands swarmed all over Monk and the man he was grappling with.

"What's this all about, T. Ray?" Molotov stepped closer as Marcus, Lionel, and those in windbreakers with SECURITY stenciled in yellow on their backs separated the manager and the private eye. A space age plastic Glock was held loosely in the attorney/manager's right hand.

• • •

"So T. Ray capped Bell and Hanson to make money?" MC Molotov shook his head in disbelief as he paced about Monk's office.

"It had to be a psycho, or for revenge, or for one of the oldest reasons there is, like when Cain slew Abel." Monk reared back in his creaking swivel.

Molotov and Marcus gave him a blank stare.

Lionel, his back to the door, said, "To get something."

"For gain," Monk seconded. "I'd searched through some news services for articles that would give me background information. In one of the pieces from the *Wall Street Journal* on the economics of rap, it mentioned Bell's suit."

"Yeah, so?" Molotov said.

"The piece also had a quote from Beatrice Klanski, one of the Latham Grand lawyers."

"She and T. Ray go out together," Molotov added.

"I learned that from Marcus at breakfast."

The big man looked surprised, not recalling the cell phone conversation Monk had overheard at the Boulevard Café.

"But how did you know that she was Hanson's lawyer?"

"It was mentioned in the *Journal* piece." Monk put an elbow

91

on his desk. "That Friday morning I went back to his office. I'd talked with his secretary before, like I'd talked to Bell's. But my questions had been about whether Hanson had received any death threats, any disgruntled clients, the things the cops had already asked her. This time I asked her about his finances. I'd remembered what Candy Jack Lee had said about the audit sheet in his car."

Molotov was getting it. "Beatrice and T. Ray was ripping him off."

"Yes. Or at least he'd come to suspect that, the secretary admitted. He'd been having the independent audit done, Klanski found out, and that's when they figured to do *him* in, too."

"Shit." He sat down bewildered on one of Monk's Eastlakes.

"I think he's been ripping you off, too, Randy," Monk continued. "I know," he flicked a hand toward Marcus, "that you let him handle your money. You've earned millions and have you bothered to ask for a balance sheet?"

His sheepish countenance was his answer.

"They killed Bell because his suit might have exposed their financial shenanigans. T. Ray and Klanski fostered the crazy fan rumor, then brought me in, knowing I'd pick up the Illson angle. Either way, it obscured their moves."

"Why try to plant my man?" Marcus spoke up from Monk's couch.

"That wasn't in the original plan, at least not so soon," Monk answered. "But when I mentioned the other day I'd been talking to Lysa, Randy started thinking."

"I was going to talk with her," Randy "MC Molotov" Irvin admitted. "I told T. Ray that."

"But if you did that, invariably she would have asked you about your finances, since she's hands-on in every aspect of her career. If you started asking Pierce questions. . . ." Monk held up his hands. "With you dead, and I gather like most young folks you don't have a will, who better to administer your estate than the man already doing it?"

"Damn. But none of us went through the metal detectors, why use the Glock?"

"A metal gun would point to one of you. The mostly plastic Glock, though it can be detected on certain devices, would keep the premise alive of the crazed fan or that Illson had snuck in, and escaped in the pandemonium after you were shot."

"T. Ray or his girlfriend cop to anything?"

"Not yet, they're going to try to not have separate trials, but the DA will push to do them separately, that way you put pressure on one to testify against the other."

"Goddamn," Molotov exclaimed. "You sure earned your money." He smiled. "Course you might have to wait a bit, I don't even know where T. Ray kept the check book."

"Talk to Parren, he'll help you get your finances in order."

Molotov extended his hand. "You aw-rite, Monk."

He shook the young man's hand. "You still ought to give Lysa a buzz."

"Maybe try to get right with Greg, too."

Monk said, "Now you talking."

'53 Buick

Barreling out of Amarillo, the sandstorm swooped in as Dolphy Ornette steered the black and red 1953 Buick Roadmaster directly into its path, his foot steady on the accelerator. Route 66 lay flat and hard and open before him like a whore he knew back home in Boley, Oklahoma. Some Friday nights men would be stepping all over each other in the service porch off her rear bedroom waiting their turn.

He'd bought the car when he'd cashiered out of Korea with his corporal's wages two years ago. He'd fought another war like his older brother had not more than a decade before against the nazis in Europe. Of course just like that war, the downtown white men suddenly got a lot of "we" and "us" in their speeches, and told the colored boys it was their duty to go protect freedom. That was the war his brother didn't make it back from. The enemy were krauts and nips then in '42, and goddamn gooks in '51. White man always could come up with colorful names for everybody else except himself. Dinge, shine, jig, smoke, coon; even had dago, wop, mick, kike for those whites who maybe talked their English with an accent or ate food they didn't serve down at the corner diner.

The NAACP also said negroes should fight, prove they were loyal Americans and that they could face 'em down with the best of them. So they soldiered up. Surely that would show the ofays back home, things would have to improve in housing

94

and jobs once our boys got back. The black soldiers returned after losing lives and blood and innocence, like the white men had, and they had the nerve to demand what was theirs from the big boss man. Naw, boy, things is going back the ways they always was. Sure, Truman integrated the troops in Korea, but that was war time. This was peace.

A steady hammering of sand rapped against his windshield. Earlier, before the break of dawn, he could tell this was coming as he stood gassing the Buick at the dilapidated station in McLean. The old Confederate who ran the place wasn't inclined to sell him gas, but business wasn't exactly knocking down his weather beaten door, so a few colored dollars had to do him.

The wind off the Panhandle drove the sand at the glass with a fine consistency like his mama's frying cornmeal. But the car's road devouring V-8 and the Twin-Turbine Dynaflow torque converter kept the machine steady and on course across the blacktop. He was glad he'd paid extra for the power steering, even though at the time he did think it was a might sissified. The 12-volt charging unit was doing its job. The dash lights didn't dim like his Desoto's used to do.

He drove on and on through the sandstorm and its raging around his car like the song of one of those sea mermaids luring you. Like you'd get so hot to be with her you wouldn't notice until it was too late as a giant squid popped the eyes out of your head as it squeezed your ribcage together.

Dolphy Ornette kept driving, periodically glancing at the broken yellow line dotting the center of the two-lane highway. The pelting sand a lullaby of nature's indifference to humanity outside his rolled-up windows. He drove on because he had to put enough distance between where he'd left, and because he badly needed to get where he was going. Not that he thought they'd suspect him. No, the big boss man couldn't conceive of a black man being that clever. A couple of them might wonder what had put in his head to quit. But he'd waited weeks after filching the doohickey to announce he was going back to Boley.

Anyway the generals and the chrome dome boys would be too busy trying to figure out how the dirty reds had stolen the gizmo. A blast of wind like being backhanded by a giant caused the front end to swerve viciously to the right. His hands tightened on the wheel, and he kept the Roadmaster under control. Ornette slowed his speed to compensate for the turbulence. It wouldn't do to flip over now.

He should'a rotated the tires before he left, but he had other matters to deal with. Up ahead, an old Ford F-1 truck with rusted fenders weaved to and fro. The trailer attached to it shimmied like one of those plastic hula girls he'd seen in the rear window of hot rods.

Ornette slowed down, watching the taillights of the trailer blink through the sheet of brown blur swirling before him. It sounded as if a thousand snares in a room full of drums were being beat. The red lights before him swayed and jerked.

On he drove through the gale until it was no more, and all that remained was a night with pinholes for stars, and a silver crescent of a moon hanging like it was on a string. He pulled over somewhere the hell in New Mexico. Using the flashlight, he checked the windshield. The glass was pitted and several spider web cracks like children's pencil marks worked at the edges down by the wipers. But the metal molding seemed intact. He tapped the butt of the flashlight in several places against the windshield and it held.

Popping the hood he checked the hoses and cleaned away grit off the front of the radiator with a whisk broom from the glove compartment. Looking toward a series of lights, Ornette figured he'd take a chance and see if he could get accommoda-

96

tions. He had a copy of the *Negro Motorist Green Book* in the glovebox. This was the guide that told the black traveler where he might find a guest house or hotel that would be hospitable, and which ones to avoid.

At the moment, Dolphy Ornette was too tired and too ornery to give a damn. He drove closer and could see and hear a humming neon sign of a cowgirl straddling a rocket with a saddle around its mid-section. Blinking yellow lightning bolts zigzagged out of the rear of the rocket. The motel rooms were done up like a series of movie rockets had landed tail first in the dirt. The place was called the Blast-Off Motor Lodge. Beneath the girl on the sign was a smaller sign announcing cocktails. If they rented him a room, they'd probably take his money for scotch, he wistfully concluded. He patted the trunk and walked inside.

• • •

Ivan Monk looked up from the sepia hued postcard of the Blast-Off Motor Lodge to the elderly woman. They were sitting in her cramped kitchen, the door of the oven that was set to 350 degrees open. Its stifling heat making the sitting, talking, and listening to the woman's story that much more difficult. Outside, the temperature was in the comfortable low seventies. "Mr. Ornette liked to keep mementoes. Know where you been, and look forward to where you going, he was want to say." She tapped the postcard with her delicate fingers.

"And you want me to find his Buick?" Monk repeated, to make sure he wasn't getting delirious from the heat.

She nodded. "1953, Roadmaster Riviera hardtop coupe, yes sir. It was like something out of Flash Gordon, that car. What with that bright ol' shiny grill like giant's teeth and those port holes, four of 'em, lined along the side." She shook her head in appreciation. The black wig she had on slipped a little and she adjusted the hairpiece in a deft motion.

"I remember it so vivid, that Tuesday he drove up in his beautiful car to the rooming house. Had us a wonderful three story over on Maple near 24th. All that's Mexican now." She tucked in her bottom lip, willing herself not to go on about the old days.

"Those cars were a classic," Monk agreed. "But Mrs. Scott, why do you want to find Ornette's Buick, and why now?" The heat was too much. His shirt was plastered to his back like it was stapled to his skin.

"It was a gorgeous car, you said so yourself." She touched her head and looked over at a kettle on the stove. "Tea, Mr. Monk?"

Was the old girl part Iguana, so in love with the heat? "No thanks."

She got up in the quilted house coat she had on and poured herself some tea. Standing at the stove she said, "Mr. Ornette kept that car in fine running condition. He could hear anything wrong with the engine and he'd get it down to the mechanic lickety-split." She stirred and sipped. "There were a couple of mechanics he particularly liked going to. One of them had a shop over on Avalon." She inclined her head. "Had some kind of royal name, you know? The Purple Prince, no that's the skinny child who runs around with the butt cut out of his jeans."

"Kings High Auto Repair," Monk supplied.

"Why yes, that was it. But he couldn't still be around, could he?"

"No, my father died some time ago."

She halted the cup at her cracked lips. "My goodness, that was your daddy's business?" She laughed heartily. "The Lord sure moves in his ways, doesn't he? It's providence then that

98

I got to talking to your mother after church last Sunday, and she getting you to come here and see me about my need." She laughed some more.

Monk's father had won the stakes with a kings high full house poker hand to make the down payment on the garage. The rest he'd borrowed from a gambler he'd been in the Army with in Korea.

"Mrs. Scott, I'd still like to know why you want to find this car. Did Dolphy Ornette skip out on his rent years ago and now for some reason you want him to make good?" He had to find a way out of this silly business gracefully so as not to offend her or his mother.

"Child, Dolphy Ornette died in 1968."

"And he' kept the Roadmaster all that time?"

"Yes he did, he wasn't living with us by then. But my sister, who knew some of his friends, used to see him around town in it. Oh yes," she said animatedly, "he kept that vehicle in good running condition."

"And what happened to the car after Mr. Ornette died?"

She raised her head toward the ceiling, the steam from the cup drifting past her. Momentarily, Monk had the impression her head existed detached from her body. "When we heard about his getting killed, my sister and—"

"Killed?" Monk exclaimed.

"Yes, didn't I tell you?" She sat at the table with its worn Pionite topping again.

Details definitely weren't Mrs. Scott's thing. "How'd it happen. Don't tell me it was because somebody wanted his car."

"No, nothing like this car jacking foolishness we got today, no. When Dolphy got back from Denver, he had more get up and go. We'd known him before the Korean action. My sister had gone around with him before. But when he came back to town, he seemed more focused, I'd guess you'd say. Before, he was just interested in fast cars and club women." She made a disapproving sound in her throat.

"But when he came back to Los Angeles in 1955, he was like a man afire. He got himself into community college while he waited tables over at the Ambassador Hotel on Wilshire. He soon had a delivery service operating for colored businesses in town and on up into Pasadena. He did all right," she said proudly.

"His death?"

"Shot in the face one night as he came out of his office on Western."

"The police find the killer?"

"No. Some said it was a jealous business rival, Others said it was white folks who had delivery services and couldn't abide a black man taking business away from them."

"And the car?"

"I was raising a family and working part-time at the phone company, Mr. Monk. I couldn't rightly say."

Was she ever going to explain why it was she wanted this car so much now? If there'd been rumors of money hidden it, like Ornette didn't trust banks? Surely she didn't believe it would still be hidden in it after all this time. The Buick was probably long since recycled metal, and was part of a building in Tokyo by now.

Mrs. Scott, anticipating his next question, rummaged in the lidless cigar box she'd plucked the Rocket Motor Lodge postcard out of a few minutes ago.

"Here," she finally said, "this is a picture of the car. You can see Dolphy with his foot on the bumper, right over the license plate. My sister Lavinia took that shot right in front of our place on Maple."

• • •

"Come on, baby, snap that damn thing," Ornette growled. He pulled on the crown of his Flechet.

"Take your hat off, the shade from it's blocking your face."

"Maybe I don't want my face in the picture."

Lavinia Scott put a hand on a packed hip.

Ornette complied. He put one of his new two-tone Stacy-Adamses on the Buick's bumper. His foot directly over the black license plate and yellow numbers and letters. The first thing he'd done coming back was to re-register the car in California. It wouldn't do to get pulled over by the law for out-of-state plates.

She wound the film in the Brownie camera, held the thing against her stomach, and sighted his reflected image in the circle of glass. She snapped off two shots rapidly.

"Let's go now," he ordered. Ornette plopped his hat back on and got in behind the wheel of the Buick. Lavinia squirreled the little camera away in her purse and joined him on the passenger side.

"You been back a month now and you still haven't told me about your job in Denver."

"I told you I'm planning on going to school 'fore I get my ideas set up." He steered the car onto Maple and headed south toward Jefferson.

"See, that's what I'm talking about, Dolph, you all the time ducking the question." She studied her lips in her compact's mirror, applying a thin coat. "You know perfectly well what I'm talking about. What was it like working at that PX? It had to be exciting what with everybody returning from the war."

He grinned, showing his gold side tooth. "Like any other slave a colored man can get, sugar honey. Punch that clock and hit that lick."

She gave him a playful slap on the arm. "You so bad."

"That's why you dig me."

She giggled. Then she leaned over and kissed him on the neck. He took a hand off the big steering wheel and rubbed her leg.

"Don't you go getting too frisky, mister, I'm a church-going woman." But she didn't remove the hand.

"Don't I know it. Got your nosy sister askin' me when it is I'm going to get down to church every Saturday evening since I been back."

"She's concerned for your welfare," Lavinia Scott teased, touching his shoulder.

"Soon, if things go right, we ain't gonna have none of those worries. I mean money or our future." He piloted the Roadmaster west along Jefferson toward the Lovejoy Fish House.

"You been hinting around about something since you been back. What is it?"

Ornette beamed at her and chuckled. "Maybe I'll show you. You keep riding with me, sugar honey, you won't have to ask for no more. For nothin'."

She squinted at him not convinced, but intrigued nonetheless. She was about to speak when the car suddenly lurched to a stop. Behind them, a Mercury slammed on its brakes, its front end meeting the rear of the Buick.

"Goddammit, kid," he yelled.

A boy of about nine looked aghast into the windshield of the Buick, standing in the middle of the lane. His ball had rolled back to his feet, but he was too frightened to move.

"Oh lord, I think he's going to cry." She unlatched the door.

Ornette had a hand to his face. "Goddammit, Goddammit."

Lavinia went to comfort the child.

Ornette also got out to talk to the Mercury's driver. He was a small, stout man in horn-rimmed glasses and a beret.

Influenced, no doubt, by the fashion fad among be-bop jazz men.

The man was looking down at where his bumper had gone over the Buick's and was now pressed against the trunk.

"Looks like we can get them apart. How 'bout you get your trunk open and let's use your tire iron for leverage."

"Ain't got no spare," Ornette said hurriedly. He gritted his teeth, staring at the trunk. "I'll get on it and push, you put your car in reverse."

"You might dent it."

Ornette just stared mutely at the trunk.

The man hunched his shoulders and got back in his car.

Ornette got on his trunk and planted his Stacy-Adams on the Mercury's bumper. His weight sank the Buick's rear enough that the bumpers came free with little effort.

"I'm prepared to call it square if you are," the small man said.

"Yeah." Ornette absently stuck out his hand, still glaring at the trunk.

The other man shook the limp hand and left in his car.

Lavinia had calmed the child down. Ornette dabbed at his forehead with the sleeve of his camel hair coat. He parked the Buick, taking care to lock the doors.

By the time he'd done that and walked to where Lavinia stood, the kid was on his way with his ball. The child waved at the nice lady.

"Happy?" He sounded nervous.

"Don't like to see anyone disappointed," she said.

He shifted his shoulders beneath his box coat. "That's what makes you so special."

She hooked her arm in his and together they entered the Lovejoy Fish House, right beneath the huge plaster and wood bass suspended over the entrance.

• • •

Monk carefully refolded the brittle newspaper clipping from the *Eagle* newspaper. It was an article and photo of the Lovejoy Fish House. The occasion had been the visit of young starlet Dorothy Dandridge to the establishment in November of 1952. Mrs. Scott had told him about the incident with the child when she'd chanced to open the clipping. She said too that not soon after that, Lavinia and Ornette had broken up. The sister would never say why.

Mrs. Scott had loaned him the box of small knickknacks, postcards, photos and clippings, some of which had apparently belonged to Ornette, or had been sent by him, and some of which she wasn't sure *how* they'd gotten into the box. But it was all she had, she'd told him in that Hades of a kitchen, and couldn't he for an old woman, a friend of his mother's, spend a few days looking for the Buick, please?

Listlessly, he shifted through the contents of the box that now sat on his desk. There was part of a Continental Trailways bus ticket, more photos, a couple of rings, some buttons, an old fashioned skeleton key, and another postcard. This one depicted a landscape shot in the Painted Desert in Arizona. It was blank on the back.

Monk threw the postcard back into the cigar box and shoved the thing aside. What a pain in the ass.

• • •

Delilah Carnes, the fine all-purpose administrative assistant and researcher he shared with the rehab firm of Ross and Hendricks, entered the room. She wore a mid-thigh length form-fitting black skirt and shocking blue silk blouse.

"Here's what I got from a check of the license plate number you gave me, Fearless Fosdick."

From the National Personnel Records Center in St. Louis, Monk had obtained Dolphy Ornette's service record including social security number. The SSN, the magic number to open up the doors to one's life in the not-so-private modern world.

"Let me guess, somebody filed a certificate of non-operation with the DMV sometime in the mid-eighties, and that was all she wrote."

"Indeed," she said, sitting down and crossing well-defined legs on the couch. "Yet a call back I got from New Mexico showed the car was registered again in Gallup in 1988. Nothing after that."

"Registered to who?" Monk didn't hide his displeasure. "So now I'm supposed to go on my own dime to Gallup and prowl around junk yards for this car?"

Delilah laughed. "Your client said she'd pay you with three fresh-baked sweet potato pies. After all, she's on a fixed income, Ivan."

"All her money must go for her heating bill," he groused. "Who re-registered the car?"

Delilah checked her printout. "A Delfuensio DeZuniga. I called the number matching the address, but it's been disconnected. I've got half a white page of DeZunigas currently in Gallup.

Monk groaned. "How about any moving violations?"

"Yeah, I ran that, too." She leafed through a couple of sheets, then settled on a page. "DeZuniga got a ticket for having a taillight out in 1989. Here, in town."

She got up and handed him the sheet, pointing at the location of the infraction. Monk recognized the area as near Elysian Park where the LAPD's academy was, and where cholos and their rukas kicked it in the park. Bordering the park was the Harbor Freeway, the 110, as it became the Pasadena heading north.

"The 110 used to be part of Route 66," Monk noted aloud.

"And?" Delilah asked.

"Nothing, really. Ornette had driven Route 66 into L.A. though."

"The address listed for DeZuniga at the time of the infraction is the one in Gallup," she added, walking out of the office.

"Maybe he was in town visiting relatives," Monk called out. He was not going to drive or fly to New Mexico on this vehicular McGuffin of a favor. His phone bill was going to be on him though, as he knew he was going to have to run down as many DeZunigas as he could to satisfy Mrs. Scott that he'd done what he could. His mother, he told himself, was going to hear about this for years to come. He marched into the rotunda to retrieve the white and yellow pages, and got busy.

Later, tired of getting answering machines, nadas, and busy signals from DeZuniga households in Gallup, he was glad to take a break. He drove his midnight blue 1964 Galaxie with its refitted 352-cubic-inch V-8 east on Washington Boulevard from his office in downtown Culver City. The carburetor had been running sluggish, but he hadn't had time to fool with the fuel mixture screws. At Cattaraugus he cut over to the Santa Monica Freeway and headed east. Driving in the fairly unobstructed early afternoon flow, he was happy to find the car's engine smoothed at a higher sustained speed.

Eventually Monk was on the 5 and took the exit in the City of Commerce. Following the directions, he wound up at the Southern California Buick Association headquarters a little before two in the afternoon. On time for the appointment he'd made. The headquarters was also the business address of Willy Serrano, a machine shop operator where they rebuilt car and truck engines. A boss black-and-white 1955 Special Riviera hardtop with the sporty mag rims sat in the slot marked owner. During the early to mid fifties, the Special Buick was the car to have among true believers.

Monk chatted with Serrano in his parts and paper-cluttered

office in the rear of the machine shop. Through the door the muffled sounds of lathes turning and metal being ground could be heard.

"I looked back in our membership records there, Ivan." Serrano was a large gregarious man who favored pointed cowboy boots, a western style shirt, and a buckle with his initial on it. A white Stetson with three 'Xs' on the band rested on top of a file cabinet.

"Sure enough, there was a Jessie DeZuniga in the club in the early 90s. He didn't renew for '94. I recall talking to him once or twice, I think. But I couldn't tell you why he didn't re-join."

A machinist stuck his head in, and said something in Spanish to Serrano. He answered in the same language and the door closed again.

Monk found out Jessie was in his early thirties and got the last known address for him. It was on Callumet in the Echo Park section, near Elysian Park. He thanked the man and drove back into Los Angeles. Nobody was home at the small frame house on Callumet.

He went over to Barrigan's restaurant on Sunset and had a late lunch, topped off with a Cadillac margarita, one made from the good tequila. Then he called his office from a pay phone. Delilah told him their back check on Ornette's SSN had turned up his employment record. She'd leave the report on his desk.

Afterward, he wandered along the shops on north Vermont, the happening avenue for this season. In the window of a clothing store called Red Ass Monkey, the female mannequin had larger than usual breasts straining her top. She was in a latex mini and thick soled studded boots astride a stuffed wild boar. Around six, he went back to the house. A cherry 1971 Camaro with fat rear tires was now in the driveway.

"Sorry, my friend," Jessie DeZuniga said, taking another swig on his beer at the door. The younger man had been home ten minutes from work, and was in his undershirt and blue work khakis. "Somewhere around here I kept the paperwork, but yeah, I sold the Buick about four years ago. It was a sweet car, I'll tell you, homes. But you know I already got one honey," he indicated his rebuilt Camaro, "plus two kids, and the old lady always going on about how I'm putting more money and attention into my dad's car than her."

He took another pull, then tipped the can at Monk's Ford. "But I guess you know something about that."

Monk nodded agreeably. "My old lady is always yapping about that too, but these are classics, right? A man has to have a hobby." Monk was lying. His significant other, Judge Jill Kodama, liked his Galaxie.

"Yeah," DeZuniga commiserated. One of his children, a young girl who must have been a third grader, popped up. "Pops, when you gonna fix dinner?" She averted her eyes from Monk when he smiled at her.

"Wife works nights," DeZuniga explained

"I'm going to let you handle your business, Jessie. Do you remember the name of the guy who bought it?"

"It was a woman, young, hip hop Chinese chick. Can't say what her name was now. She answered my ad in the Auto Trader, and made the best offer."

He'd already mentioned that his father had died. Monk asked as he stepped from the porch. "Do you know how your father acquired the Buick after Dolphy Ornette was shot?"

Jessie DeZuniga looked at Monk as if he'd grown a second head. "Don't you know? My father and Mr. Ornette knew each other from this Army base—I think it was in Alamogordo. Dad worked in a bar in town, and Mr. Ornette worked at the base, janitor or orderly, something like that. This wasn't the bar the Army people went to, either. This was the one the townspeople went to."

"Ornette must have been the only black man in there."

"He got along." DeZuniga opened the door wider and gestured with the can. "Look at this."

On a tan-colored rough-finished living room wall were several photos in what appeared to be hand-made wooden frames. DeZuniga pointed at one. The shot captured men and women, Chicano, white, and one black man who Monk presumed was Dolphy Ornette. All were sitting or standing at the bar.

"That's my father." He touched the can to a smiling bartender leaning on the bar, looking in the direction of the camera's lens. Ornette was a couple of stools down, raising his beer to the photographer. It was an afternoon because through the bar's windows Monk could make out the Buick and several other cars parked at an angle in front of the place. Beyond the cars in the distance were white gypsum mounds.

The backwards script painted on the front window was discernible too. Monk stared at it trying to decipher the Spanish words.

"Flor Silvestre," DeZuniga aided. "The Windflower Cantina.

"Anyway," DeZuniga continued, "the car was at our crib in Gallup months before my dad heard he got shot. Mr. Ornette had brought it there. At least that's what my dad had said; I wasn't even two when all this went on."

His daughter called him again and if he could find the papers, he said he'd call Monk. The PI returned to his office and Ornette's job history. The official record backed up what Mrs. Scott had related to him, that Ornette had worked in a PX supply depot in Denver. Yet there was that picture and what the younger DeZuniga had said. And Monk was no geographer; Denver might have white hills like New Mexico for all he knew.

At ten-thirty that evening, he had an answer for the discrepancy.

"Who was that on the phone?" Jill Kodama asked, handing him a tumbler of Johnny Walker Black and ice. They were in the study of the house they shared in Silverlake. Her name on the mortgage. One day, Monk figured, he'd get used to calling it his home, too. "One of your chippies, darling?" She turned on the TV.

"Information broker I use from time to time. His specialty is out-of-date locations. He confirms that the Flor Silvestre Cantina was in Alamogordo in the '50s, the time period Ornette told Lavinia Scott he was working in Colorado."

"What do you make of that?" she asked, interested.

Monk crossed his arms. "Maybe he left behind another girlfriend he didn't want Lavinia to know about. According to the sister—"

"The one that's going to pay you in pies."

"Uh-huh. She said her sister and Ornette broke up one afternoon after he'd returned from an errand in Pasadena. Whatever it was, it set something off, and Lavinia came home swearing she'd never have anything to do with that crazy man again. Her exact words."

Kodama flipped through channels. "She, that is Lavinia, say what was so crazy?"

"No; Mrs. Scott says she'd never talked about it, even when the two would be out and would chance to see Ornette."

"What happened to the sister?" She settled on the History Channel.

"You know, I never really asked her that? I assumed she died."

On the screen a mushroom cloud shot through with

colonized oranges and reds blossomed on screen as an off-screen narrator droned on about America's love/hate relation-ship with nuclear power. This image dissolved to one of '50s downtown L.A. fantastically backlit by a nuclear blast in the Nevada desert some 300 miles away as the narrator continued.

"The stealth bomber flies out of White Sands now," Kodama said, eyeing the explosion. "But in the '50s and '60s, nuclear testing used to go on there."

Monk made an exasperated sound. "And Roswell's in New Mexico, Jill. You think Ornette was a space alien? Was the car his disguised flying saucer and Verna Scott needs to go home?"

"Okay, smart ass, then why does the old girl want the car? Sentimental reasons? Why did Ornette conceal where he worked? Why take Route 66 when the way to drive from Alamogordo to here is a different highway. Unless he was backtracking to throw somebody off his trail. And why is it the Buick hasn't shown up on any of your checking since Jessie DeZuniga sold it?"

"Whoever bought it never bothered to get it registered. The Buick's probably sitting in some garage now, the tires going to rot, the gas in the tank turning to gum. The proud possession of a weekend shade tree mechanic who keeps telling himself any Saturday now he's gonna get back out there and get this bad boy running," Monk pontificated.

"Anyway, why does he fill in the gaps for me with that bit about his father and Ornette knowing each other and Ornette leaving the car with his dad?"

"Don't be naive, baby," Kodama responded. "You've done that with the cops. Give them enough of the truth you figure they'll find out one way or the other, but also hold back. That way they believe you, and don't look twice in your direction."

"And," she went on, "why didn't the DMV check you told

me you did when you got back to the office this evening produce a release certificate from Jessie DeZuniga?"

'It was a spot check going by the license plate. I don't have DeZuniga's social security number."

"He's the last known owner."

"You're much too suspicious for a judge."

"Press him for the paperwork. Because all the potential bugging your mother and Mrs. Scott are going to do if you leave it hanging will be curtailed."

Monk had to concede her logic.

Over the next several days he called DeZuniga several times and it was one excuse after the other as to what might have happened to those papers. As much as he bugged the younger man, the older Mrs. Scott was bothering him. Repeatedly asking about any leads. On Friday, Monk broke down.

"I'm concentrating on a guy named DeZuniga, okay?" Monk rubbed his face as he held the receiver to his ear.

"Can you spell that, dear, my hearing's not so good."

He could just picture her standing in her hot kitchen in her quilted house coat. He spelled the man's first and last name for her. And he assured her he'd have something to report by the end of the weekend. Like he was done with this one way or the other.   Monk had considered staking out DeZuniga in the evenings. But that meant again coming out of pocket and renting a regular car or at the least borrowing his sister's Honda civic as he'd done in the past. His '64 Ford was not what one would call a car that blended. Plus there was the impracticality of being a black man sitting night after night in a car in a Latino neighborhood, and not expect to get noticed.

Lastly, he hoped DeZuniga was being on the level when he said his wife worked nights, and that would curtail any movement by him until the weekend.

It did work out like that.

DeZuniga, the wife, and kids drove out to a small frame house in Whittier early Saturday morning. There, he went inside as his wife and kids waited in her Camry. About fifteen minutes later, he was backing out of the driveway behind the wheel of the 1953 red-and-black Buick Riviera Roadmaster. It sounded and looked new. The family then drove back to Echo Park. Monk following in the Civic belonging to his sister, a public high school teacher.

"Look man," he began, approaching a surprised DeZuniga in front of his house. "What you do with your car is your business. If you would just let this old lady, my client Mrs. Scott, see the car." Monk stopped walking so as not to be perceived as a threat. "I don't know why, but she's been—"

A Bell Cab pulled up to where they were. The driver got out and opened the door to let Mrs. Verna Scott out. She paid him and he departed.

Mrs. Scott looked in awe at the Buick.

The children were bothering their mother for something, and DeZuniga waved them inside.

"I didn't want to tell you I had it 'cause some others had been around asking about it around a year ago," Jessie DeZuniga said. 'They offered me all kinds of money, but something about them." He frowned. "I told them I'd already sold the car. They said they'd been away but had made it back and needed to have the Buick."

DeZuniga looked at the car longingly. "My dad made me promise for him to keep the car. Not to sell it, ever. Normally, I keep the Buick in my neighbor's garage down the street. But I moved it out to my cousin's that first night you were here.

"And my constant calling got you jumpy."

"Yeah. That time a year ago when these dudes showed up, the car just happened to be out at my cousin's pad."

"Where you went this morning?"

"Uh-huh. At that time he was redoing the upholstery. I knew they didn't believe I'd sold the car. I spotted them keeping watch on the house. But I out-waited them, and finally they went away. Now, I was going to drive it to Moreno Valley, and leave it with my sister-in-law."

Monk was thinking about Ornette's unsolved murder. And that he'd given the car to DeZuniga's father as if he'd anticipated someone would be coming after him. "What did these men look like?"

"X-files types, you know. Creepy, pasty-faced white boys. Big overcoats, hands in pockets, lips didn't move and shit."

Monk was about to ask more questions but the gun in Mrs. Scott's hand got his and DeZuniga's attention. It wasn't much of a gun, but it could sting.

"Open the trunk, please," she asked forcefully.

Bemused, DeZuniga did so.

"My sister would lay awake nights telling me—" Verna Scott didn't finish her sentence. Like a mouse to cheese, she went to the now open trunk compartment. Monk and DeZuniga got in position to watch her.

"Ain't nothing back there but the spare and a tool box," DeZuniga offered.

The old girl was halfway in the trunk. "Dolphy showed it to her and it scared her. It was too much for her then. Years later," she grunted with effort, "she always regretted she didn't help him sell it."

"Sell what?" Monk moved forward to get a better look.

"But who would buy it?" she said to herself. "He found out the thing was more trouble than it was worth. But by then, he couldn't turn it in either without going to jail forever. Here it is, here's the latch."

Monk and DeZuniga moved forward to see what she was doing.

Suddenly a brilliant glow shot from the trunk. Mrs. Scott's wiggling form was swallowed in the light. Tendrils seem to be snapping like whips from the pulsation.

"What the hell is that?" DeZuniga shouted, shielding his eyes. Sound seemed to be evaporating.

"Your dad never mentioned this?" Monk tried to move but it was as if some kind of heavy gravity were weighing him down. He and the other man sank to their knees.

"What the hell's going on?" The scintilla throbbed in his ears and he felt as if his heart was going to stop. Monk's world was a white hot essence where he couldn't tell up or down, back or front.

There was an even brighter flash, then birds could be heard chirping again in the morning air. The two got their orientation back; the Buick and Mrs. Scott were gone.

The uniforms who questioned them peered at them doubtfully. The story was they'd been car-jacked by an old lady with a peashooter. Later, the plainclothes went over and over the story with them separately at Ramparts Division. Unswerving, they kept to their version of the truth. Each had agreed before DeZuniga had called the law not to mention the light thing. They didn't directly talk about it when they were finally let go seven hours later.

"Sorry about the Buick, that was a beautiful car, man." Monk shook DeZuniga's hand.

"Yeah. Think my dad and Mr. Ornette knew this would happen?"

Monk didn't have an answer. Didn't want to even consider one.

• • •

Route 66 stretched before them, the stars overhead like tiny

115

pin pricks of light in an ebony cloth. The moon full and incandescent. Ornette Dolphy, his Flechet perched at an angle, was at the wheel and Lavinia Scott rode beside him. In the back seat of the '53 Buick Roadmaster were Verna Scott and Delfuensio DeZuniga. On the roadway some had called the mother, and others *Camino de la muerte,* the four drove on and on. Before them lay hope and knowledge and the road. But they didn't drive with haste; they went as if they had all the time in the world to get there.

The Desecrator

"I should'a doubled down on the queen."

"That's right, baby."

Irked by his shallow solicitousness, Jill Kodama replied, "You weren't exactly seven against the house yourself, Ivan."

"Sure you right."

Monk and Kodama waited for the light at the crosswalk as a shuttle bus rounded the corner in front of them.

"But I did win enough tickets in the New York, New York arcade to get you this, baby." He jiggled the small purple and white Koala Bear in her face.

She gave him a peck on the cheek and they walked across the street to the Park One lot stationed on the periphery of the Los Angeles International Airport.

"And we did catch Tony Bennett's show and he was swinging to the rafters," Monk said glowingly.

"It was sweet, this getaway." She smiled and patted his butt as they walked with their bags to her Saab convertible. "It was definitely a surprise you suggesting we get away for a couple of days in Vegas. Not that you're predictable so much as you're, well, steady." She glanced at him quickly.

"Steady." He said the word as if it were new to him. "Is that a way of calling me boring?"

The couple arrived at her car. "No," she said slowly. "You know you're the rock, honey."

"Gettin' to be the old rock," Monk said, grunting some as he hefted the luggage into the trunk after she undid the lock.

Kodama mushed his lower jaw in one of her hands, putting

her face close to his. "Yeah, I have noticed more grey whiskers in the morning."

"Who's driving?"

"I guess I better, Pops, so you can rest."

He patted her butt with his left and closed the trunk with his right.

"Kick on the AC," he said getting in the passenger seat. "That damned heat wave is still in full effect."

"You ain't never lied," she said, flipping the air conditioner on after turning over the engine.

They came out of the exit after paying and Kodama took a left down a curving two-lane path.

"I think you should have gone right to get us onto 96th Street," Monk observed, hunkered low in his seat, his eyes half-closed.

"I hate it when you're right. Well, we'll wind through this part of the airport and I'll whip us out onto Century." She proceeded to do so, the Saab passing by the Theme Building located in the center of the busy airport. It was a structure like something out of an old Jetsons' cartoon, an enclosed saucer-shaped upper portion supported by four equidistant columns that rose from the ground, reaching an apex above the circular part. Inside the saucer was a restaurant called the Encounter that was a hip spot for the retro crowd complete on club nights with a mix-master DJ.

"That looks cool," Kodama commented as they drove past. She was referring to the purple and soft blue floodlights that illuminated the underside of the arching columns.

Monk allowed his resting eyes to flutter open, but it wasn't the effects of the lighting that made him more attentive. There was a tall gaunt figure moving out from behind one of the columns. The man paused, looking up at the blood red lights playing on the underside of the Theme Building, one hand held to his chest. The figure was dressed in a light grey pullover with large silver buttons in a diagonal along the front and matching pants. His brush-cut hair was the same hue as his outfit. His other arm and hand were outstretched in the direction he was looking, like he was grasping for something in the hot, still air.

"Whatever," Monk mumbled to himself, summing up the odd tableau as Kodama guided them away from the man and the building, the seeming object of his desire.

Two days later Monk was on one knee replacing the left front inner bearing and race on his '64 Ford Galaxy. The front end of the car was up on jack stands in the grease bay of the Alton Brothers Automotive Repair and Service garage. Curtis Armstrong—no relation to the long deceased trio of Alton Brothers—current co-owner of the establishment, tapped Monk on the shoulder.

"Moms," Armstrong said in a small voice that did not go with his over-sized body. He held a cordless phone. Monk wiped his hands on a shop rag and took the phone.

"Hey," Monk said into the instrument.

"The bastards have done it, Ivan."

Forty minutes later Monk saw what the bastards had done to the Biddy Mason Salon on East 76th Street a few doors west of San Pedro. The Salon was a club house located in a converted two-story Spanish Colonial Revival with angular touches set back from the street on a wide lawn behind towering poinsettia bushes. The individuals who belonged to the club were older black women who, like Monk's mother, an RN, had worked in some trained professional capacity: mid-level bureaucrats who worked for the city, fellow sorority members, and the like.

"One of your members want revenge from the last bid whist tournament y'all had?" Monk was poking around in what

119

remained of the built-in sideboard the sledgehammer had demolished. A sideboard like the house, that was, or had been, more than sixty years old. The intruder or intruders had used a sledgehammer to bust up the china cabinet, punched ragged holes in several of the plaster and lathe walls, and destroyed the ancient tile in the upstairs bathroom.

"That's not funny," his mother advised him in a sharp voice. Monk was crouching down now, examining the locks on the front and screen doors. "I'm sorry." He straightened up, pointing at the lock mechanism. "The cops said the doors hadn't been forced and the alarm had been by-passed?"

His mother was staring at the pieces of the now useless Beleek china set. A collection older than the house. "Yes," she said distractedly, kicking at a chunk of plate. "We've maintained this place a long time, Ivan. It's survived both riots and had only minimal damage during the Northridge quake. Now these gangbangers or crackheads or whoever just come strolling in and for no good reason tear up somebody else's property."

"Jealous little punks," Paula Caldwell piped in. She was the current club president and had been upstairs, looking at the damage to the bathroom there.

Monk wanted to say something comforting, but knew it would come out wrong.

"The officers who took the report this morning, after I insisted they send one of their lazy butts out and not write it up over the phone, said there was probably little that could be done." Nona Monk put her hands on her hips in a disgusted manner.

Monk had his arm around her shoulders. "I know it's rough, mom."

"Vandalism, they said; not that big a priority, they said."

Caldwell shook her head for sympathy from her sister club member.

Monk had to agree, but again silence was the smartest move. He turned his head, hoping for something to break the tension. He noticed the cylindrical showcase cabinet standing in the corner of the front room. The cabinet contained various memorabilia and photographs of Biddy Mason. She had been born a slave, but had successfully sued for her freedom upon coming west to L.A. Subsequently, she did quite well in real estate, and her sons ran a stable out of her property in what became downtown on Spring Street.

"They didn't mess with this though." Monk pointed at the cabinet.

His mother and Caldwell shrugged their shoulders in unison. "Only because they didn't have time," Nona Monk replied. "Mrs. Lewis next door heard some noise from over here and had set Beasly, her German Shepherd, out into her yard. While he stood at their fence barking this way, she hollered she was calling the police."

"Good thing them fools was probably high on malt liquor and weed and whatever," Caldwell declared. "They must have gotten nervous and lit out of here."

"Yet they remained calm enough to go back out the way they came. You told me the back door was still secure when you two came in this morning."

"Liquor and dope makes you do funny things," Caldwell concluded. "You must know that."

Monk took in the downstairs again. One of the walls next to the cabinet had been plowed into, less than five inches from the showcase.

"I guess there really isn't much you can do, Ivan," his mother said in a resigned voice. "I just wanted to feel better by asking you to come over."

"Who knows?"

Caldwell bored fatigued eyes into him as if he were slow-witted. "That's all you can come up with, mister private investigator?"

He slunk away, suitably chastised and chagrined.

Two days after that, a woman in a Liz Claiborne ensemble was found taped to the south wall of the Odd Fellows Temple Building No. 3 on Oak Street near downtown. Her name, according to the news reports, was Helen Mouton Abell and she was a resident of Newport Beach, a tony Orange County enclave some sixty miles away from the Odd Fellows Temple.

Abell was alive and had been found by a janitor on his way home to Pico Union early in the morning. The *L.A. Times* piece in the Metro section related that she'd apparently been drugged and taken from a restaurant's parking lot in her community where she'd been dining with friends the previous evening.

"It says that as far as she knows, the dazed and confused woman can think of no one in her family who is an Odd Fellow." Kodama continued to read the piece. "A social and benevolent society that originated in England in the 18th Century."

"Maybe the Odd Fellows are hooked up in the nefarious history with the Masons and the Illuminati. And this woman is really their high priestess." Monk swirled the Johnny Walker Black in his tumbler, grinning.

Kodama slapped his leg with the folded Metro section, and tossed the paper onto the coffee table. The photo accompanying the article showed the cordoned-off area where the woman had been plastered with massive amounts of duct tape. Shreds of the material still clung to the wall. An outline around her body had been delineated by holes punched into the wall of the building with a sledgehammer.

Monk wasn't paying attention as he settled on the couch to watch a rerun of "Hawaii 5-O" on the Family Channel. Steve McGarrett had his hair thing going on.

The following late afternoon Monk was helping Elrod, the six-foot-eight solid mass of man manager of Continental Donuts, finish the batter for the devil's food donuts to be deep fried in the early morning hours. In the front of the shop, an establishment Monk owned next door to Armstrong's garage, he could hear the TV going. It was a small portable that Elrod had installed on a shelf he'd erected over the front counter.

"Gotta stay up with the times, boss," he'd opined to Monk a few weeks ago. "The regulars say it adds a nice, friendly touch."

"They could show their gratitude by buying something once in a while other than taking up space and generating hot air," Monk had countered.

"Aw, chief, you ain't gone capitalist, have you?"

What could he say to that? The TV remained.

Monk and Elrod finished and put the mixture away in the industrial refrigerator. They wandered up front. Andrade, a sometime accountant and full time horse handicapper and boozer, was perched at the counter. He had a folded racing form before him, several possibilities circled in heavy pencil. Abe Carson, carpenter and contractor, was also in attendance.

Both men were watching "Final Deadline," one of the daily tabloid shows that had fully realized the Huxleyan concept of infotainment. On screen, an attractive woman in a lacy black bra and hot pink panties was bent over a disassembled computer hard drive, an electronic meter in her purple nailed hand.

"What the hell?" Monk exclaimed.

"A new computer repair service called Beauty Bytes," Andrade absently commented.

123

"Uh," Monk grunted as he and Elrod also became enraptured by the fascinating angle of the segment.

There was a commercial break and Kelly Drier, the aging surfer boy anchor of the five o'clock news, offered a few teasers for what was coming up on his broadcast.

"Last night in Boyle Heights, the birthplace home of famed Southland Chicano labor leader Joaquin Accero was partially destroyed by an intruder. And we will check in with the five honor students from Muni High. All this plus sports and weather in less than a half hour."

Monk was talking about that incident with Kodama after dinner at the house they shared in the lower Silverlake Hills.

"They could be hate crimes," Kodama commented, slipping effortlessly into her judicial tone. "Abell, the woman who was abducted, is Jewish."

"A threefer," Monk commented coldly. "But this guy or guys don't scrawl any epithets or spray paint nazi swastikas on the places they've hit. If it is the same people."

"There is one way to find out, Chester Drum."

"And redeem myself in the eyes of my mother and her doubting club president."

"Most important," she laughed.

The next morning, after an introduction by Paula Caldwell, Monk had a leisurely chat with retired principal Mrs. Hattie Lewis. She was the woman who lived next door to the Biddy Mason Salon.

"Yes, Nona has mentioned your sister is a teacher, too." Mrs. Lewis shifted her thin frame in a sun bleached wing-chair.

"Yes, she enjoys her work despite the heavy-handed bureaucracy of the school district."

"I know what you mean," she empathized, sipping her coffee.

"Mrs. Lewis," Monk went on, setting aside his own cup, "did you see anything the night of the break-in?"

"As I told your mother and Paula, honey, I was too scared to stick my head out, hearing that commotion like I did."

"You acted, Mrs. Lewis, that's much more than many."

"Well," she demurred at the compliment.

"How about anything that day? Anybody hanging around out of the usual?"

"Oh, I saw a few young men hanging near the corner when I drove back from the market," she pointed west, "but I know one of them works at that Staples in Culver City." She shook her head. "They're not the hoodlum type if you know what I mean."

"I understand." He rose, "I may be back, Mrs. Lewis, once I've talked to a few others."

"Sure," she said offering her hand. Something else passed behind her eyes.

"What is it, Mrs. Lewis?" Monk asked delicately.

"The young men, that is why they were hanging around, what they were looking at."

Monk stepped closer. "Yes, Mrs. Lewis."

"Honey, they were looking at a pristine hope-to-die clean as a preacher's collar LaSalle."

"You sure about that?"

"Mister," she began, leaning forward, "my late first husband Robert Qualles had inherited a LaSalle from an uncle after the war. We had that car for more than ten years. I'm telling you, that was a '39 or '40 LaSalle parked right here on 76th Street that day. I believe forty or forty-one was the last year they made them."

Nineteen-forty, Monk knew. "And you haven't seen it since?"

"No," she answered, shaking her head.

Monk tried to reach someone from the small museum inside

125

the frame house Joaquin Accero's birthplace had been turned into, but had no luck. The house had been declared a historic landmark by the National Registry after several community organizations on L.A.'s Eastside had demanded recognition for the home through petitions and demonstrations. But full time staffing was a luxury the place could not afford.

Next he tried vainly to reach Helen Abell. After his third call, the last two to her home machine whose number he'd obtained backtracking through federal tax records, he got a call back from her lawyer Elliot Morgenthau. He stated unequivocally she would be unavailable for some time.

"Before she passed out, did she get a glimpse of what kind of vehicle she was taken away in?" Monk asked the lawyer, grasping for anything.

"What is it that you know, Mr. Monk?" The lawyer tried to hide his inquisitiveness behind his demanding tone.

"Okay, you don't want to tell me, that's fine, Mr. Morgenthau. Though I'm sure her vague description wasn't enough for the cops to go on."

Monk pretended to be hanging up but was actually listening silently.

"Mr. Monk," Morgenthau boomed.

"I'm here."

"There is something, not much, but maybe something. But you must guarantee to me that if you find anything out, I am to know immediately."

"Without hesitation."

"Helen was groggy you understand, about to go under as this mumzer dragged her away."

"I understand."

"Helen told me as she gamely struggled; she thought he was taking her toward a car behind a row of hedges like one from an old movie premiere." A few beats went by. "She said

126

too his hair was grey, cut like he was in the Army, she said, or at least what she surmised such haircuts to look like. Well?"

"You've been a great help, and maybe you'll hear from me soon." He hung up.

On top of the empty filing cabinet in the corner of his office he'd placed an oak cigar box detailed in pale yellow ivory. He opened the container and removed and lit a Jose Marti torpedo. Monk sat on the batik-cloth-covered couch, smoking and ruminating. Okay, the nut drove around in a LaSalle. He doubted if there were enough of the classic cars left around to have an association, though he would check anyway. The other consistency was the fact the man had hit racially specific landmarks.

No, correct that, two of the targets fit that explanation. The Odd Fellows hall was, for all intents and purposes, a "white" establishment, although maybe because of their inclusive policies that's why the place was on his list. And for some reason Helen Abell had been specifically taped to its wall. Whatever system of convoluted logic this dufus was using, the Odd Fellows fit in his scheme.

What then, among the numerous designated and unofficial historically significant places in and around Los Angeles, would the man, this desecrator, hit next? How to whittle down the possibilities. Monk puffed and blew smoke at a fly buzzing near his head. He smoked some more. What had Morgenthau added? He'd said Helen had mentioned the guy's brush cut grey hair. Monk got off the couch and walked over to the window. It wasn't much, but what else did he have in the way of a lead?

• • •

The Los Angeles Airport went through a post WWII

modernization from 1957-61. Among the innovations the design team of the offices of architects William Pereira, Welton Becket, and Paul R. Williams came up with was the saucer and spidery curved columned Theme Building and the since-demolished Standard Service station that repeated the look.

Interestingly, Paul R. Williams was a black architect who enjoyed a successful career designing work for clients ranging from First African Methodist Episcopal Church to Frank Sinatra. He even did homes in areas where he wasn't allowed to live. Monk had a lot of time to read material he'd gathered on the places previously attacked and the one structure he'd seen the grey-haired man adoring. It turned out the house that his mother's club was in was designed by Irving Gill, an architect of local reputation in the formative years of Los Angeles. Three nights of reading by a Sharper Image book light and staking out the Theme Building at LAX in his car finally came to fruition.

The heat wave had broken and it was a cool night with winds off the nearby ocean as Monk spotted the man coming from around one of the columns of the Theme Building. He was dressed in a conservative grey suit and matching shirt, and black tie. The stranger gazed at the underside of the building's saucer as if he'd just discovered a new star in the firmament.

Monk had gotten out of the car because maneuvering around the circular parking lot in his Ford would be too unwieldy and obvious. But the man was already moving away across the parking lot, going in a north-east direction. Beyond the lot was a parking structure with short-term meters. Monk had to hope he guessed right because he turned around and got back into his Ford. He piloted the Galaxie along a lane next to the Theme Building's parking lot after he'd paid at the exit. There were a Blazer and an Infiniti coming out of the metered lot and he fought disappointment and anxiety as he looked around. There, on the roadway toward Sepulveda north, was the LaSalle. Even from the rear, the classy car's sloping rear was unmistakable. Particularly since he'd taken time to study a 3-D model he'd located on a website.

They drove north down the wide thoroughfare of Sepulveda, neon announcing liquor, nudes, and bowling flashing by. Monk was not too concerned if the man spotted him now. He'd already made a note of the license number and he planned to turn it over to Morgenthau and have him work the cops to follow up.

At Manchester the LaSalle went left and Monk hung back four car lengths after making the turn. Heading west, they passed the barren stretches and industrial parks of Playa Del Rey. At an unlit side street the La Salle took a right. A jet clamored off the LAX runway not too far way, angling over the blood dark Pacific. Monk followed the LaSalle to a three-story squarish building on the edge of the Ballona Wetlands. It was a narrow street of threadbare trees, small frame houses with overgrown lawns and pieces missing from leaning picket fences. And this building at the end of a steel and concrete overhang looking out on the Wetlands below.

The LaSalle parked under a leaning carport on the side. The man got out and entered the front through a steel door he unlocked. Monk had parked diagonally across from the man but was sure he'd been made. He got out, zipping up his light windbreaker against the damp wind wafting off the nearby sea. He walked across the street. All right, he'd come this far. The building looked like it'd been a hotel at one point, a faded name in paint unreadable across the top floor of the thing. Its residents were long gone or long dead.

The front door had been re-locked. Unlike TV detectives, Monk had no idea how to pick a lock. He went around back and then to one side of the place. There was a painted over window behind a set of bars. The bars were old-fashioned, the bolt heads facing out from the brick they were screwed into. Monk used a socket set from his trunk and got the bars off as quietly as possible. An oblique light showed through a window on the third floor. Using a screwdriver with a long shaft, he worked the doubled sash window and pried it loose after knocking a small hole in the top pane.

He came into what had once been the joint's heat room. There were several non-functioning gravity furnaces with asbestos covered tubes snaking from them up into the floor. There was also a row of rotting water heaters along one wall. But Monk could hear one furnace going on this cool evening, the light from its burner quite evident in the gloom. He moved toward the door, snapping on a pen light. He undid the door and in the same instant felt the tug of the wire on the knob. Counter-intuitively, he went forward through the opening, not backward. A glass container shattered where he'd been standing. It was acid and it bubbled voraciously on the concrete floor.

"Slick bastard," Monk rasped, breathing hard. Cautiously, he proceeded toward the stairwell at the end of the hallway he'd stepped into. He got to the stairs and used his light to shine on the wooden steps, a worn carpet ascending along its center. If he had a devious mind, one or more of those steps would be booby-trapped. Of course it was the only way up, so he had little choice.

He took the screwdriver with its long shaft out of his back pocket and used that as a probe. It wasn't much, but it was what he had. Each tread of the stairs groaned and sagged from age as he went up. Monk was crouched low, the small flashlight shut off. No sense giving his adversary too clean a target. He was about half way up, the screwdriver jabbing at the next immediate level of the stairs. This plank felt springier than the others had been. Monk jabbed down with the screwdriver, trying to exert enough force like it was his foot coming down.

He heard a whoosh and his arm fell through an opening, the screwdriver dropping from his now loose hand. The PI clicked on the light, and there, beneath the swirling dust motes was a rectangular maw where part of the stairs had been. Inside the maw, about three feet down, was a platform of metal spikes. A taut grin pulled his lips back and Monk stepped over the opening and continued his ascent, trying his best to feel his way with the toe of his shoe.

Almost to the landing, he briefly clicked on the light, sweeping it side-to-side and up and down. There was a hallway with a railing going right and left, doors marked with numbers along each way. He switched the light off. Anyway, for all he knew the man had hidden cameras with night vision capabilities trained on him at that moment. But such speculation would only freeze him up and he needed to keep moving. Concentrating, he visualized something that had . . . flickered when the light had shined.

Using both hands, the light tucked under his arm, Monk scraped and scooped dust from the stairs into his palm. With the light back on, Monk blew the dust into the air over the landing. There was a brief gleaming of a silver wire at chest height. He stepped back down and snapped his light windbreaker at the wire. Twin shotgun blasts took out the corner of the banister.

Monk bounded up the steps and dove to the left. Given the layout of the place, he figured the next set of stairs would be in that direction. He got up and went slowly along the hallway, the flooring very solid. No trap doors, yet.

Monk turned on his flashlight again.

131

Hung between the room doors were framed photographs, head and shoulder shots of men and women. He paused, looking the black and whites over. From his recent studies of buildings and architects, he recognized Paul R. Williams, Gregory Ain—who designed portions of affordable housing in Mar Vista after the war—and Alice Constance Austin, who designed Llano Del Rio in the high desert of the Mojave.

Del Rio was a planned utopian community that Job Harriman, the man who was cheated of being L.A.'s first socialist mayor in 1911, and others intended as a grand experiment in cooperative living. Intercine politics and the *L.A. Times* saw to its demise. Realizing he was spending too much time contemplating an unobtainable past, he turned and, in the same instant, switched off the flashlight at what he saw. It didn't matter, a dog's sense of smell is what?—a hundred, two-hundred, times greater than a human's? It doesn't need to see him that well to get at him.

The animal, a pit bull, had been standing in the hall, next to the room it had walked out of, glaring at Monk. The dog's goddamn eyes seem to catch the weak moonlight through the window at the end of the hall. The pit was unnaturally calm. Monk didn't have his jacket, as it had been blown to shreds by the shotgun blasts. His screwdriver had dropped into the trap on the stairs. And his gun? That was back at the house. How much trouble could a guy with a sledge hammer be?

The dog scrambled forward and Monk kicked at it, trying to drive it back. That only made the little bastard angrier. The thing's hinged jaws snapped at his lower leg and Monk ran toward the end of the hall. The dog was on him, its teeth raking his calves. Monk had been working his belt loose and got it off. The pit bull was barking and snarling and it leaped at his groin. Monk cracked his belt like a bull whip on its head.

Of course the belt didn't really hurt it, but it did get the dog's attention. He whipped at the pit some more, the leather stinging the dog's thick muscles. The animal got its teeth locked onto the end of the belt, as Monk hoped it would. With both hands he swung the belt and dog up and over the railing and let go. The mongrel dropped down onto the first floor.

Monk went up the second set of stairs. Fuck the traps, he was going to get this over with. Seriously sweating, he got to the third floor landing. There was a light under room 302. He hesitated touching the knob. Maybe it was coated with a fast-acting poison. Maybe on the other side was enough C-4 rigged to blow him and the building to Sri Lanka. Maybe, maybe. He twisted the brass knob and he stepped into another city.

Or at least it was a cardboard and balsa wood model of a city created from the imagination of the man sitting on the far side of the model. Only the lower portion of his legs were visible in the circle of the overhead light.

"I never did like that dog." His voice was without inflection, sheet metal smooth.

Monk moved more into the room, his eyes alternately examining the model and straining to see the grey man.

"She barely tolerated me, turning her nose up at the special meals I prepared for her like they were table scraps."

"Pits have been known to turn on their owners." Monk went to his right into semi-darkness, calculating if the other man had a pistol trained on him.

"Still," the man flicked a wrist and hand, "dogs on the whole are so much more trustworthy than humans."

The city was laid out in much the same way Thomas

Jefferson had helped diagram D.C. But at the center of this design was the Theme building of LAX. Radiating out from that was a radius of tall angular structures, a ring of park land, mid-sized structures, a disk of a lake, then the outer area done in what Monk presumed were single family homes. The whole of it seemed to have been inspired from the likes of Frank Lloyd Wright, Richard Neutra, and Wallace Neff.

"All clean and orderly," Monk noted, walking around the saucer of a city on the floor. There were no model cars on the streets, and only a few miniature people. "That why you wanted to destroy the landmarks, not part of your plan?"

The man stood up and Monk's jaw bunched. "They were corrupted from their true purposes."

"The Odd Fellows Hall was built to be just that."

"Her father was the lawyer who robbed the true builder of that edifice of his inheritance."

"And the Theme Building? It's a restaurant these days." He wanted to keep him talking as he got closer.

"That too shall be made to right."

The man clicked on more lights. The room was bereft of dividing walls with only the large model in the center of the floor. A futon was located in the corner, and black scrim had been adhered to the windows. The only other furniture was an old schoolhouse wooden chair the man had been sitting on. He barely blinked as he stared at Monk.

"I shall be realized." The man stepped to one side to reveal two heavy pry bars leaning on a side wall.

"Fine," Monk said softly.

The man picked up one of the pry bars and stepped back several paces. Monk picked up the other one.

"I must be younger than you by at least ten years," Monk said, readying himself. "Plus I'm heavier. How about we just go without fuss or muss?"

134

"Hah," and an overhand swipe at his head was what he got for a reply.

Anticipating that, Monk was already ducking and countered with an upward thrust at the man's breadbasket. But the cocksucker was quick and dove out the way.

Monk swung like Mark McGwire but the man was reacting too. Their pry bars met, the clangs reverberating up each of their arms. The grey man was first to recover; clearly he'd been practicing. He caught Monk on the side of his deltoid with the pry bar as the detective tried to get out of the way.

Monk sank to a knee, the pain spreading through his body like fever. He felt more than saw the iron coming for him and went flat at the last moment. The bar banged down on the back of his legs and he let loose with a howl. He twisted around and blocked the follow-up swing arcing toward his head. On sheer will he pushed back and forced his way up, his arms and legs shaking with effort. The grey man bore down, a single-minded desire guiding his actions.

The pry bars came apart and the gaunt man did a fast uppercut with the flat end of his. The edge gouged Monk's chin as he reared back. Doing his best to compartmentalize the burning sensation engulfing his face, Monk bent his torso and leveraged the pry bar like he was using a rifle butt. He caught the other man in the chest, staggering him back.

Sweat was stinging his eyes and his heart was beating too fast, but Monk pressed his advantage. The pry bars shook as they met again. Monk unexpectedly relaxed his hold, the other man suddenly off-balance. As he stumbled closer, Monk delivered a blow to his kidney, then a punch to the side of the man's face. He then jabbed him with the round end of the bar right over the bridge of the man's nose.

Dazed, his eyes blinking rapidly, the grey man dropped the

bar and toppled over onto his city, demolishing the Theme
Building.

• • •

"They say his name is Sirus Gerhardt, and he used to work
for the Department of Building and Safety as a senior
inspector."

Monk leaned his head back as he sat in the sauna of the
Tiger's Den, willfully soaking the moist heat into his bruises.
Tiger Flowers, a former Golden Gloves champ who'd served
in Korea with Monk's deceased father, peered closer at the
folded newspaper he was holding. He stood in the cracked
doorway to the sauna. Beyond it were the sounds of hopeful
young men and one woman pushing their bodies to attempt
careers in the fighter's game.

"The article say why he nutted up?" Monk rubbed the arm
that Gerhardt had banged with the pry bar.

Tiger read some more. How he could see the page given
the swirling steam amazed Monk. "They don't seem to be
sure. He was always a good worker, never missed a day, all
that shit." He looked up at Monk, a seriousness composing
his features. "You did good, Ivan. Seems the court appointed
psychiatrist is of the opinion Gerhardt was getting bolder and
bolder. Pretty soon, they figured, he would have started killing
anybody who got in his way of his . . . dream."

Monk nodded imperceptibly.

"This article also says Gerhardt never seemed to have many
friends from work or a woman in his life." Tiger slapped the
paper against his thigh. "Man gets too much, like say Clinton,
or he don't get enough, either way I guess it's gonna trip you
up or make you go off your rocker."

With that cogent observation, Tiger left, closing the door behind him.

Monk stretched out on the wooden bench, laughing softly.

The Sleeping Detective

M onk wasn't quite himself. His arms swung loose at his
sides as the heels of his brown wingtips echoed in the
long hallway. The corridor stretched underneath Los Angeles
International Airport. It was the last old part of the sprawling
facility, constructed in 1961 and still connecting the TWA
terminal with the outside. Wait, he asked himself, what year
is this anyway?

His heels clacked a rhythmic pattern as Monk, no, it was
McGill, yeah, his name was McGill, and it was 1967, strode
confidently along the tiled passageway. The walls were also
covered in tile, done in multi-colored linear designs.

McGill cared nothing about style or theories of architecture.
He cared nothing that he'd been double-crossed and left for
dead in a wind-blown shack in the Tehachapis. He projected
little about what willful fate had spared him the grave after
being shot twice, point blank. No, the only thing McGill cared
about was getting back the $67,000 owed to him. And if he
had to do it over the bodies of his best friend Veese and his
wife, Jill, so be it.

McGill's tie herked and jerked as his tall fluid frame pounded
toward the end of the corridor. His face was as empty of
emotion as the hallway was devoid of other passengers. His
close cropped prematurely grey hair complimented his crisp
Brooks Brothers suit. The muscles in his legs flawlessly

propelled him toward the end of the passageway and closer to his goal.

'S funny, but he didn't ache from the wounds, the holes his dear darling had lovingly put in him, while her boyfriend, Veese, the guy he'd saved once on a job gone wrong, looked on, licking his lips. If McGill were the chatty sort, and he wasn't, he'd be vague on the details of how he got out of that below-freezing cabin that night and got himself healed up.

Suddenly he was no longer in the airport. The echo of his shoes now blended in with the sounds of mid-day traffic. The sun was bright and glinted off the windshield of the new Biscayne he'd stolen as he parked on a rise. He removed the hand shading his eyes. Up there past that wall and shrubs was the door to their love nest. If he could've still remembered how to smile, he would have.

Now he was moving across the threshold, the .357 Magnum in his right hand. His left hand was in Jill's face, pushing her back and out of his way. She'd been so shocked upon seeing him that all she could do was whisper his name over and over. Not that it mattered to him if she called out Veese's name. He wanted *him* to step into the crosshairs.

Everything–his motion, her falling, the door banging back –happened in slow motion, defying logic and the laws of gravity. He kicked in the door to the bedroom, aiming and firing in the same heartbeat that thudded in his throat. The recoil of the pistol made his arm twitch. It wasn't his .45, and absently he wondered why he'd traded that for this bruiser. He emptied the gun's six bullets into the unmade and unattended bed. He whirled as real time jumped back on track.

"A ghost, an avenging specter." Jill had a hand to her forehead as if she were fevered. "McGill, I–" she couldn't finish, didn't dare to offer an excuse.

He stood there, spent, close on her, and despite himself that familiar feeling flooded over him, if only momentarily. He pointed the gun barrel at the bed. "Where?"

"Gone."

"How long?"

"Months. He stops by every so often. Sends money by courier each month."

"When?"

"Today, later."

He glanced back at the bed. Behind the headboard was a floor to ceiling mirror so Veese could watch himself as they made love. On the nightstand was a box. It was open and on its side he read Continental Donuts.

He turned back to her as they sat on the couch. For some reason, his eyes were closed and he couldn't get the lids to lift. . . .

"Ivan," she said, kissing his ear. "Ivan, when did you get in, baby?"

He yawned, his arms encircling the pillow. "Ummm," he drooled, "after five." He lay half-awake, the details of the dream fleeing his conscious mind.

Jill Kodama got off the bed, rubbing the back of his head. "I didn't hear you get in. You must have driven straight from New Mexico after I talked to you yesterday."

"Wanted to get home, sleep."

She leaned over and kissed his cheek. She smelled like flowers. "Aren't you a bit perfumed up for a judge?"

"You want me to smell like cigars and Old Spice like *you* do?" She slapped his butt under the blanket. "I'll call you later, see if you want to come downtown for dinner. Let's try Ciudad. The Veese case I'm trying is about wrapped up."

"Is he guilty?"

"That's for a jury to decide, citizen Monk."

He opened an eye, a kraken awakening from the depths. "Is he guilty?"

She was at the door to their bedroom. "I'd say he has blood on his hands. Call you." She left and he tried to get back to sleep. After some effort, as his body wound down again, the phone rang, and rang, and rang.

"Boss, somebody's been puttin' the nab on our donuts."

It was Elrod, the manager of Continental Donuts, the small business he owned in the Crenshaw District. Elrod's bass was an indication of the size of a man who'd give Jesse Ventura palpitations.

"You mean some cat broke in and took our donuts but not cash?" he breathed into the handset. Why wouldn't they let him sleep?

"No," the manager boomed, irritated. "For the last week glazes, fancy twists, maple and chocolate crullers and jellied-filled have been gettin' filched while the shop's been open. Sixty-seven, I counted. Sixty-seven donuts have been taken."

Monk was going to question just how the big man could be so exact in his count, but he didn't want to encourage a long discussion. He coughed, clearing his throat and rolling onto his back. "You have suspects?" He scratched himself.

"Well," Elrod rumbled on the other end, "I hate to say it, but it has to be one of the staff. The inventory has been gettin' filched off the racks as the goods cool in the back."

"You mean the new guy, Moises, right."

"Aw, see, I don't want to say that for sure." Elrod, like Monk, had been born and raised in the 'hood. Unlike Monk he was also an ex-con and was sensitive to the notion of disparaging someone trying to be responsible.

The new guy was a young man from the area where the shop was located. For the last two months, since he'd begun, there had been no suggestion of problems with him. If

141

anything, Monk had noticed the young man had looked more harried and thinner the last week or so as he'd been diligent working with Elrod in learning how to perfect his doughnut making.

"It ain't mutant rats, is it?"

Elrod didn't deign to answer such a ridiculous remark.

"Okay, how about you see if you can correlate the times you've noticed donuts missing with Moises' shifts. If the times are the same, then I'll have a talk with him. You haven't said anything to him yet, have you?"

"No, you're the private detective. I was kind'a figuring you'd want to take over this investigation."

"Carry on, my swarthy cohort."

"I'll let you know."

Monk hung up and lay on his stomach. Of course now the missing donuts intrigued him and he had to concentrate to stop himself from thinking about them. He put on the radio, the volume low. If nothing else he'd get filled in on a few current events, and hopefully the drone of voices would be an electronic lullaby to put him back in slumberland.

He switched from FM and National Public Radio to AM and KNX, the all-news station. He settled under the covers once more, tamping down deep whatever angst he might be developing about missing doughnuts. There was a report about a tie-up on the 101 in both directions. Monk smiled inwardly, feeling superior, in that he didn't have to be out there with those poor bastards today.

Tom Hatten, the entertainment reporter, came on after a commercial. "I'm saddened to report today the passing of Jack Denning, one time '50s and '60s leading man of such neo-classic tough guy films as *Prison Cell 99* and *Desperation Alley*. Younger listeners attuned to TV Land reruns will no doubt remember Mr. Denning in later years as the mysterious reclusive millionaire Raxton Gault in the cult '70s TV show *The Midas Memorandum."*

Monk began to drift off, an image of Denning in snap brim hat and trench coat punching out some crook slipping past his eyelids. Hatten went on, his voice seeming to come to Monk through thick glass. "And of course the older crowd out there, like yours truly, have fond memories of Jack Denning as half of that sleuthing man and wife team, the Easterlys, a late fifties, early sixties TV show that. . . ."

Alex Easterly was walking Sergei, the silver-tan Afghan hound, through the park. It occurred to him that the grass in the park was awfully green, more like carpet than real blades. There were places where the grass bulged, as if it somehow weren't lying flat upon the earth. And the park bench where the man waited for him, what of those bushes behind him? Wasn't that glint a jiggling wire leading from the greenery, shaking the limbs as if there were a slight wind?

"Mr. Easterly?" The man looked off, past Easterly's shoulder. He stood and they shook hands.

"Yes," he said, sitting next to him. Sergei rested on his haunches, his head regally erect. What kind of dog didn't pant? "You said over the phone there was a matter you could only talk to me in person about, Mr. Jones. Or should I say Mr. Masters." He took out a cigarette case inlaid with whitish jade tinged with green. When the hell had he started smoking those? "Care for one?" he asked, snapping the case open as if he'd done it a thousand times before.

Nolan Masters declined, showing the flat of his hand. "I guess you're as sharp as they say you are."

"You're not exactly unknown, Mr. Masters." He lit the cigarette and placed it in his mouth. In doing so, his fingers brushed against his chin—where was his goatee? But damned if that cigarette wasn't smooth as he didn't know what. "I peruse a number of publications, Mr. Masters, including *Business Today.*"

"Yes, well," the other man began, uncrossing his legs, "it's my business that I need help with, unfortunately. Someone has been stealing some of our, well, let's call them plans, shall we? This is hush-hush stuff we've been keeping under wraps until the right moment to introduce it to the market, you see."

He was about to reply but turned his head at a sound. Was that someone watching them over there, beyond the ring of light from the street lamp next to the bench? "You know I'm retired now, Mr. Masters?" The damned dog hadn't looked their way once. He just stared off in the direction he heard the sound coming from, "Any of this have to do with the space race, Mr. Masters?"

Flustered, he blurted, "How— Why did you ask that? My company makes tubes and transistors for radios and TVs."

"As I said," he dropped the cigarette, "I read various publications." He ground out the butt, a black area appearing in the supposed grass beneath his toe. "Our new President Kennedy in his last speech made it clear we need to be doing more to reach the stars for the U.S.A. This Sputnik satellite the Russians put up caught a lot of us sleeping." He winked at the man but he wasn't sure why.

"And your company has done work for the State Department before." Finally the dog looked at him, panting. There was the snap of a finger and the dog stopped, then resumed his previous rigid stance.

Masters leaned forward as if a great weight were upon him. He stared at the ground, his hands pressed together. "As per your reputation, Mr. Easterly, I knew you to be the man for the job."

He then stared intently at Easterly. Oddly, he seemed to be

suppressing a smile as he did so. "An experienced sleuth, and someone from outside who could easily go undercover in my company to ferret out what may be spies in my organization. Because of the press to get our work done, I've made several new hires. And, Mr. Easterly, in less than three days, 67 hours to be precise, I need to deliver a top secret device to the government. I must know if I've been compromised or not. Of course, you can name your price."

"This is for my country, sir." Yeah, but didn't he have a mortgage he had to help pay? "How will you introduce me?"

"As the new accountant."

"What happened to the previous one?"

"He was murdered."

Kettle drums suddenly boomed, and a guitar and horn joined in. Easterly frowned as the camera came in tight on his face. Things went black and when the lights came up again, he was dancing with his wife, Jill Easterly in their posh living room. Now a swinging jazz number played on the stereo unit, a lot of vibes and strings. Ice melted in two tumblers amid amber liquid on the wet bar.

She murmured in his ear. "I thought you said walking Sergei was excitement enough, Alex?"

"I'm just helping out an old friend, dear. Nolan and I were in the Army together. And he's asked me to look into how to better the security at his company, that's all." He spun her around. She was a gorgeous woman.

"Uh-huh, how come you've never mentioned him before?" She came back into his arms. She smelled like flowers.

"I don't talk about everybody from my past." They danced slowly, his face near hers. He turned to kiss her.

Her lips were on his. "This wouldn't have anything to do with the fact Masters Electronics is rumored to be aiding our space effort, does it, darling?"

Alex Easterly frowned, pulling his face back from hers. "Yes, well, that's so, only—"

She put her arms around his neck. "Do you think I while away my days reading Jane Austin and getting my hair done? Not that you noticed my new hairstyle." She lightly touched the ends of her coiffured locks.

Alex Easterly suddenly didn't feel like romancing his wife. As if someone were reading his mind, the music abruptly ceased too. But he was so flustered, he didn't notice that it had happened. "It's not that, dear, really. It's simply I didn't want you to be concerned, that's all."

She walked to the bar and shook a cigarette loose from his pack of Lucky Strikes lying there. She shook two loose and lit one, inserting the thing in his mouth. "Don't you think I might want to know if my husband is facing danger, going up against what may be a spy ring?" She'd lit the other cigarette for herself, talking over it as it dangled from her lipsticked mouth.

Jill Easterly then sipped from her drink. "Did you think I'd sit home and weep and be hysterical?"

"No, I know you're an independent woman." He felt as if he was in the docket, and she was cross-examining him. This must come from reading that new magazine, *Cosmopolitan,* and what not.

"And didn't you think I might be of some help in this matter considering some of my investments have been made in Masters Electronics?"

"I didn't know that," he reluctantly admitted.

"Of course you didn't, honey." She blew smoke at the ceiling and belted down more alcohol. "You seem to believe that because I inherited money, I just trot down to the bank now and then and draw out some and don't think about where it comes from."

She sat down and crossed her legs, her foot bobbing up and

down. "I admit, when daddy died, I was befuddled as to the whys and whereofs of his steel and shipping empire. Of course his law firm was very solicitous, helping the little woman figure out all those complex contracts and business relationships." She fluttered her eyes dramatically.

Alex Easterly sagged against the bar, his hand blindly seeking his own drink. "It's as if I'm seeing you for the first time," he muttered. He drank deeply.

"Sweetie," she said, "I haven't been hiding anything from you. But you work so hard solving cases–the Gaunt Woman matter as a good example–and trying to keep me from helping you, you haven't noticed that I've focused my inquisitiveness on other things, too."

Easterly came over to his wife. "And how was it that Masters came to call on me?"

Jill Easterly inclined her head and puckered her lips. "A word to a friend of a friend. That's how business is done. You know that."

He had to smile. He sank to one knee beside her chair. "I may be getting long in the tooth, but maybe I can learn a few new tricks, huh, partner?"

Her fingers played with the nape of his neck. "Yes, that is so, Mr. Easterly." She kissed him tenderly. Then, "I think you going undercover is a good idea. While that takes place, I'll use my entrée from the financial end to investigate some of the board members."

"Any particular suspects?"

"Oh, not exactly the fellow travelers you and Nolan might be thinking about, my love. There's this Shockman on the board who is brilliant in electronics, but dreary in human understanding. In fact, during the war years he was a youth member of the German-American Volksbund. And I have it on solid background he's maintained his crypto-fascist ties.

147

The East may be red, but there are plenty of those with brown shirts still in their closets."

"You're full of surprises, Mrs. Easterly."

"Ain't I though?"

He rose to fill their drinks. In doing so, he happened to catch their reflections in the mirror on the wall. Absently, he noted the grey that seemed to have increased since breakfast in his temples. At the bar he had to look around again, a troubling notion gnawing at him.

"What is it dear?"

"Ah, ruminating on our next steps." In the mirror he blinked at the middle-aged Negro, or was it "colored" now? He was dressed impeccably: monogrammed sleeves and creased pants. This fellow's arm lifted when Easterly lifted his arm. By George, he *was* this fellow and he was mixing drinks for himself and the woman in the chair. And damned if he hadn't paid attention before, but she was Oriental. That was his wife, right?

"Alex, are you okay? You look distracted."

"The case, the enormity of it, I guess." As if he were an automaton, he brought her the drink.

"Umm," she said, taking her glass. She put it on the floor beside the chair and stood. The mellow jazz score started again.

Hearing the signal, Easterly put his drink down too and began dancing with her again. "He said we had 67 hours," he whispered in her ear.

"As I said, love," she began, "the answer might not be what you think. The missing donuts may be missing because the thief is looking for something else."

He looked hard at her as a knock sounded at their door. The knock persisted as the fire alarm also went off. Easterly seemed to be moving through hot tar to reach the door. The bell's ringing drowned out all other sound. . . .

"Elrod," Monk slurred into the receiver.

"Yo, you're still sleeping," he noted innocently. "I called over to the office and Delilah said you'd probably be taking the day off. I guess she said why, but I guess I wasn't listening. This doughnut thing's got me worked up."

"The times that Moises has been at work don't jibe with the times you've counted doughnuts missing, do they?"

Elrod was quiet on the other end for several moments. "Damn, that was pretty good, chief."

"Then it doesn't look like he's our man," Monk amplified. "He doesn't have a key, right?"

"No, and he couldn't have had a duplicate made either."

"Then when the probable has been eliminated, my dear colleague, all we have left is the improbable. Or words to that effect."

"Meaning what?"

"Has to be one of the regulars." He yawned.

"Yeah, I was afraid of that."

Through the walls Monk could hear a power motor starting up. He was doomed. "Who's been around?"

"Let's see," the big man rumbled, "Abe Carson, Peter Worthman, and Karen Osage." He snapped his fingers. "And Willie, Willie Brant stopped by, too."

Osage was a defense attorney who Monk had done some work for. "She's not a regular," he pointed out.

"No, but I remember her 'cause she asked about you. This was yesterday and you were still out of town." He got quiet again. "You just drove back this morning, didn't you?"

"Don't sweat it, El D. You've got me curious about the missing doughnuts, too."

"Aw, man, I'm sorry, I should have realized," he apologized.

"The game is afoot. Okay, from your list the one that doesn't fit is Karen, but she only showed up yesterday. Yet the doughnuts were gone before she showed up."

"That's right," the big man said on the other end of the line. "She didn't tell me what she wanted, but said she'd try to get a hold of you today."

"That leaves us with the, hey, what the hell did Willie want? He hardly ever comes by the doughnut shop. I always see him at Kelvin's." Monk referred to the Abyssinia Barber Shop and Shine Parlor on Broadway in South Central Los Angeles that he and Willie, the retired postman, frequented.

Elrod said, "You know, now that we're talking about it, I'm not sure, but I think Willie was here more than once in the last couple of days."

"Just to hang out?" Monk wondered aloud.

"The first time he came in after Abe showed up. They just seemed to be shootin' the shit and all. Willie broke down with his cheap ass and bought a small coffee and then complained about having to pay for a second refill. And," he added ominously, "that was the night I first noticed some chocolate twists had been taken."

Another power motor joined the first—must be gardener day in Silverlake he glumly concluded. "Why would Willie steal our goodies, Elrod. He can't be selling them on the side."

"He might. Should I question him on the sly like?"

He didn't have to activate much of his imagination to see how that might go. "Hold off, all right? How could he be sneaking the donuts out? If you're not there, Josette or Donnie or Moises is around, right?"

Unless one of them is in on it with him." Elrod sounded like Jack Webb drawing in his dragnet.

"I tell you what, before you start hauling everybody in and

150

putting them under the hot lights, let's sleep on this, dig? Let me catch a few hours of zees, then I'll come over and we can formulate a plan."

"A plan is good," the other man concurred.

Monk, despite his interest in the doughnut caper, could feel the lead weights pulling his eye lids down. "We'll figure it out, Elrod, you'll see."

"Okay. Get some rest."

The line went fuzzy, and Monk stretched and scratched himself like a domesticated bear. The mowers were still going but their engines were like a motorized melody to his over tired body. He lay still, curled up under the covers again. The world went about its business outside the bedroom, and no doubt bad actors were out there doing bad, bad things. And apparently one of them was a reprobate scarfing down his ill gotten doughnuts. And he was probably washing down Monk's meager profit margins from the shop with cups of exquisite coffee.

The answers, he reminded himself, would have to wait until he joined the waking again. Although, he advised himself, a cup of coffee would be just the right nectar of nourishment right now. And for him, he could drink the stuff day or night and go right to sleep. He got up and traipsed into the kitchen. Kodama had left the coffee maker on and he poured a cup. He walked back to the bedroom carrying the morning *L.A. Times* .

Propped against the headboard, he leafed through the paper. In the Calendar section he saw a piece about a new film version being made from Ferguson Cooper's last book, *Platinum Jade.* This novel was the final in the series of sardonic and surreal tales Cooper had written about two South Side Chicago cops called Tombstone Graves and Hammerhead Smith. Cooper, a black writer who would later reinvent himself with "mainstream" novels about race and class in the '70s and early '80s, would subsequently disavow the hard-boiled books as merely ways to meet the rent while living in Kenya and Cuba.

But toward the end of his life, Cooper admitted he'd had a lot of fun writing about Graves and Smith, and thus published *Platinum Jade* in '83. The book was both running commentary on the co-opting of the civil rights movement, women's lib and the Reagan-led backlash against social safety nets as well as a pretty solid mystery. Monk sipped some coffee and put the paper and cup aside. He stretched and soon his head sagged against the headboard, blissfully sleepy.

"Carson is a carpenter—Honest Abe they call him. Ain't that sweet?" Hammerhead Smith snickered in his basso profundo voice and tossed aside the bio and photo printed on card stock of the man. He pushed the aged bowler back on his large head, crossing his size seventeen Stacy-Adamses on the desk where he'd propped them up. His hand, as large as a car engine's fan, held up the next Criminal Investigations Division print off the desk.

"Peter Worthman, longtime labor organizer and general rabble rouser," Smith's partner, Tombstone Graves illuminated upon eyeballing the photo. "He's operated in some interesting circles over the years; backroom deal making with pols, getting thousands of workers to strike and stay united on the picket line, and been married to more brainy, good-looking women than I can shake your dick at."

"You the one the chicks go for, man," Smith said, not without a touch of jealousy. "Here I am, all six feet eight big dark burnished inches of me, and with thumbs that are, shall we say, longish." He winked, chomping on the smoldering cigar in his mouth. "But no, you with your Savile Row and Saint Laurent suits, alligator and ostrich skin ankle boots. . . ."

The dig was coming, but Graves didn't mind so much, now, anyway. It was his gruff partner's way of saying he liked him. "But to top it all off," Smith flapped the file card in the air, that bullet scarred mug of yours actually seems to turn the ladies on. They love to feel your scars, Je-sus."

"Back to the case," Graves said, hiding his ego boost. "Worthman can be ruthless, so we can't rule him out."

Smith unlimbered his brogans from the table and straightened in his chair. "He's no pie-card union fat cat sitting on his can collecting his worker's cut from their dues check offs."

"Spoken like the son of a city hall clerk that you are," Graves said, adjusting his gold chainmail cuff link.

"My point, fashion plate, is why in the hell would Worthman—hell, *any* of these supposed suspects—be involved in the theft of 67 assorted doughnuts? In fact, why the hell did the captain assign this goofball, penny ante misdemeanor to us anyway?"

"Because there's more to it than what's apparent, Sergeant."

The new voice belonged to Captain Mitchum. Phones rang, perps and cops bustled and argued, yet there was a quality to his baritone that cut through the institutional din. He was standing near their desks, his lidded eyes at once giving nothing away yet taking in everything. He shoved his hands in the box-style coat he always favored. His barrel chest strained against the coat's buttons.

"Word just hit the streets that the shop owner where those doughnuts were swiped is offering 67 grand for their return."

"A thousand dollars a doughnut?" Graves asked rhetorically, gazing at his partner.

"It would seem," Mitchum confirmed. "Could be there's more missing than icing and jelly."

153

"Like something hidden in the doughnuts." Smith shoved the bowler even further back on his broad forehead.

"And, ah," Mitchum moved the file cards around on the desk, "don't forget that our good counselor Osage also legally goes by the name Kodama." He tapped the woman's card for emphasis.

Smith was staring at the photos, then suddenly clapped his mammoth hands together. "And she defended Willie Brant."

"How do you know that?" Graves asked.

"I was down at the courthouse last week on that Veese matter. So I'm strolling down the hall and who do I see all huddled up on the bench outside one of the courtrooms but Osage and Brant. Me and her nod at each other and I keep going. But I recognize Brant from his picture here."

"We got to get out and circulate," Graves said.

"Keep me posted." In that particular gait of his, Mitchum stepped back into his office, whistling a tune.

The next thing Graves knew he and Smith were tooling along Quincy in their big, beat-to-hell looking Ford. Underneath the hood, the gas guzzling 425-cubic-inch V8 performed like a champ. It was night time, but Graves couldn't remember what he'd done after the conversation in the squad room. Presumably, he reasoned, he and his partner had been busy working the case.

Smith guided the car along several rain slick streets. Lit neon announcing everything from cocktail lounges to 24 hour shoe repair was reflected in the shallow puddles. Odd too, Graves reflected, he didn't recall any rainstorm either. Must be working too hard. The car pulled to a halt across the street from an office building that was old during the Warren G. Harding administration. From the upper floor, the chiseled eyes of stone gargoyles looked down from their perches.

"She's in," Smith stated, glaring up at a lit window on a

particular floor. He blew white cigar smoke into the ebon sky.

As he extricated himself from the passenger seat, Graves said, "Let's see what our beautiful defense attorney has to say about missing doughnuts."

The two men made an imposing pair as they crossed the narrow thoroughfare, cars of various eras cruising by. The hems of each man's rumpled top coat came to mid-shin and flailed behind them like dusters worn on the plains a century ago. Smith towered over most civilians, but people tended to forget that Graves too was large, six feet two and built like an aging linebacker. Together, the duo reached the vestibule of the building.

"How long we been doing this, partner." Smith flicked the butt of his cigar into the street. As it bounced, it gave off orange and yellow sparks.

"You thinking of retiring?" Graves replied. He didn't know how long they'd been chasing criminals. It seemed to him this occupation of theirs, if that was the right term, had been a forever job.

"Just making small talk," Smith deflected. His pale grin gave away his true feelings, but he didn't pursue the matter further as the night watchman let them in. Their flat cop feet slapped against the marble floor of the lobby, the sound bouncing everywhere in the cavernous area.

In the elevator, Smith said, "I was wondering, that's all, Tombstone. I've been trying to figure out what it all means, ya know?" He adjusted his bowler, shading his deep set eyes.

Tombstone Graves said, slumped against the far wall, "Our lives of absurdity, you mean?"

The elevator stopped and the doors opened on an opulently appointed reception area. "Exactly, my man, exactly."

"Gentlemen." Karen Osage, a.k.a. Jill Kodama, greeted them

from a doorway to their right. She was a handsome woman of average height and a build belying her forty-something years. Her hair was of a moderate length with auburn highlights. She wore a dark blue power suit and a magenta blouse underneath. Her look told them she was formulating several moves ahead of their questions even before they spoke.

"Come on in." She made a gesture with a sheaf of papers toward her inner office. They hung their topcoats up.

"About these missing doughnuts," she said after everyone was settled. She grinned and lit a thin cigar after offering the two of them one from her humidor. "I can be unequivocal in that my client Mr. Brant had nothing whatsoever to do with these items being eaten."

"How do you know they were eaten?" Smith jabbed. His bowler rested on the mound of his knee.

"Why else would an obviously hungry person take food?" She looked from the big man to his partner. Her eyes stayed on him for more than a beat.

"We think there may have been something hidden in one or more of the doughnuts," Graves put in. "We know that the doughnut shop owner has been involved in some questionable activities in the past."

"Allegations, not convictions," she averred.

"And we find it interesting that your other client happened to come to the doughnut shop at or around the time the doughnuts went bye-bye." Smith worked his tongue on the gristle stuck between his teeth from the pastrami sandwiches they'd inhaled for dinner.

"What's your point, detective?" Again, she did a sideways glance at Graves. As she did so, she repeatedly touched a ring on her finger. A particular kind of ring Graves had seen before.

"Of course," Tombstone Graves suddenly blurted.

"What?" Smith glared at him.

"Of course," his partner repeated, snapping his fingers. Kodama too was standing, and he felt an irresistible urge to kiss her. So he did. And to his pleasure, she kissed him back. "You're terrific," he told her.

"So are you, big boy. I knew you could do it."

"You two mind telling me what the hell's going on?" Smith was now dressed in a chef's apron with streaks of flour on it. He adjusted his chef's hat as he sank doughnut dough into the industrial deep fryer.

The oil crackled and popped to a beat that hummed in Graves' head. He and the attorney slow danced to Nat King Cole singing "It's Only a Paper Moon." The fish in her aquarium sang the melody. As the great crooner went on, the sound of the doughnuts frying replaced his voice and Monk woke with a start.

He rubbed a hand over his face and looked at the time: a few minutes past eleven in the morning. Scratching his side, he dialed Elrod. Idly, he considered mentioning to the big man how he looked in a bowler in his dream.

"I know why the donuts have been missing," he announced after pleasantries. "And why Moises did it."

"You talked to him?"

"Nope." He didn't explain further. "I'll be there around three, Elrod. See you then." With that he hung up and finally slept soundly.

Moises had been destroying doughnuts because the one material thing in his life, his high school ring, had disappeared. He was sure it had somehow been sucked off his thin finger by the sticky doughnut dough. He was also replacing the doughnuts as he learned how to make them by working with Elrod. His accomplices in this deed were the other employees

Josette and Lonnie, who he'd enlisted, swearing them to silence. He didn't want to seem like a flake to Elrod, his immediate boss.

Moises had figured once he knew how to make the various styles of doughnuts, he could sneak in and replace all of them.

As it turned out, he'd left the ring on the shelf above the wash basin in the back. The young man had taken it off one time before cleaning up and had forgotten it was there. Subsequently, a can of cleanser had been placed in front of the ring, putting it out of sight.

Monk had recalled on a subconscious level that the last time he'd seen Moises, the ring had been absent from his finger. While days before that, he'd observed the kid was very keen on keeping the ring clean. The private eye had seen him use a cloth to rub it after he'd laid down the chocolate on a rack of French Crullers.

Karen Osage finally caught up with Monk. She wanted him to look into a matter for a client of hers. It seems this Nolan Masters was plagued by industrial thefts from his high-tech electronics firm.

And Monk soon tired of the regulars at his doughnut shop calling him the sleeping detective.

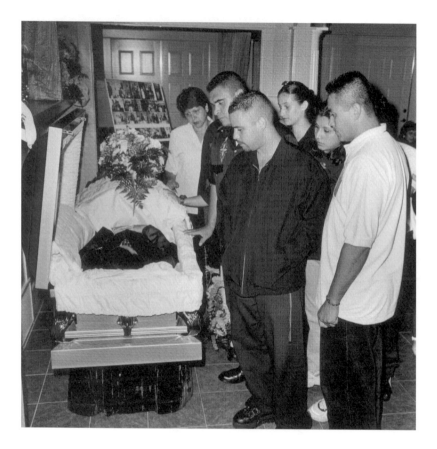

171

174

Lowball

Sweat collected in his goatee, and Monk could feel the stuff gather along the rim of his collar. A heavyset white guy, the upper portion of his shirt wet, and sported out in lime green suspenders, munched on a pear in the corner. Near him, a water fountain leaked coolant. The were only three people sitting in the oppressive atmosphere of the lunch room. Everyone else was outside eating on the lawn and at lunch tables.

"The police said I should forget it. My husband was killed for $73. It happens every day, they said." The room's humidity didn't bother Betty Patrick. She had more important matters to contend with. "I don't want to forget it, Ivan."

Monk shifted his gaze from her to the beefy man in the corner, then back. Patrick's fellow worker seemed genuinely immersed in the Super Bowl highlights edition of the *Sports Illustrated* he was leafing through.

"I hate to sound like Larry Elder, Betty, but you and I both know meaningless death can be too much of life in South Central L.A."

A tiny smile eased the tension on her handsome face. "I know." Her eyes fixed on him and they were like twin pieces of hardened amber. There was a resolve mirrored in them, and there was no letting it go.

"Marcus is coming home from work after an overtime shift on Friday night," Monk began, hoping to show her how hopeless it was by going over it again. "He stops at a liquor store to get a six-pack and also buys three Lotto tickets."

Patrick nodded affirmatively.

"He leaves with his beer, rounds the corner where his car is parked, and is shot. No witnesses, no apparent motive other than a stick-up." He closed his steno pad.

Betty Patrick touched Monk's arm. "We were married for eight years. Had no children because we were saving our money to put something down on a house. Marcus and I had been sweethearts since our junior year when I transferred to Locke High."

There was no pleading or wheedling in her voice. Just the finality of a woman who wanted some reason in a chaotic universe. The bell rang signaling an end to the half-hour lunch the employees of Tycor Brake Company received each day. The young widow rose but didn't leave as the man in the suspenders exited.

"I have over nine thousand in the bank. I've got nothing to spend it on now, Ivan. I can pay you your rate for whatever you can find.

"The police figure it's just one more young black man in a never ending assembly line of them snuffed out in the low level genocide we practice on one another daily. Solving his murder is not a priority with the law, but it is with me."

A supervisor stuck his head in the room, then withdrew it at a withering look from Patrick. She went on, "Reverend Tompkins gave me your name, he's the pastor of my . . . my mother-in-law's church. He did the service. He said you were to be counted among the wheat, not the chaff."

Now it was Monk's turn to smile. "Okay, Betty, I'll take a run at it." He got up and shook her hand. "I'm not promising anything."

"I understand," she said gratefully.

He walked with her onto the shop floor toward the work bench where she assembled truck calipers. "I'd like to swing by your apartment around seven to go through your husband's things and drop off a contract."

"Good, I'll see you then." She returned to her duties and Monk got into his restored '64 Galaxie parked on the lot. He left the industrial city of Vernon – population some 10,000 by day and less than 300 actual residents at night – and got to his office in Culver City in less than thirty minutes.

Sitting at his antique Colonial desk, he dialed Wilshire Division and got his only cop friend, Detective Lieutenant Marasco Seguin, on the line.

"Home deduction," Monk joked.

"Hollywood Dick, what up?" Seguin drawled in that unique inflection of his, a combination of East Los vato and professor.

"Make a call for me to the Southwest Division and put in a sterling recommendation to the cops handling the Marcus Patrick killing. I'd like to know what they've found out so far."

"Por que?"

"Because I'm your fuckin' ace and gave you a good tip which helped you break a murder case you took the credit for a couple of weeks ago."

"Well, hell, if you're going to be that way," Seguin laughed. "Hang by the phone for a bit, I'll see what I can do."

The connection severed and Monk re-read the notes he'd made at his meeting with Betty Patrick. The late Marcus Patrick had worked at Academy Litho in Gardena as a four-color film stripper. The man drank socially, not to excess, played poker now and then with a group of friends, and fixed the leaky faucets around the house. The couple lived in a duplex on Van Buren, and used to get out to the movies or a club maybe once a month. Betty Patrick knew he wasn't in debt to any gambler, and was positive her husband hadn't

181

been robbed by a prostitute as one of the cops had suggested to her.

Monk looked at the next page in his note pad and saw where he'd written that the liquor store was across the street from a quickie motel. But it did seem that angle on the crime was wrong. Prostitutes or their pimps had been known to rob a customer, but usually when they were in a more compromising situation.

Sitting and waiting, Monk puffed on a Jose Marti torpedo and spun various theories around in his head. If you discounted the obvious, that it was a common but tragic random street crime, then it was planned. After all, the robber had taken the wallet, but not the watch nor the gold band on Patrick's finger. Of course the thief might have just been in a hurry.

Maybe Patrick was working with a printer who was counterfeiting and got bumped off by his partner. Monk liked that idea and wrote it down. Or maybe Patrick was having an affair. The picture Betty gave him showed a sharp featured, muscular man. Counting their time with each other in high school, they'd been together nearly eleven years. Yeah, he could have gotten the itch. Jealous boyfriend or the girlfriend herself shoots the philandering husband and makes it look like a robbery.

Monk looked at the list of the late man's friends. If he was fooling around, one of them was sure to know. Man had to brag to his running buddies about gettin' some on the side. Monk reflected on his own relationship with his long-time girlfriend, Judge Jill Kodama. Before he could dwell on such matters too long, the phone rang.

It was a detective named Switt assigned to the Patrick murder. He was curt but answered Monk's questions. From the cop Monk got nothing new except the names of the managers of the New Experience Motel, and the owners of the liquor store. Switt abruptly ended their call with the pat "If you dig up anything, let me know."

The New Experience Motel was on south Hoover near Vernon. It was a graffitied yellow-and-black cinder block low-slung wonder. Two women, one black, the other Latina, and both dressed in outfits even Fredericks of Hollywood would find risque, traded jokes with each other in front of the joint. Monk parked across the street in front of Diamond Star Liquors and went inside the store.

"No man," Wilcox, the co-owner of the establishment said to him and the twenty on the counter.

"You didn't see or hear anything, huh?" Monk asked dubiously.

Wilcox, an older black man in starched white shirt and pressed khakis, stared blank-faced at Monk. "Look here, I've been running this business for thirty-two years. Two riots, several earthquakes, do-rag wearin' gangbangers, and them no-smilin' Koreans ain't put me out of business yet.

"And the reason is because I don't worry myself in the affairs of my fellow man." With that, he put his back to the money, Monk, and the world, and continued setting his bottles in order.

Monk walked over to the motel. The two women were gone, no doubt having acquired some five minute company. He went to the closed-in booth with the word "MANIGER" incorrectly spelled in press-on letters forming a crooked line across its heavy glass. A curtain of dark material loomed behind the glass, and a thin Indian woman appeared from around it.

She shoved a registration card and a stubby pencil at Monk through the space at the bottom of the glass. Monk put the twenty into the metal recess beneath the slot. "I'd like to ask you some questions about the shooting that happened across the street three weeks ago."

She considered the bill, then said. "What shooting?"

Monk added another twenty.

Her hand descended on the money like it was manna. "All I heard that night was the shot, then a car leaving in a hurry. Same as I told the cops." The forty was snatched up.

"See what kind of car it was?" Monk tried.

"No, no, didn't see." She turned to go back behind the curtain.

"You heard only one shot?" Monk repeated.

"Yes, yes." She went away.

A door to a room opened, and Monk turned to see the Latina who'd been out front stroll onto the courtyard. She was young and pretty, but the cynical cast of one who plied her trade in human loneliness was already distorting her features. She walked past where he stood, her mini-skirt hiked high over one of her hips. She gave Monk the eye as a middle-aged white man also emerged from the room, then scurried off to his late model Thunderbird.

"Did you see anything the night of the shooting?" Monk asked the young woman, coming up alongside her as she lolled on the corner of the Experience.

"You ain't no cop, you're too cute" she complimented. Monk produced another twenty, holding the folded bill tight between his thumb and his hand balled into a fist. "I pay better than the cops."

"You mean the thing that went down 'bout a month ago at the liquor store?" She inclined her head to indicate the store across the street.

"That's right. Were you around that night?"

Coyly she asked, "What if I was? There some kind of reward being offered?"

Monk was inclined to lie, figuring she was just stringing him along. If she did know anything, probably Switt had already sweated her. Still. "If your information leads me to the killer, it could mean something substantial for you."

She puckered her red lips and her baby browns disappeared behind slits. She seemed to be considering her answer when the black hooker walked up.

"If she's arguing price with you, big man, see about my rates for dates." The second one gushed, placing a hand on Monk's arm. "Goddamn," she said, squeezing his triceps, "you work that iron steady, huh?"

The Latina pulled her friend over and whispered to her. Then she said, "You got a number, man?"

Monk gave her one of his cards. "Think about it. There's more than a twenty in it for you if you produce something of value." Yeah, a good citizen's award.

The black woman nodded at her friend. "Okay."

In the evening Monk went through the few artifacts representing the too-short life of Marcus Patrick. As he did, he asked the widow more about his habits and hobbies and took more notes. Afterward, he thanked her and went home.

His abode these days was a split-level overlooking the reservoir in Silverlake. The mortgage had Kodama's name on it, who was out of town at a conference until Sunday. The fact the house wasn't his bothered him less and less, particularly as they talked more and more about having children.

He dismissed fretting on the implications of that as he constructed two smoked turkey sandwiches, added a side of cole slaw, and a dark Becks for lubrication. Eating his meal, Monk watched C-SPAN which replayed an address by Senator Jesse Helms at a Heritage Foundation function. Helms was going on about the connection his researchers had uncovered between homosexuality and nuclear terrorists.

• • •

Johnny Briggs nudged Howard Washington and laughed heartily. "Shit, Marc wasn't no macker. That boy was as square as a box of sugar cubes."

Washington drank more of the beer Monk had bought the two of them for lunch at the 5C's seafood restaurant on 54th Street. "Damned if that ain't so, brah. Marc might smack his lips at pussy same as all of us, but, naw, he didn't dip his skeeter where it didn't belong."

"Yeah," Briggs agreed, "he wasn't no Cleavont."

The two laughed again, then looked at each other. Washington said, "Don't mistake our foolin' around for what it ain't, Monk. We like to remember the good times with our friend, not the fact that some cowardly motherfuckah shot him down in the street."

"I understand. Who's Cleavont?" Monk signaled for the waitress to bring two more beers.

Briggs' shoulders rose and fell. "Dude I know. He and I used to work over at the Greyhound depot in Santa Monica 'fore it closed. I invited him to a couple of our poker games and he's always goin' on about what chick he's doin'—"

"All talk and no fact," Monk opined.

"Oh, I've met some of his honeys," Briggs offered. "I guess it's fair to say he did most of what he said he did."

Monk talked more with the two, getting the names of other men Patrick and the two had played poker with on different occasions. Later, he called Briggs at his home and got their phone numbers and addresses.

As afternoon lengthened, Monk met Cleavont Derricks at his apartment off Stocker in the Crenshaw District.

He was large in the torso, slim in the hips. His do was done in a semi-Jheri Kurl forming oily ringlets of his dyed hair, and he wore too much cologne. Crow's feet were beginning to form in the corners of his bright eyes, and Monk had the impression that as the years descended on him, they would not be welcome.

"No, Monk, I haven't got any idea who would off Patrick." From a CD outfit on a bookshelf, Anita Baker's voice soothed in the background. "I only talked with him at Johnny's."

"You two get to conversing about anything in particular?"

An imp's grin creased Derricks' smooth face. "Women and money, you know how it goes."

It went like that and over the next few days Monk talked to all the men who'd been involved in the poker games at Briggs' house. It was looking more like Betty Patrick would never have an answer.

Then he got a call from Marcy, the Latina hooker.

"Can you meet me down at the Experience tonight? Room four."

"What time?"

"Around seven." She hung up.

Monk knocked on the right door at the appointed time. The Indian woman was behind her glass, a box from Kentucky Fried Chicken at her elbow. She went back around her curtain quickly.

"Come on in, baby," Marcy said sweetly, and he stepped inside. Pain blossomed across the upper portion of his back and he staggered forward. Gritting his teeth, Monk sank to his knees as he dully heard the door slam shut.

A shadow contorted across the filthy shag carpet and Monk got his body around in time to see the round end of something plowing the air over his head. He got under the swing but the batter adjusted and brought the wood down on his shoulder.

"Yeah, mutherfuckah," the man wielding the timber

seethed. "Think you can come around here flashing money and my ho's not tell me?"

Monk blinked, compartmentalizing the pain as he sized up his opponent. The pimp was dressed in a tailored sport coat, open collar shirt, over-sized cotton shorts, no socks, tasseled shoes, and a derby atop his small head. He was hefting a large wooden mallet like something Tom would chase Jerry with in one of their cartoons. The asshole was an escapee from a Master P video.

The man began another attack, but Monk buried a straight left into his stomach.

"Sheeit," he exhaled, doubling over.

Marcy, who'd been sitting on the edge of the bed, launched her body and landed on Monk's back. "Get him, Snow, get his money, baby."

Snow, darker than Monk, had his mouth open like a hanger, the mutant mallet held loose in his gloved hands.

Monk worked to get to his feet, but Marcy was punching him in the side. With her other hand she was yanking on his ear. He gripped her leg and spun his body, crashing down on top of her with force.

Marcy swore like a drill sergeant but Monk was already in motion and rolled off as Snow struck again with his weapon. The mallet smacked against Marcy's thigh with a mushy thud.

"Fuck," she screamed.

"Shut up," Snow warned, bringing the mallet back into play. He swung it again at Monk's head.

Now back on his feet, Monk snatched up the room's sole chair to block the weapon's descent.

He shoved with the chair, getting his two hundred plus behind it. Snow's body cracked against the cheaply made door in the confining room. The pimp's head dipped down.

Monk kicked him in the jaw. The derby flew off as the clean shaven head snapped back resoundingly.

Monk looked down at Marcy, who was rubbing her bruised thigh.

"Big punk," she said in a little girl's whine.

"Sorry to spoil the surprise." Monk stepped over a groggy Snow sitting on the floor and picked up the mallet. Instinctively, the pimp covered his head with his arms.

Monk showed his teeth and went out into the air carrying the thing. Gathering himself in the courtyard, he heard a familiar sound and looked across the street at the liquor store. He saw something he hadn't before and smiled.

• • •

He hit him hard alongside his head with the folded newspaper.

"Goddammit," the other man swore, wheeling around at Monk. Recognition tempered his anger. "What'd you do that for?"

Monk heard the wariness in the man's voice. "You know why," he snarled.

The other man sagged against the side of his van. "It's not like I meant to kill him." Workers filed past the two.

"Bullshit," Monk retorted.

He looked at him, searching for relief but there was none to give. "How'd you find out?"

"There're two Dumpsters rented by Diamond Star Liquors and a shop next to them. Every other Friday at 7:15 or thereabouts the truck comes to empty them. The driver remembered seeing your black and tan van that evening. The one I'd seen you drive up in when I took you and Johnny to lunch."

Howard Washington's head did a little movement. He looked way past where Monk was standing. "Nobody filled out a summer dress like Jenny. Only she looked on marriage as merely words on paper. She figured her beauty would make me so desperate for her, I'd keep letting anything slide."

A meanness crept into his voice, and it was clear Jenny stood before him in his mind. "One night I waited up for her. We had a place outside of Galveston where I worked at a boatyard. It wasn't much more than a fancy lean-to, but it was clean and comfortable. For two at least. She came in, hadn't even bothered to wash the smell of sex off of her."

Monk swallowed.

Washington went on, "She was high and passed out on the bed in her clothes. But I could see her panties were missing. I cleaved her head in two with a claw hammer and left her body on the edge of the interstate." The violence drained from him and a purity calmed his face.

"Nobody suspected you?" Monk inquired.

"No. She had a couple of boyfriends who got the go-round but they were let go eventually. Sheriff figured some other dude she'd picked up had done it." He rubbed his chest like something burned inside of him. "She was part Seminole, man. She was beautiful."

Monk took Washington over to Southwest Station to make his statement to Switt. Pulling into a parking space on the street, Monk asked him, "Why'd you kill Patrick?"

"It was one of the few times we played poker at my crib. Afterwards, me and Marcus was the only ones left. We both got a buzz on and we get to talkin' about women, you know how it gets."

"Sure," Monk said.

"I don't know how I got on to it, but he was talking about how he couldn't cheat on his old lady even if tempted by a stone fox. Said too it would kill him if Betty ever did it to him." He snorted at the irony.

Two uniforms passed along the sidewalk, staring at the two. No doubt assessing if they were wanted, Monk ruminated.

"For some reason, I told him. I guess I wanted some kind of understanding. Once I started, I couldn't stop. I told him how I'd put up with Jenny's foolin' around until I couldn't tolerate it any more." Washington wiped at his eyes. "She clowned me, man, over and over. Wasn't trying to be discreet about it, you know?"

They got out of the car. Washington's body stiffened as he took in the police station. Monk got sharp, but the other man compliantly marched forward.

"What did Patrick say when you told him?"

"Nothing. I mean he kind of looked at me and then laughed. I tried to make it a joke and said I wished I'd killed her."

"But it wouldn't leave you alone?" Monk wondered aloud. His hand was on the door handle.

The man plucked his lips with his fingers. "What if he got to thinking I wasn't foolin'? What if he made a call down to Galveston?"

Monk was pretty sure Patrick had rationalized Washington's confession as a sick joke. Otherwise, given how close they were, his widow would have mentioned it. "So you followed him from work that Friday night to kill him." They went inside. Civilians and uniforms moved about in pre-ordained patterns.

"No, man, that's not how it was," Washington pleaded.

"You had the gun on you," Monk amended.

"I kept in the glovebox. Everybody's strapped in L.A. I'd worked myself up so bad over it I just had to talk to him." He paused, gnawing on his lip and kneading his knuckles. "The piece was in my hand without me thinking about it."

Yet he'd tried to make it look like a robbery, but Monk would let a jury decide how premeditated Washington's mind-set had been. The duo went to the front desk.

191

Washington worked his hands like he was molding clay. "I always knew women would do me in," he lamented.

Monk's mouth was too dry for words.

Washington stared ahead, then said: "Lowball. That was the last hand we played. Marc had a natural wheel: ace, deuce, three, four, five. He won big that night."

Later, Monk drove to Betty Patrick's house. He played a Muddy Waters cassette. "You're Gonna Miss Me" finished as he pulled into her driveway.

Wild Thang

She was chunky in the hips. This only added to the sensual quality of her shapely body. And given the nature of the venue the dark and very healthy lovely woman was showcased in, notions about ideal weight weren't bothering the various audience members ogling her.

The woman wore a mauve bustier with matching lace panties that peaked from below. Initially she was viewed from behind as the camera's shot opened on the middle of her back and panned down to the sway of her hips. The camera tracked her and the firmness of her wondrous butt as she entered the bedroom, swathed in candle light. She homed in on her destination.

Lying stomach up on the king-sized bed with its massive headboard was a brother who even Stevie Wonder could see hadn't been shorted in the shaft department. He wore only a pair of boxers imprinted with cartoonish grinning devil heads. His one-eyed beast lay outside the slit and was fast coming aroused as he grabbed that bad boy in one hand and started working his tool.

The shot switched from the hand-held to an up-angle side view as the woman sank on the bed next to the man, helping him along with her purple-nailed hand. The shot cut again as the camera pushed in slowly on her profile. She ran her tongue across her bright lipstick, making its pumpkin hue wet with anticipation.

"Day-um," Elrod, the six-foot-eight ship's-container-built manager of Continental Donuts, exclaimed. "That is *her,* man."

Ivan Monk, the proprietor of said house of sweet breads and licensed private investigator, kept silent. The two men were anchored before Monk's PC monitor watching the downloaded video clip unfold. Beyond the open door to his file room, the phone rang.

"That's the judge," the big man joked. "Her radar has gone off and she knows you're in here watching some homegrown porno."

"I'm looking for clues."

"If you need a clue to what she's doing, I feel sorry for you. Really."

Now those orange lips parted as she descended on the man's penis.

"Yeowww," Elrod said.

The veins in the man's enlarged member stood in rigid relief as he methodically, and gently, pumped her mouth. Her head bobbed rhythmically.

"Buddy, buddy," Elrod said. "And this has been up since this morning?"

"Yeah," Monk said hoarsely. "Willie Brant was talking about it this morning at the barber shop."

Elrod's laughter was like rocks tumbling in a clothes dryer. "That's the first time that old crow has been right about anything."

The camera shots alternated from the stationary view to the hand-held. Then, as the woman changed position, so too did the hand-held. The shadow of the person taking the shots was briefly thrown against the headboard as one of the candles spat liquid wax. The man took hold of her panties and slipped them off her, kissing and nibbling her stomach as he did so. In her three inch heels that were now visible, the famous woman straddled the sprung man, inching up until her legs smothered his face. She grabbed the top of the headboard and bucked as the man's head shook from exertion.

Monk gulped. "You damn skippy."

The woman then eased back and inserted the man inside her. She bent over and they kissed as she began to ride him. The muscles in his legs tightened and he matched her stroke for stroke.

Elrod and Monk watched transfixed.

"Ivan," Josette called from the front.

"Huh?"

The clip ended on the woman arching back as she shuddered with pleasure. The screen blinked to black.

"Phone's for you."

"I'm coming." He and Elrod chuckled. "I mean I'll be right there."

"I got to see it again," Elrod proclaimed.

Monk got up from his seat and left the room. Elrod, who'd been sitting next to him on a stacking chair, fooled with the mouse.

"Thanks, Josette," Monk said, picking up the handset after stepping into the front.

She wagged a finger at him. "I'm going to tell Jill."

"The dude in the video is fine."

Josette made a face.

He answered the phone. "I bet you've seen it," the voice on the other end of the line said.

Josette finished taking care of a customer's request for three maple crullers.

"Pardon?"

"This is Alicia Scott."

Josette walked toward the file room.

Monk listened, then said, "Well, yes, I have heard about this steamy video you're supposed to be in." He lied because he was embarrassed at being found out, like when he was 14 and his mother found a copy of *Playboy* under his bed.

"Then you know what I need." Her voice was without inflection, yet the stress was just beneath its surface.

At that moment, Monk realized how it was she'd called him. He occasionally did work for, and was represented by, an attorney named Parren Teague. Though criminal law was his specialty, like his law school colleague Johnnie Cochrane, his firm had branched out into entertainment and sports. And more and more in the big bad city, those areas always seemed to be overlapping.

"There's not much of anything I can do for you, Ms. Scott. The video is out there on the internet. Whoever shot it," and he paused, catching himself. "That is, I understand this took place inside a room." To admit more would let on he'd seen her and the stud getting very busy.

"Can we meet? I'll pay you your day rate."

"That's five hundred seventy-five." That price wasn't for everybody. But he knew the three-time Grammy-winning, multi-platinum-selling singer/songwriter could stand the freight.

She put some sugar in her voice. "At my house cleaner's crib in half an hour? I'm hiding out from the press. She lives in Inglewood."

"Sure." Too bad, he'd wanted to see her house and maybe get to see the bedroom where the alleged penetration took place. Monk grinned and went to tell Elrod where he was heading to make him envious. Thirty-three minutes later, the bemused PI was sitting down with the worried singer, cups of coffee on the table

"Thanks for coming."

Be cool, man, he warned himself, don't make everything into a double entendre. "No problem."

They were sitting in a breakfast nook in a modest house on 6ᵗʰ Avenue near Hollywood Park, the race track. Inglewood was a mostly working class city of blacks and Latinos that other people drove through on their way to the airport. Save for those years the Lakers used to have their home games at the Forum, no one from Hollywood, not even the hookers, trod its streets. As this was Saturday, the animated mayhem of Courage the Cowardly Dog drifted in from the living room where Monk had stepped past three youngsters watching his exploits.

"I need you to do one simple errand, that's all." She was sitting sideways at the table in jeans and crossed her legs.

It took all of Monk's discipline to shut down the image of those bare muscular legs clamped around the man's head as her ass gyrated in the video.

He shrugged. "I don't do beat-downs. That is, I don't set out to do thug work."

She frowned.

He spread his hands. "Take care of the cameraman."

"Camerawoman, actually."

It just kept getting better. "Lay it on me . . . I mean—"

She held up a hand. "I know."

Olga Salas stepped into the kitchen. "You two okay? Want more coffee?"

"We're the ones imposing on you," Alicia Scott responded. She crossed her hands to her chest. "I'm just so thankful."

The house cleaner, in her mid-thirties, smiled. "You know I owe you, too. More than," and she choked up, unable to go on.

Scott got up and went to the woman and they hugged. Monk

waited. The woman mumbled that she was just going down to the store and would be back in a few. Scott responded she would make sure the kids didn't torture each other—much. Salas exited through the back door in the kitchen.

"Olga was in an abusive situation," Scott began, sitting back down and answering the question on Monk's face. "He was a motherfuckah from the word go," she said, lowering her voice so it didn't carry into the living room. "This bastard wailed on her while she was pregnant with Rudy, their third one."

He nodded.

"I got Parren to not only get a restraining order against him, but to use some of his connections to get the D.A. to pay him a visit, too. He split and now's shacked up with some ho down in Santa Ana."

Monk liked her. She was real, "Okay, so tell me about this 'director'."

Alicia Scott put a hand to her pretty face and shook her head. She looked at him through open fingers, then took the hand away. "She'd recorded other . . . things I've done. We've done."

"Well, well." It had occurred to him that personalities like Rob Lowe, Pamela Anderson, even sorry-ass Tanya Harding, had survived their sexcapades being the subject of public titillation. But those were one-time tapes, and conventional in a certain way. "There's more than just the usual on these other episodes."

She looked off, then back at him. "Unfortunately."

He almost blurted, "You been muff diving?" but managed to maintain some decorum. "So this camera woman, she's a friend, is she?"

"The bitch used to be," she said. From the living room one of the kids yelled at another one and Scott went in to see what was up. She returned in a few moments. "Look," she resumed, going to the refrigerator and taking out a carton of orange juice. "Let's just say there's other stuff that I don't want, can't have, out there, okay. Can we leave it at that?"

She poured some juice, then said, "Maybe me getting it on with a dude hung like a stallion might be good for sales." She replaced the carton.

He had to ask. "She not only taped, she participated?"

Scott winced. "I'll tell you this, me and homegirl, her name's Yolanda Marie, well, that's what she calls herself now. The name her mama gave her is Mary Stevens. Anyway, me and her go back a long ways, junior high, okay?"

"For me that's decades. For you it's what, seven years?"

"You're cute. It's more than ten even for me." She paused. "The two of us been through a lot."

He helped her take the three glasses to Olga Salas' children. Back in the kitchen Monk said, "So now she's blackmailing you?" He leaned against the tiled counter.

"Yep. Got a little note in my e-mail last night 'bout twenty minutes before the video dropped." Scott snickered. "Damn, I'm talking about this like it was an album. She said in her note she'd release this mild one to make sure I understood she wasn't playing."

"And the rougher tapes would show up if you didn't come across," Monk finished.

"No doubt."

"Tell the police. It's illegal to extort money."

She shook her head. "The less who know, the better. Plus just let me go to the po-po and this mess will leak out for sure." She looked evenly at him: "I need your help, Ivan."

"I'll do what I can. But you don't know the bloodletting may never stop," he cautioned. "And I'm guessing this sudden manifestation of greed your girl's exhibiting is due to some personal static between you two."

She regarded the dude built like an aging linebacker. "Parren said you're good, and nosy as hell."

Monk wiggled his eyebrows.

"Fine," she smacked a hand against her thigh. "We were lovers and partners in her music video business. We had threesomes and foursomes going on, all colors and all persuasions gender and sexual preference-wise." She crossed her arms. "Happy now?"

"Exceedingly," he said as Olga Salas returned.

Soon Monk was guiding his fly '64 Ford Galaxie up one of the numerous twisting inclines of Silverlake, not too far from the house he and Jill Kodama, his old lady and a superior court judge, shared overlooking the eponymously named reservoir. He'd recently installed a CD unit and was listening to his client's latest album, *Lot 47*. Scott's material was a mixture of R&B interjected with hip-hop flavor. In particular the song playing as his car wound along Berkeley was entitled "Nightfall." The cut set the mood of the case.

Scott and Stevens/Marie had had a parting over the last music video the latter had shot for the former. But, as Scott told it, this was merely the last in a long line of fissures erupting between the two. The problem, she concluded, was not having enough distance between their personal and business lives.

"And," she'd added, placing those purple nails on Monk's arm in the kitchen, "I like dick too much." Her kilowatt smile boiled his heart. "Mary just don't swing that way and was mad-bothered that I did. You feel me?"

He was glad she couldn't tell he was blushing. Now at Ms. Stevens' house, Monk took in an understated California bungalow of angles and fluted panes reminiscent of Gregory Ain's designs. No one answered the door, and there was no car in the driveway. Monk's job was to scope out the situation, part stake-out and part tailing the blackmailer if need be.

The message Alicia Scott had received last night hadn't been from Stevens' usual server. And also funny, Scott had told him, she was to deliver the cash tonight to a drop in Wilmington.

"Why's that so odd?" he'd remarked, halting at the kitchen door.

"Girlfriend's all that with computers and high tech shit. Got little cameras, fiber optics, knows CGI." She hunched her shoulders. "I figured she'd just have me wire the benjamins somewhere."

Recalling that as he stood on the side of the house, Monk was happy the view from the street was partially blocked by a hedge not trimmed for months. Breaking in could at least cost him his license—if he admitted doing such a deed. Like his work for Teague, he was given certain parameters, and how he accomplished those goals, well, Teague and his current client had plausible deniability if he got jammed up. After all, they never said to do anything illegal. But it was understood that walking the straight line didn't always produce results.

And who was to know if no one's home? He had no lock picking skills, but in this case it didn't matter. Like a lot of side doors in houses of this age, this one wasn't as substantial as the front and it was loose in the frame. A few leans of his heft against the door, and the lock popped out of its socket. Inside, the house was still. On a ledge over the sink, a clock ticked off the time.

There was something else, and it took Monk a few seconds to realize the number he'd been listening to in his car was on in the house, too.

A Rod Serling moment, he told himself, and went forward. The living room was populated with tasteful furniture: North

Vermont Avenue trendy. Stevens' home office, Scott had told him, was a second bedroom off a short hallway to his left. On his way there, he took a right to see the master bedroom where the nasty had been done, as Scott had also mentioned.

The door was closed and the old instinct slipped into gear. He withdrew his hand hovering just above the old-fashioned glass knob. Aware that prints could be made of his ear, he leaned in close to the door without pressing the side of his head to the wood. As far as he could tell, nobody was in there getting their swerve on. From inside this room the music emanated. The prickling on the base of his neck wouldn't stop.

"Shit," he swore softly. He couldn't help himself, he just had to get a peek in there. Alicia Scott was a fool for the freaky-deaky as he was for snooping. John Lee Hooker was right, he mused. "It was in 'em, and it had to come out." Monk retrieved a potholder from the kitchen and twisted the knob. Sure enough, Yolanda Marie, born Mary Stevens, was lying on the bed, face up, eyes on the ceiling and dead as Jimmy Walker's career. She was in a terry cloth robe that was tied at the waist.

Looking at the corpse closer, he could tell there was an object in her pocket. Some sort of remote control he guessed. He was also cognizant of the woman's rigidity and estimated she'd been dead since last night. There was a red stain on the robe's side, near her waist. She'd been stabbed through the kidney, probably more than once. A particularly painful way to die. The repeat button had been punched on the CD player. He took a look around, then walked out of the room. He didn't shut the door, as he'd need it open to go along with his story of coming to the house, finding the back door unlocked, and this room open.

In the kitchen, Monk replaced the pot holder on its hook, next to the phone. He began to dial the cops, then replaced the receiver. The picture of Alicia Scott working overtime on the hung brother's tool suddenly snapped into his mind. But he wasn't fixating on the act; it was the point-of-view of the shot that intrigued him. He went back into the bedroom.

Crouching alongside the bed, he pivoted from the still body of the filmmaker toward the far wall. There were two parallel built-in shelves and on them were some retro toys made of sheet metal. He went over there, then looked back. Monk nudged a couple of the items, then picked up a blockish robot replica from a '40s sci-fi serial. There was a clear lens in its chest. The toy also had a rear cavity for batteries. Upon opening it, Monk smiled broadly.

• • •

Horace Edwards was arrested as he left his apartment in Gardena for his drive out to Wilmington. He was the love machine who'd been doing the wild thang with Alicia Scott.

Edwards was a calendar model and bit part player used by Kelly Marie in a few of her music shoots. He and Scott got to talking during the shoot of her music video, exchanged e-mails, and so it went. But Horace had ambitions and shared those ideas with Marie, aware of the pair's recent rift. He figured if she'd filmed him sexing Alicia Scott down that one time, there had to be other tapes.

"But that stupid lez couldn't see what I was talking about," he griped during interrogation. He snorted derisively. "How she and Alicia had a split, but she'd never do that to her friend. Now look here," he added, "that crazy broad came at me, hear? I had to defend myself."

The two detectives interviewing him gave each other the big eye. What jury would go for that bullshit?

It turned out that Kelly Marie had wisely hidden previous tapes elsewhere. She had only the most recent one in her home because she was doing an edit of it on her computer.

Edwards got a friend of his who knew something about computers to send the tape he stole, after killing Marie, onto the 'net. Edwards had moved Marie's car several blocks over to make it seem she was away on assignment. He'd collect the big payday from Scott, then bounce out of town.

"So Yolanda Marie had one of those micro-surveillance devices in the robot?" Jill Kodama unbuttoned her shirt.

"Yep," Monk said. "She used shots from that and the hand-held digital video recorder to make her masterpiece. Horace hadn't seen the video and so didn't know Marie had two cameras going. When he cornered her at her house, she palmed the remote control that triggered the camera hidden in the toy robot." Monk unbuckled his pants, folded and hung them up.

"She probably got him into the bedroom so she could catch him threatening her on tape and tell him later to have him back off." Kodama unzipped her skirt. "But he must have gone off and stabbed her." She stepped out of it.

"All captured in living color. He put her on the bed and took off." He stepped out of the closet. She came over to him. Her breasts, encased in a silky bra, rubbed against his back as she reached around, her hands exploring a body very familiar to her.

"And how did you surmise all this, master sleuth, if you hadn't seen the video?" Her fingers latched onto his stiffening rod.

"Aw, baby, you know me."

"I sure do."

He turned around and kissed her as she walked backward to the bed. They flopped down, he on top of her. "Okay, your honor, you caught me. I did see the thing. Elrod made me watch it."

She laughed. "You must think I believe that like I believe the backdoor to her house was open."

"How about we concentrate on what we're doing right now?"

"Depends on how hard you try to convince me."

They kissed and her hand massaged his balls. And Monk did the best he could to please the court.

The Raiders

Oh, baby, that's it . . . um, yes. Uh, uh, that's sweet darlin'.
Oh yes,. Damn, oh, oh . . . God, we're going to break
the bed you big thing you. Yeah, uugh . . . huh? How come
you're stopping, sweetie? Oh, you kinky dog, shooting it all
over these nice panties you bought me.

"So now you're pulling them off, a little late isn't it? Hey,
where you going, lover? Gonna go in the bathroom and sniff
them? Untie me so I can watch. If you're going to the kitchen,
bring me some peach tea, okay, Derek?

"My rear's sore from all that scooting around we did, honey.
First on the damn rug, then on the dining room table. I guess
you got my number when I agreed to let you tie me up with
these satin sashes to the bed. Oh Lord, hope you don't tell
my mama about this. She's a God-fearin,' upright deaconess
woman, you know.

"Derek, baby? what's keeping you out there? If you'd be so
kind, master, I'd like to be released now if you please . . . .
Derek, can you hear me, or has all our slappin' skin made
you deaf? Derek . . . shit . . . Derek, you didn't drop dead out
there, did you?" *Damn, better keep my voice down. Wouldn't do
for the neighbors to call the law and they roll in here to find me
trussed up. My butt naked paramour lying on the kitchen floor holding
onto a bottle of Snapple.*

I can see the tabloids now, Congresswoman Jean Gregory kills lobbyist with her snapping coochie.

Okay, girl, get it together, you ain't had that much Hennessy. Gotta get an arm loose. Damn, he knotted them pretty good. Uggh, dammit, I'm starting to get cold as I cool off. Damn. Alright, rather than try to get one of my wrists loose, maybe I can get one of the ends free from around the bed post. If I can do that, I could stop being so nervous and mumbling to myself.

Okay, a little more, a little more. Yeah, now once I'm up from here, "You'd better be passed out on the toilet, knee-grow. That's the only excuse you've got for keeping me hog-tied, Derek.

"Derek?" *He's not in the kitchen . . . not in the back room office. He wasn't in the dining room either. Only other place is the bathroom . . . damn, that fool is gone. And, goddammit, where's my clothes and purse? I left them on the couch. Except my panties, which he insisted I put back on when he tied me to the bed.*

. . . Oh shit, a fuckin' set-up. That horse-dick bastard done set me up. Fuck. I'm in the company apartment, all my goddamn clothes are gone, and it's the middle of the goddamn night.

Fuck me.

Okay, do something, Jean, do something quick . . . Tina, she's the only one I can call.

"Tina? Sorry to bother you at home on a Friday night, but girl, this is serious . . . You have company? Sorry, like I said, this is a political emergency . . . Girlfriend, it takes too long to explain, but what was the name of that friend of yours that's a private eye?

"Ivan, right, he's a Russian? Uh, huh? Uh-huh, he's black? Good. Is he a roughneck, Tina? 'Cause I need one right now. Tina, Tina, I'm not bullshittin'. Girl, I'm in a bad fix.

"Look, I need somebody who can find an item of value, and I mean tonight. But he's got to be trusted, understand? This Ivan's the man, huh? Frankly, I ain't got much in the way of choice. Can you call him for me, and have him meet me at the Dominguez Hills Towers out here in Carson? Room 306.

"Ah, one more thing, Tina. I need him to bring me some clothes . . . it's too long to go into now. Let's put it this way, I'm sitting here bare-assed nakkid as you please, and colder than the Republicans are to welfare mothers.

"But listen, maybe he can bring me a pair of sweats or leotards and a top. Oh, and uh, shoes and socks too, all right? Jesus Christ the Almighty, Tina, don't start on that now, please."

• • •

"This Derek Jackson is a lobbyist for Byzant Industries?" Monk suppressed a smile, getting his cherry '64 Ford Galaxie onto the 405 Freeway south.

Jean Gregory worked her jaw muscles, her hands slicing the air like an automated scythe. She was now wearing tights and an over-sized sweat top with the logo of Hastings Law School on it. It was the property of Monk's significant other, Superior Court Judge Jill Kodama. He appreciated that she was an understanding woman who had willingly, if howling with laughter, lent the clothes. A hefty California Penal Code book lay on the back seat. Monk had needed it to look up a statue for a case he was working on. And was going to return the borrowed book to the offices of his lawyer, Parren Teague, but hadn't done so yet.

Ten minutes ago Gregory had been in a towel when she answered Monk's knock. "Yes, for the second time," she blared impatiently.

"And Byzant, among its many endeavors, is looking to get a variance signed off by your sub-committee to build a solid waste plant in your district," he went on rhetorically. "On top of that, to use the expression, you and Jackson were going at it hot and heavy like soldiers on leave for the last month or so."

"That wasn't influencing my position on the merits, or lack thereof, concerning the project."

He checked a wry comment. "Why are these articles of clothing so important to retrieve?" A late model maroon Cadillac Eldorado suddenly veered into their lane in front of them. Monk had to pat the brakes to prevent rear-ending the inattentive driver.

Gregory, a woman still earning a second look in her early fifties, tenderized her bottom lip with evenly capped teeth. Her dark skin glistened with a varnish of panic sweat reflecting the passing lights of cars. "It's the panties I need to get back," she finally admitted.

"Well, well." This time he didn't stifle a hearty guffaw.

"Listen" she said, fixing her wide ambers on him. "I'm not apologizing for shit, hear? I'm twice divorced, grown children, and can manage to wiggle into a cocktail dress now and then."

Monk glanced at her muscular legs, testament to hours on the treadmill. "The panties," he repeated.

The Congresswoman slumped against the Ford's vinyl upholstery. "I was very circumspect."

"Just snapshots? you guys didn't burn a CD?"

"Are you going to help me, or did you come out here to satisfy your prurient interests?" she flared.

"Self-revelation is the nature of the external investigation," Monk remarked.

She straightened up and jabbed a lavender nail at him. "Look here, Deepak Chopra, during the gymnastics Derek and I performed in the apartment, he asked me to keep those panties on at one point, understand? He said it made him really hard. He'd bought them for me last Valentine's Day. Anyway,

209

lemme make it clear to you. Those panties are soaked with my body fluids and his. And thus proof positive of our tryst."

Monk pictured a press conference wherein Jackson would dangle aloft the soiled goods in a Ziploc baggie as video cameras whirred. "So Byzant wants to blackmail you into okaying this variance?"

"We don't need to go into all that. What you do need to be doing is plotting how you're going to earn that thousand I'm paying you for a couple of hours work."

Angrily Monk said, "Just 'cause I voted for you last time doesn't mean you have carte blanche with me, Ms. Gregory. The only reason I got out of a warm bed with the woman I love watching the original version of the "Glass Key" with George Raft that I've never seen before is because of Tina. You want my help, I don't go down blind alleys. Now what's up? Or what corner would you like me to let you out on?"

For several ticks she stared out the window as the Galaxie rode across the sparsely populated freeway. It was as if they were traveling through a concrete desert. "Not surprisingly, Byzant has met organized opposition in trying to build this plant."

"I read that in the *L.A. Times* a week or so ago." Monk exited and got on Slauson east, heading toward Windsor Hills and the home of the gone-missing Mister Jackson. "The residents in that neighborhood don't buy the company's claims the solid waste process won't cause health problems."

"Byzant's regional head of operations out here, a man named Hollis Rand, swore things like run-offs and airborne toxins were rectified at previous facilities. So I talked with the city attorney down in Decatur where Byzant built a similar facility. Also a reverend who'd been part of a community opposition group in Lexington to another of their plants. They both said that after organized pressure, Byzant fulfilled their promises.

The city attorney even faxed me a few op-eds attesting to that." Her attention was miles away, the words having little shading.

"But you know different?" Monk ventured, driving past the Fox Hills Mall.

She explained. "On the down low, my staff found out the right reverend had suddenly acquired a wondrous, two-story brick home and boat."

"And the city attorney in Atlanta?"

"Byzant was a big contributor to his last campaign race. His cousin's the editorial writer on the paper."

Monk took Angelus Vista into the Windsor Hills section. Thereafter, he had to follow her specific instructions to negotiate the winding avenues of the enclave.

The two arrived at Jackson's address on Orinida. The home was a comfortable looking ranch house with an expansive porch framed in Ionic pilasters. A light tucked underneath the overhang cast a weak glow.

"Naturally I don't see his car." Gregory was already moving out of the Galaxie before it came to a complete stop.

Monk caught up to her on the porch. "You have a key?"

"We hadn't progressed that far." She pushed against the solid door forcibly. "Come on, looks like you work out, we can get this thing open."

Monk folded his arms and leaned on one of the pillars. "This place is wired."

"Huh?" She fumed at the door.

He pointed at the security company's sticker stuck in the corner of the oval leaded glass set in the door. "Besides, you're making way too much noise."

"Goddammit!" She jerked hard on the latch, turning and snarling at him. "If the only use you have all night is to spout your little fucked-up homilies and sputter sarcasm, why the hell do I have you along? I need someone who can give me results." She stalked off around the corner of the house.

Monk moved out of the light onto the side of the porch. He was acutely aware that this neighborhood of Lexuses and BMWs berthed in driveways framed by well-tended lawns was apt to be keen on two strangers prowling about.

Momentarily Gregory returned. "What the fuck are you doing?" Her voice was high, and her eyes wet with desperation.

"What do you suggest we do, Jean? I didn't bring my Star Trek matter transporter to get us inside."

She rushed at Monk like she was going to tag him. "I've got to get those panties back," she shouted.

"He's not here. Jackson is moving around or he's sitting in one of Byzant's labs running up an analysis of your love juices. Which reminds me, how is it your precious body fluids are a matter of public record?"

Gregory clasped her face in her hands. "Do you have something resembling a plan?"

"Not particularly. But how about we try a few of y'all's haunts? You never know who might be around, and what they've seen or heard."

"That's useless." Gregory panned her head back and forth along the street, as if employing telepathy to snare Jackson's lingering thought patterns.

"We damn sure can't get into Byzant's offices, and we can't get into his house. What're the alternatives?"

Gregory didn't have an answer as they left. They tried one spot not too far away on La Tijera but gained nothing. Then the pair headed toward downtown to a club called Little J's.

"My sexual appetite has been the subject of several files of oppositional research." Gregory had calmed down or had resigned herself to a bleak outcome, and spoke quietly. "A couple of years ago, a challenger, you know that crazy-ass Hatch Nelson, made his robust health a campaign issue. It was a strategy to force me to disclose my medical records." Gregory shifted in the seat, gazing at Monk.

"If I were a man, I'd be one of the guys the others always clap on the back and buy him a round so he could regale them about which chick he banged that week. But be a woman with an active. . . ." She shook her head at the contradictions of sexism.

"Anyway, I had to have a full physical, which naturally included screening for AIDS and other STDs." Gregory massaged her head beneath a tangle of curly brown hair. "I was clean as a cue ball, so that undercut Nelson's bullshit. But this time, even if I say Jackson is a liar, I'm sure the press would demand I prove it by having a DNA screening like Clinton had to do."

"Yeah," Monk acknowledged, "but you could allege Jackson used Rohypnol or a similar date rape drug on you, and didn't know squat until you came to."

"That's not bad. I'd have to ingest some so it would be in my system."

"We'd have to be careful. That stuff's killed several unsuspecting women. Plus there are witnesses who've seen you two together. Fraud ain't as easy to pull off as people think." He smiled.

She touched his upper arm. "Thanks for the effort, Ivan."

He got the car onto Olive Street, near their destination. Unlike cities such as San Francisco, Chicago, or New York, downtown L.A. at night was a gigantic movie set awaiting the return of the extras during the daylight hours. Nothing stirred except the few places like the Staples Center with its sports teams, a few 24-hour eateries, and Little J's. The establishment was a red-bricked two-story building tucked halfway down the block on Olive.

The place was open daily and served a buffet lunch to the nearby office drones. But on Friday and Saturday nights, it jumped with canned and live music. J's was a gathering place for mid-level bureaucrats, secretaries on their way to being producers, a few off-duty LAPD detectives, and even a smattering of proletarians looking to bump up in the catch chain.

"I see a couple of people who know Derek," Gregory said after they paid the cover and wedged their way into the club. "Let me see what I can find out."

She went off and Monk stiff-armed his way to the bar to order a beer. Looking around the packed throng that sipped and bopped its collective head to the Ohio Players "Roller Coaster," he knew he'd have a better chance finding Madonna at a chastity rally than Mr. Jackson. Tina Chalmers would owe him a pretty favor for this fool's errand. And it didn't hurt to have an ambitious politician, currently a councilwoman but running for a County Supervisor seat, beholden to you. At least his beer was cold.

A Slavic-looking blonde, built like a WWF wrestler, was on the end of the bar posing with a martini glass. She was in a tight black mini that five grown men would beat each other stupid to help her put on. The woman was talking to her friend, a Latina Monk guessed, who was less bulky, but also buffed. There was a wide gold band encircling one of the blonde's over-developed triceps.

He noticed the two because the lighter-haired one would look at him, then whisper to her pal. He could also feel the back of his neck getting warm from the two black women boring heat vision from their narrowed eyes into his back while the white babe checked him out.

It got worse because the Slavic one approached. One of the black women audibly mumbled, "Goddamn, why don't you just use a rope to lasso him, shit."

"You're not a regular," the blonde bruiser said over the start of Los Lobos' "Down on the Riverbed."

He couldn't attach the accent to a country. "Well, sheriff, I'm just passing through." He didn't dare look around.

Her dark eyes sparkled over the rim of her glass as she took a drink. "My name's Jara."

"Oh please," one of the women behind him groaned.

She pronounced the 'J' softly, a melodious contrast to the deft configurations of her body. A bit of honest flirtation was good for honing off the dull edges he reasoned feebly. "Ivan."

"Nice. You look like an Ivan." Her husky voice pronounced the 'I' like it was an 'E.' She engulfed him with her smoldering agates.

Gregory came back, breaking the spell. "Let's bounce. I didn't learn a damn thing and there's another lead I just remembered. Derek's mother lives on St. Andrews near Washington. She might know something."

Monk waved goodby to the pleasantly smiling Jara. Outside, he was unlocking the Ford in the parking lot when his street senses kicked in. He turned as the two robust women were almost to them. He smiled like a goof, and was on his back before he realized Jara had laced his jaw with a short left. She then calmly and methodically aimed her three-inch spike at his groin. Monk rolled, the end of the heel clipping him on his thigh. He yelped, but didn't slow.

Like an old-school break dancer, he spun himself on his shoulder and latched a hand onto one of the woman's corded legs and yanked. She went down and he got to his feet, the friend rushing him from his right side. His overhand blow landed flush, dazing but not dropping her. Gregory leapt on the friend's back, the two sliding across the hood of a maroon Caddy.

Gregory and the woman went at it as Monk concentrated on the big blonde. Jara reared up, grunting and flexing her rock hard upper arms, and got them around Monk's waist, driving him like an NFL tackle. He slammed against the side of the empty attendant's booth.

"Fucker," she railed, burying a fist in his kidney, and flattening her other set of knuckles along side his nose.

Monk's vision went momentarily off-kilter. Desperately, he unlimbered an elbow into the flat of the woman's face. He followed with a punch up and under her rib cage. She went limp, and he delivered an upraised knee to her jaw.

Blood streamed from one of his nostrils. Their fight had attracted a small crowd leering on the sidewalk in front of Little J's. Jara's dress was up higher and tighter across her exquisitely hewn backside, exposing thong underwear. Men and women were hooting and clapping as she circled in on Monk. The two black women who'd been commenting weren't sure who to root for, and stood watching, hands on hips.

The strong woman flung herself on him as if they were performing a tango choreographed by the Marquis de Sade. She grabbed his head and her horse teeth clamped on his cheek, grinding into the meat. Monk bellowed in pain and put her in a bear hug. She tightened her powerful legs around him. But he'd hoped for that so he could use their combined weight to tip the two of them over onto the ground. They slammed down on her back, her mouth thankfully releasing his face.

He punched his way loose and straddled her, pinning her arms to the ground. The crowd, now in the middle of the street, sent up a cacophony. Jara bucked but Monk's 220 plus kept him in place. "Neeri," she called out to the other one as if enticing a familiar.

Monk felt elated; a lurid sense of control made him light in the head. But that was merely a passing sensation when Jara's partner tackled him.

He went sprawling while Neeri rocked and socked his back and sides. There was clapping and booing, the Romans having decided their favorites. Monk managed to get himself around and half way up just in time to get clacked on the jaw. He reeled and she took full advantage. Neeri liked close action and went to work on his body. Jara, back on her feet and in full effect, gleefully gouged him in the face with a heel when she got an opening.

Neeri laughed and it was a bitter wind across fallow land.

Her malice gave Monk motivation. Damned if he was going to be beaten down in the street by woman or man. He rushed forward and plowed Neeri into Jara, sending them off-balance. Losing blood and strength, Monk unloaded a right and left into Neeri's six pac. It didn't double her over, but it did give her pause. He closed in but Jara clipped him flush on the chewed side of his face and it hurt. He staggered back against a Navigator. Bumping it, one of those talking alarms went off. A sweet grandmotherly voice advised, "Step away from my ride, motherfuckah."

"Let's finish this fool, so we can get the rest of our money," Neeri said contemptuously. "I want to get some sun in Palm Springs." Her accent matched Jara's.

The two came in on Monk from either side. The crowd was silent, excited by the anticipated climax. Except the two black women had made up their minds.

"Come on, man, get your fists up," one extolled.

"Be like Lennox," the other advised. "Don't let them crazy broads do you in."

217

Monk blocked a punch from Neeri but wasn't fast enough to prevent Jara from busting him one in the gut. He started to sink down under a rain of blows and had the premonition that he wouldn't be getting back up any time soon. But then Neeri's head went sideways with a pop. She pole-axed into the Navigator, her forehead bouncing off the rear quarter panel.

Congresswoman Gregory huffed from the effort of hitting the dark haired woman upside the head with the law book from Monk's car. And Jara, momentarily distracted by concern for her friend, looked back at Monk in time to be drilled on one side of her face. Like in a boxing movie where the director uses slow motion to heighten the drama of the blow, Monk saw her face turn as a reaction to his punch, then followed that with short twisting jab. The bodybuilder went over onto her side.

"Nice work," a thankful Monk said to Gregory. He sucked in air, bent over with his hands on his knees. Quickly getting himself in order, he scooped up Jara's purse and dumped out its contents. He couldn't help but notice that the woman's dress was way up over her magnificent buttocks. He got closer.

"We don't have time for any freaky-deaky, Monk," Gregory rasped.

He didn't respond and soon returned his attention to the stuff from Jara's clutch bag. Both women stirred and moaned. He snatched up a cell phone and thumbed its readout on and smiled. The two hurriedly departed in his Ford. He drove on, his body beginning to stiffen and ache.

• • •

"I've got trouble," Gregory said in a passable imitation of the big blonde's throaty voice. She spoke to the man who'd answered on the other end after they'd hit redial on Jara's cell. She listened, grunted, then clicked off.

"Now we're in the game," she said elatedly. "I'm pretty sure that was Rand on the other end. We're supposed to meet at the Pacific Dining Car on 6th Street. From what I could gather, those two were supposed to put us in the hospital to prevent me from doing any counter spin to control the story once it broke tomorrow morning."

Monk tenderly massaged his swollen face, his curious mind active even as his body wanted to shut down and rest. "Why the hell is Byzant so hot to get this plant built, Jean? Rig a blackmail scheme against you, and have a couple of Xena's running buddies out gunning for you?"

"I really don't know, Ivan."

"Jara had a tattoo on her upper thigh. It was a bayonet spearing a gear. There was Cyrillic writing encircling the design."

Gregory kept mum.

Monk drove further, then spoke. "Look," he began, his hands trembling as he gripped the steering wheel tightly. "I've been bit, beat, and drop-kicked, and I swear by the plastic Jesus I ain't got on my dash, you don't start talking, our next stop is to a bar containing a couple of reporters of my acquaintance."

She knew it wasn't a bluff.

"Byzant, through overseas cut-outs, has contracts to clean up nuclear waste in former areas once under the Soviet Union. My office verified that their plan was to surreptitiously ship some of this material into parts of the U.S."

"The inner city and the south in particular," Monk added dryly.

"Yes," she uttered softly.

"Places the major tree-hugging types don't always get all

goose pimply for," Monk noted. "How'd you find out about this?"

"I had a new planning deputy who, it turned out, had a sister who worked for Green Now, the international environmental organization. When she heard about Byzant seeking a variance, bells and whistles went off for her. She got us reports through Green Now's European branch not widely circulated over here. They alleged what Byzant was attempting to do."

Monk caught sight of his puffy features in the rearview mirror. "In the words, almost, of the late politician Jess Unruh, if you can't fuck their men, drink their liquor, take their money, and still vote against them, you shouldn't be in politics." They were getting close to the restaurant. It was open 24 hours.

Gregory sagged like she'd been hit. "Yes, I took their money, the bribe," she croaked. "Only my deputy's sister, who obtained the information for my office, had hinted about the reports to some friends of hers in the alternative press here who smelled a big story. If I went through with my yes vote, I'd be cooked. It would look too suspicious, and would be sure to trigger an investigation."

"What a fuckin' shame." He coughed. Monk was having trouble breathing through his nose.

Gregory started to respond but didn't.

"So meanwhile, you're still banging Byzant's boy toy. And he swipes your panties to keep you in line. 'Cause he can tell you're starting to get cold feet. Jara and her pal were supposed to get me out of the way and make sure you understood what was what." He pulled the car into the Pacific Dining Car lot. He parked and the two got out. Gregory was moving slowly, as if going through a pool of thick oil.

"Inside," Monk came close to her, "we're going to find Jackson and Rand. And Rand will offer me some sweetener for my coffee, won't he, Jean? 'Cause the other rule of politics is, if you can't beat 'em, buy 'em."

"He's willing to go one, two hundred thousand for you to keep quiet, he told me when I made the call," she admitted. "Rand knew it wasn't Jara calling him."

"You know, once upon a time, you used to stand for something, Congresswoman. I remember you out there on the front lines leading the fight to divest the state's investments in any company doing business in the then apartheid regime of South Africa. Or the time you and a few other colleagues went on a hunger strike to symbolize your opposition to the three strikes law."

Gregory gave him a wan smile. "You get tired of tilting in the wind, Monk. You win some, but you lose most."

"That may be so, but you still need a reason to get up in the morning." He held the door open for her. "Come on, your buddies are waiting for you."

• • •

That Monday, Congresswoman Jean Gregory held a press conference announcing her resignation from office. Her last act was to vote down a zoning variance for Byzant Industries. And the report alleging their dumping scheme was leaked to several press outlets.

After about a week and half, Monk could breathe through his nose again.

Bring Me the Head of Osama bin Laden: A Hollywood Fable

FADE IN:

ON SCREEN: Sometime in the near past.

INT. ALAN ROSS' OFFICE – DAY

ALAN ROSS is thirtysomething, a vp of development at
Ten-Shun Productions. He is built like the runner he is,
wears tortoiseshell glasses, and is in shirt sleeves and
suspenders. Ross sits behind his stressed antique desk in his
tastefully appointed office. Absently, he fools with one of
his Mont Blanc pens as he listens to:

WALSH KAGEN, late fifties, sitting across from Ross.
Kagen is craggy-faced, thick in the middle, the product of
too many scotches for lunch for too many years. He is a
director-writer with a track record of cult features and cable
movies.

ROSS: I'm going to take a pass on the interstellar doctor
transporting medicine for sick alien kids, Walsh. It's cute
and touching, but not blue sky enough, you know?
"Hardball," now that was a heart-tugger and we could

identify with those kinds of kids, their problems, what have you. See what I mean? (beat; fools with pen) What else?

Kagen leans back in his chair, a satisfied smile spreading his cracked lips.

KAGEN: "Bring Me the Head of Osama bin Laden."

ROSS: Pardon?

KAGEN: You ever see that flick by Peckinpah?

ROSS: The old dead western guy?

KAGEN: Yeah, but he did other sorts of pictures, too. Though you could argue they all had western sensibilities. Anyway, this one, "Bring Me the Head of Alfredo Garcia," was released in 1974.

Ross says nothing, jiggling the pen in one hand. Kagen leans forward again.

KAGEN (cont'd): Alfredo Garcia starred Warren Oates—

ROSS (interrupting): He was in that other movie of Peckinpah's, "The Wild Bunch."

KAGEN: Right. Anyway, in this one I'm talking about, it's set in present day, and Oates is hired by this Mexican crime lord to bring back proof that the scum punk who seduced his daughter is dead.

ROSS: Wasn't this already re-made with Joe Pesci?

Kagen swallows a caustic comeback, instead he says:

KAGEN: Not really. That was "Eight Heads in a Duffel Bag," and it was a comedy.

ROSS: Oh. I'm sorry. Go ahead.

KAGEN: No sweat. Okay, in Sam's picture Oates goes through all manner of turmoil to get this Garcia's head. And his character arc is each step of the way his psychological state deteriorates faster than the head he's bringing back.

Ross says nothing. The pen is held motionless in his hand.

KAGEN (cont'd): I mean, Oates at one point is talking to this head, in this crummy stained canvas sack, flies whizzing all around it, as it sits on the seat next to him in his car.

ROSS: So in your picture, what, your protagonist is riding around in a jeep in the hills of Afghanistan yakking it up with the world's number one terrorist's head next to him in a Trader Joe's shopping bag?

KAGEN: Not exactly. The idea here is a group of guys, men and women, who have failed at one thing or another, led by a disaffected vet, hunt bin Laden down—who's now fallen out of favor with his other *al Qaeda* pals.

Ross absorbs this.
KAGEN (cont'd): Remember this guy has been called the

"venture capitalist" of terrorism. He's got an extensive network and has been working out his strategies for a long time. He would have prepared for the contingency of capture.

ROSS: This is pretty, you know, out there, Walsh.

KAGEN: Jesus, Alan, the goddamn "Producers" is a fuckin' comedy about Hitler.

ROSS: We've had decades of distance, Walsh.

KAGEN: That won't bring back the millions who died in the camps or on the battlefields.

ROSS: So your point is?

KAGEN (enthused): It's a great story, it's got action and suspense, and a certifiable bad guy. See, the subtext is about how this isn't about Islam versus the world, because of course these terrorists subvert any religion they purport to advance. This is about how an extremist of any stripe is dangerous. Because they feel they can do anything in the name of God.

Ross puts the pen down, leans forward on his elbows.

ROSS: Mideast politics is a very touchy subject, Walsh. "The Siege" and "Rules of Engagement" didn't exactly burn up the box office nor make Arab-Americans all that slap happy either. We want heat, but not that kind of heat.

KAGEN: I read that "Invasion: Iraq" has been green-lighted. And in this version of "Bring Me the Head," the hunt for this bastard takes us to Paris, London, and out West.

Ross taps his desk with his finger.

ROSS: Here, too?

KAGEN: Yes, of course, this is where the third act will take place. And I see the lead as this semi-burned out character who at first is hunting bin Laden for the money, the reward, you know. Then in the course of events, his arc is that his patriotism is reawakened. Not the stick-a-flag-on-my-car-then-put-it-away-halfway-into-football-season kind, but real, tangible.
(beat) Some of what was felt when we didi-maued out of 'Nam. Even though by then, the grunts were disillusioned with our government and its policies.

Ross says nothing as Walsh shakes a faraway look from his face.

KAGEN (cont'd): So here, try this. Our hero is a somewhat cynical, slightly burned-out veteran of Beirut or the Gulf War. This guy came home after doing his duty, wounded, you know, the whole bit. He's drifted from job to job, but now there's this opportunity within his grasp.

ROSS: Which is?

KAGEN: The 25 million dollar reward for bin Laden is reactivated when the rumors are confirmed that he isn't dead. Like Stalin and Saddam, I'm going to posit in the picture that bin Laden uses doubles to fool his enemies.

One of them is killed and at first everyone thinks the sumabitch is dead.

Ross scratches the side of his cheek.

ROSS: But we find out different. How can the hero, ah, what's his name?

KAGEN: Flagg.

ROSS (nodding head): That's good. Who are you thinking about for the lead?

KAGEN: Not sure, maybe Cage or even Snipes—who needs a hit.

ROSS: Yeah, yeah, I can see that.

KAGEN: Like I said, Flagg has been going from job to job, more bitter each time, more withdrawn. He comes to a town in rural Illinois. A friend from the service has sent him a letter, offering some kind of a vague job.

ROSS: But this friend has been tied into some shady stuff, right? Cut-out kind of work for our intelligence agencies.

KAGEN: Exactly. He's a kind of NRA/soldier of fortune borderline nutzo.

ROSS: Bruce Willis? You know, he'll work for scale if he likes the project.

KAGEN: I had in mind someone like Ben Affleck or

maybe make him Latino or even an Arab-American. Get Tony Shalob or that tall good-looking guy from "Undercover," a show that was on NBC for a hot minute. What's his name? He was in the mummy movies. Anyway, this would show we're not out to beat up the Arab community. Anyway, the friend has these on-the-ground contacts and now has a line on where to get bin Laden.

Ross holds up a hand.

ROSS: Look, I get it, all right? I know you can do this but I need to talk this over with . . . (makes vague hand gesture) the others.
(smiles)

KAGEN (rueful smile): How well I know.

Ross rises, signaling an end to the meeting. Kagen gets up too.

ROSS: We'll noodle on it and I'll get back to you. I like it, enough to maybe talk about it further. But as you're well aware, it's going to be tough to do in this market.

KAGEN: Think on it, Alan. Without going out of our way this could be entertaining but a subtle take on the meanings, or rather the dimensions, of patriotism.

Ross shakes Kagen's hand.

ROSS: I will. I'll be in touch.

Kagen exits, a noticeable limp to his gait. Ross sits back

down and starts fooling with his Mont Blanc again. He then buzzes his assistant, JOSIE.

ROSS (into phone intercom): Get me Eddie, will you, Josie?

JOSIE (over intercom): No problem.

Ross leafs through that morning's *Daily Variety*, the industry newspaper. He begins to read an article that catches his interest when Rosie buzzes him again. Ross presses the intercom button.

JOSIE (over intercom): I have Eddie for you, Alan.

ROSS: Thanks. (he picks up the handset) Eddie? I just had a meeting with Walsh Kagen. (he listens) Yeah, yeah I know he hasn't made anything in a while, but he's got this crazy idea that, well, may be something.

DISSOLVE TO:

EXT. BILTMORE HOTEL, DOWNTOWN L.A., ESTABLISHING – NIGHT

ON SCREEN: Three nights later.

Various limousines and trendy cars pull up to the valet parking at the swank hotel in L.A.'s downtown and disgorge smartly dressed men and women.

INT. BILTMORE HOTEL, CRYSTAL BALLROOM

CU – SIGN

–announcing the 9th annual Frontlines of Justice Dinner sponsored by the Legal Aid Council of Greater Los Angeles.

WIDEN

– to reveal many well-dressed guests milling about drinking and talking in the large foyer of the ballroom, the curtain still drawn as the space is readied.

ROSS

– sips his drink and spots IVAN MONK, whom he has met before.

MONK

– is black, six-two, built like an aging linebacker, but solid, despite the fact that he's a private investigator who owns a donut shop. He's casual in a dark Bironi sport coat, open collar, and cuffed slacks. His shoulders say he's relaxed, but there's an energy to him that's notched in neutral.

Near Monk is a handsome Japanese-American woman with medium length brownish hair and alert eyes. She is JILL KODAMA, Monk's significant other and a superior court judge. She is smooth in her St. John ensemble. They are chatting as Ross walks up.

Ross sticks out hand.

ROSS: Hi, you remember we crossed paths when I was with Exchange Entertainment?

Monk blinks, then:

MONK: Right, Alan Ross.

The two shake hands. Kodama looks on.

ROSS: Exactly. We had some discussions with you about turning one of your cases that got some ink into a movie of the week.

MONK: This is my squeeze, I mean, this is Judge Jill Kodama.

KODAMA (to Monk): Be cool. (she and Kagen shake hands) Good to meet you. I recall you wanted to make my character a Latina beer truck driver going to law school at night because that would make Ivan more down, more like the working man.

KAGEN: The demographics you know.

MONK: What brings you here?

ROSS: We donate to the Legal Aid Council.

Monk and Kodama look equally surprised.

ROSS (cont'd): No, really. I'm at Ten-Shun now and we were developing a show a few months ago and their attorneys provided technical assistance to the project. My boss, Eddie Mast, took a liking to them and there you go.

Ross has some of his drink.

KODAMA: I'm glad you do. The LAC fills a necessary need.

The two men nod in agreement. ROBIN LOFTON, an aging beach bunny and reporter with the *Daily Variety,* appears at Ross' elbow, butting in.

LOFTON (to Ross): Is it true you're considering doing a picture about bin Laden?

Monk and Kodama perk up.

ROSS (smiling): I shall demonstrate my usual blase indifference to you, Robin.

LOFTON: I heard this from our friends at the American Jewish Association. More than one of whom sits on your board, Alan. And it's not just Jews who will be upset if this project goes forward.

She turns to Monk.

LOFTON (cont'd): What do you think?

MONK: I'm not completely sure, but if other warped people and events aren't off limits, then why bin Laden? Wasn't there a musical about the hijacking of that ship, the *Achille Lauro?*

LOFTON (jerks head at the sign): Figures a lawyer for this group of worn out hippies and disillusioned revolutionaries with law degrees that helps welfare cheats and renters duck their responsibilities would say that.

KODAMA (to Monk): Dewy-eyed Taliban simp.

Monk and Kodama exchange shit-eating grins. Lofton is unsure what to think while Ross looks bemused and tips his drink to someone else from the Industry.

EXT. ROSS' LOS FELIZ HOME/ESCAPE ROOM BAR – NIGHT

INTERCUTTING

Between Ross' house and Escape Room Bar that Kagen exits.

Later that evening, Ross pulls up and parks his late model BMW Z4 roadster in the driveway of his restored two-story Tudor on a cul-de-sac street in the quiet neighborhood. He gets out and walks toward his home, fishing his keys out of his pocket. There is weak illumination from a nearby lone streetlight. He passes a high shrub.

ROSS
–turns toward the shrub at a SOUND.

ROSS: Who's there?

EXT. ESCAPE ROOM BAR, CULVER CITY – NIGHT

Walsh exits the bar, arm-in-arm with a tipsy middle-aged dyed blonde with frizzy hair and a dress too short for her age. They are laughing and kissing as they meander toward his car.

An SUV
– screeches around a corner.

EXT ROSS' LOS FELIZ HOME

The exec now has a anxious look on his face as an
INTRUDER, indistinct in the dim light, emerges from the
shadow of the shrub.

ROSS: What is this?

INTRUDER: Judgment.

ROSS: For what?

EXT. ESCAPE ROOM BAR

Kagen and the woman kiss and grope each other but react
to a voice yelling from inside the SUV zooming by.

VOICE (in SUV): Charlatan.

A Molotov Cocktail is tossed that breaks nears Kagen,
exploding into flame.

KAGEN: Fuck.

The woman SCREAMS as Kagen beats out the fire that
has ignited his sleeve from a splash of lit gas.

EXT. ROSS' LOS FELIZ HOUSE

INTRUDER: You know, traitor.

Ross regains his nerve and charges. The Intruder is startled and throws his Molotov Cocktail. The bottle explodes on Ross and he's ablaze.

ROSS: Oh God.

Ross has enough presence of mind to drop and roll on the ground as the Intruder runs away.

END INTERCUTTING

INT. KODAMA AND MONK HOUSE, BEDROOM, SILVERLAKE - DAY

It's the next morning and the two are in bed under the covers making love in the tastefully appointed bedroom. Morning light creeps in beneath a partially drawn shade.

CU
– on one of the judge's oil paintings hanging over the bed. The work depicts denizens of Skid Row at dusk. Some wear Mardi Gras party masks. In the background, there's a building with a lit neon sign that reads: Justice. The SOUNDS of the couple's passionate lovemaking can be heard.

DISSOLVE TO:

INT. BEDROOM

A little later and Monk exits the shower back into the bedroom. There's a towel wrapped around his waist and he's brushing his teeth. Kodama, in a slip, sits on the bed, using a blow dryer on her wet hair. The radio is on to the local NPR station.

MONK: You're meeting with the Asian Pacific Islander Caucus tonight, aren't you?

KODAMA (wearily): Yes, as you well know.

MONK: I ain't player-hatin'. I'm all for you running for the State Senate.

He raises the dripping toothbrush above his head and pumps his fist.

MONK (cont'd): I'll door-knock the 'hood till I've worn my shoes to my ankles for the one true Asian sister who'll stand up for all our rights.

Kodama makes a derisive sound as he re-enters the bathroom to finish his teeth-cleaning chore.

MONK (cont'd, from the bathroom): You said you wanted to do something different than adjudicate.

KODAMA: That doesn't mean—

The RINGING phone cuts her off. She leans over and plucks the handset up. Monk re-enters the room.

KODAMA (into handset): Hello?

She listens then:

KODAMA (cont'd): He's right here, Nona.

MONK: What's my mother want?

CUT TO:

EXT. MAGNOLIA AVENUE, SHERMAN OAKS - DAY

Monk and Walsh Kagen, his arm bandaged but not in a sling, walk along the thoroughfare in the San Fernando Valley. Monk has his hands in his pockets and Walsh puffs on a thin Parodi cigar.

KAGEN: Again, I'm sorry to have bothered your mother, but judges like cops have their addresses blocked by the phone company.

MONK: But there aren't a whole lot of people with my last name.

KAGEN: Yeah, and Thelonious ain't with us anymore.

MONK: And you're willing to see if I can find out something about this attack on you and Ross the cops can't?

KAGEN: According to the piece in this morning's *Variety*, you were one of the last people seen talking to him.

MONK: So was the waiter bringing the drinks.

Kagen snickers.

KAGEN: But you've got story potential, Ivan.

Monk halts before a bookstore. On its green awning are the words: Mysteries, Murder & Mayhem. Through the window, the proprietor, a rugged individual with a red/brownish beard, talks animatedly with a customer.

MONK: So you want to make this into a screenplay? You follow me around while I look for whoever torched you and Ross? I got news for you, Walsh. He might be all doped up now from his third-degree burns, but in a day or two Ross is going to be able to talk and that will be the end of the mystery. His attacker got up close and personal.

KAGEN: But until then who knows what can happen. What if all he has is a vague description?

MONK: You mean of some Middle Eastern perp?

KAGEN: Middle Eastern doesn't necessarily mean an Arab or Muslim.

Monk resumes walking and Kagen falls in step.

MONK: Herv Renschel of the AJA gave you grief too?

KAGEN: He hasn't been called the Jewish Farrakhan for kicks. I got a few threatening calls the day after I saw Ross. Nobody ID'd themselves, but is it a coincidence that the day of the night of the attacks, the AJA ran a full page ad in the *Journal* denouncing Ten-Shun and the purported project.

MONK: Just to be broad-minded, what if it's one of the sleeper agents of *al Qaeda* that did the deed?

KAGEN: Okay.

MONK: Shit. I've already had somebody blow up my donut shop once.

KAGEN: Come on, Ivan, you got a rep as a man who goes at it until the job is done. This could be big.

MONK: Not to mention good press for you to get a deal.

KAGEN: I'll make you a producer if we roll film. Hey, I got enough to cover your nut for a week or so. If we get bupkis, no hard feelings.

MONK: I hope I don't regret this.

Kagen beams, clapping Monk on the shoulder.

EXT. FOLTZ CRIMINAL COURTS BUILDING, DOWNTOWN L.A., ESTABLISHING - DAY

INT. JILL KODAMA'S COURTROOM

A criminal trial is in progress. The defense counsel, MS. WINTERS, is about to talk but Kodama, from the bench, cuts her off. The defendant, MR. VEESE, is white, twentysomething, dressed in jeans and a T-shirt. He has an American flag tattooed on his triceps and slouches in his chair, seemingly disinterested in the proceedings.

KODAMA: . . .hold on, Ms. Winters. (to the defendant) Mr. Hamilton, sit up.

VEESE
—glares at Kodama, then reluctantly obeys.

RESUME
—Kodama talking.

KODAMA (cont'd): Mr. Hamilton, you and your friends are charged with a serious matter. You may think that because the man you chased and, by your own admission, fought, turned out to be Guatemalan and an undocumented worker, and not of Arab descent, somehow mitigates the circum-stances, but they do not in my courtroom, sir. So I suggest you make some effort to pay attention to what's going on, because I do take attitude into account should there be a sentencing. (to the defense lawyer) And counselor, do a better job of preparing your clients.

VEESE
—frowns at Ms. Winters.

EXT. CONTINENTAL DONUTS, CRENSHAW DISTRICT, ESTABLISHING – DAY

It's late afternoon at the donut shop—with a massive plaster donut anchored on the roof—on Vernon Avenue owned by

Monk. The regulars are seen through the large picture windows sitting inside, talking, playing chess, and so forth.

INT. CONTINENTAL DONUTS

Monk selects a chocolate cruller from the case. ELROD, the six-foot-eight, muscled ex-con manager of the establishment looks on disdainfully.

ELROD: You will have to do penance for that.

MONK: "Keep up appearances; there lies the test."

Monk bites into the donut with relish.

ELROD: You can quote Churchill all you like.

MONK
—is shocked that Elrod can place the quote.

ELROD (cont'd): But that doesn't change the fact that you are backsliding, weak to the allure of butter and sugar.

MONK: Night school agrees with you.

Monk walks into the back of the shop and then takes a right along a short hall. He unlocks a heavy screendoor protecting an inner door.

INT. MONK'S INNER SANCTUM

Monk steps into the Spartanly furnished room. There's a cot, a small refrigerator, CD boom box, several old-school

241

file cabinets, a carburetor on top of one of the cabinets, a new model PC on a sturdy wooden table, and a comfortable swivel chair before it.

Monk turns on the boom box, which is tuned to a jazz station. He sits down, finishes his snack, and fires up the computer.

DISSOLVE TO:

INT. WILSHIRE OFFICE OF HERV RENSCHEL - DAY

Monk stands at a window, looking out on the city. Kagen sits on a couch before a coffee table, a fine china coffee set before him.
HERV RENSCHEL, early sixties, lean and rangy, has a crewcut topping a lined face that bespeaks of his experiences from the Six Day War to being a political infighter. He prowls back and forth on the carpet before them.

RENSCHEL: You guys crack me up.

MONK (turning): I try.

Renschel stops and glares at the detective.

RENSCHEL: I know about you, Monk, the black nationalist private eye.

MONK: I do my best to give everybody a fair shake, Renschel. I don't wear my race on my sleeve.

RENSCHEL: What, you leave your kafir in the trunk?

KAGEN: If we could stay on point, gentlemen.

Renschel leans against his messy desk.

RENSCHEL: Are you interrogating any Arab organizations in this quest for the attackers?

MONK: If that's where the case takes us.

RENSCHEL: Somehow I doubt it will.

MONK: Doubt all you like. I know you were on a radio show the day *Variety* leaked that Ten-Shun was considering the "Bring Me the Head" movie. You didn't parse your words too much when you said that a judgment should be levied against Ross and Kagen.

KAGEN: He said that?

RENSCHEL: I have a right to my opinion.

MONK: But did you put your words into action, Renschel? Like that time after the '92 riots when you and some of your more eager members jumped those kids coming out of Canter's on Fairfax?

RENSCHEL: There had been two gang shootings in that neighborhood in less than a week.

MONK: So any blacks would do, huh? Only these guys

were UCLA basketball players and you got the shit sued out of you.

RENSCHEL: I'm a big enough man to admit my mistakes, Monk.

KAGEN (gesturing): We all want the same thing here, find the guilty party.

RENSCHEL: I can say without fear of contradiction, the AJA had nothing to do with these distasteful incidents. I suggest, as I did to the police, that you and your UPN Herculot Perot here could better use your time following up leads elsewhere.

MONK: Like with Josef Odeh?

RENSCHEL (nodding): I'll give you credit, Monk, you do your homework.

MONK: Like I said, I try.

EXT. WILSHIRE BOULEVARD - CONTINUOUS

Kagen and Monk walk away from Renschel's office building and toward the latter's fully restored cobalt blue '64 Ford Galaxie parked at a meter.

KAGEN: This Odeh I gather is a leader in the Arab Community?

MONK: Yeah, he's considered a moderate, particularly compared to your boy.

Monk hooks a thumb in the direction of the AJA office.

KAGEN: So why do we need to talk to him?

MONK: It's pretty fascinating what you can find online added to some old-fashioned working the phones, Walsh. One of the service organizations Odeh sat on the board of was caught up in the Justice Department net around the hawala method of money laundering to the al Qaeda.

Monk unlocks the car and the two get in.

INT. '64 FORD GALAXIE

Monk cranks the car to life and pulls away from the curb.

KAGEN: So this charity was a front that skimmed off money to the terrorist network?

MONK: That seems to be unclear. But the point is that Odeh was tainted and did some back-peddling. He proclaimed he knew nothing of money transferring, et cetera. He wasn't arrested, but I bet he's been under watch.

KAGEN: But he could be jiving, and he really was part of some scheme to move funds.

MONK: Something like that.

KAGEN: You gonna be more objective this time?

Monk lets some silence drag.

MONK: You're right, Walsh, I was being unprofessional. I'll be on point.

Kagen winks at him.

EXT. '64 FORD GALAXIE - DAY

The car zooms along.

EXT. MASJID AL-FALAH ISLAMIC CENTER, INGLEWOOD - DAY

Monk and Kagen walk up the steps of the Center and stop at a locked door where there's an intercom located.

CU
intercom as Monk bends to it and pushes the button to speak.

MONK (into intercom): Hi, I'm Ivan Monk with Walsh Kagen to see Jabari Hatoom. I had an appointment.

WIDEN
Monk lets go of the button and the door BUZZES. Kagen opens the door.

INT. MASJID AL-FALAH ISLAMIC CENTER – CONTINUOUS

Monk and Kagen stand in a foyer. A twentysomething East Indian woman, SUNAR, in her hijab—head covered, long dress—comes out to greet them. As is the custom, she does not offer her hand.

SUNAR: Gentlemen, this way.

Monk and Kagen follow the young woman past a spacious worship area with a podium, classrooms, and into a spotless, stainless steel kitchen off a well-lit hallway.

INT. KITCHEN – DAY

Monk and Kagen are ushered in by Sunar, who departs. JABARI HATOOM is African American, tall, balding, early thirties, and dressed in slacks and a shirt with his sleeves rolled up. He has the garbage disposal unit out and on a table, working on it with a screwdriver. He smiles upon seeing Monk.

HATOOM: Homeboy.

Hatoom puts down his screwdriver and embraces the PI.

MONK: Glad you could see us.

They disengage. Monk indicates Kagen.

MONK (cont'd): This is Walsh Kagen.

HATOOM (shaking the director's hand): Man, what a pleasure. You don't know how many times I've seen "The Plunderers" and "One Deadly Night."

KAGEN: That's flattering. And how is it you know Ivan?

247

HATOOM: He busted me.

Kagen regards Monk.

MONK: Long time ago, when I used to do bounty hunting.

KAGEN (to Hatoom): And you converted in prison?

HATOOM: Exactly.

MONK: Will you set up a meeting for us with Odeh?

Hatoom is uncomfortable.

HATOOM: I have not made the call.

MONK: I know it's hard, Jabari, but you know good and well it's the Muslim community that has to step up if there's extremists in the mix.

HATOOM: Is that just another way to say we have to be good, shuffling handkerchief heads? Being a Muslim is not synonymous with being a terrorist, Ivan. And depending on the political winds, freedom fighters become rebels become evil-doers.

MONK: Odeh put himself in the mix, Jabari.

KAGEN: What am I missing here?

Hatoom and Monk exchange a look.

HATOOM: Odeh demanded and got a meeting with Alan Ross two days ago.

KAGEN: Does everybody read that *Journal* rag?

HATOOM: A possible movie about bin Laden that would invariably put our community in a bad light was bound to draw attention, especially in these times.

KAGEN: But that's the point, my idea is ultimately the film is about tolerance. I'll admit I'm exploiting bin Laden because, well, frankly, like any out-sized madman, he's great pulp material. I'm not a student of Sam Fuller and I wasn't an A.D. on a couple of Frankenheimer's films for nothing. Look guys, great villains and their acts make powerful statements about us. From King Leopold and the Congo to Pol Pot and his Khmer Rouge as depicted in the "Killing Fields" . . . that's show biz, fellas.

HATOOM: Okay. The meeting deteriorated, and Odeh, from what I understand, was removed by security.

KAGEN (to Monk): And you found this out by calling around?

Monk shrugs.

KAGEN (cont'd): Some Rolodex. Sam L. Jackson or Ving Rhames for sure, Monk. The best is what you deserve.

MONK: Lovely. Look, Jabari, you know damn will I'm not going to be part of an attempt to railroad Odeh or anybody else. But somebody tossed those hot totties.

249

HATOOM: And the Molotov is the Intifada favorite?

MONK: Maybe it's a set-up or it was done to send a message and a signature.

HATOOM: You've already made up your mind.

MONK: I'm suspicious by inclination, not vindictive, man. It comes down to this, you want it to be only the FBI that gets to talk to Odeh?

HATOOM: You drive a hard mule, Mr. Monk.

MONK: Make the call, will you, Jabari?

HATOOM: Okay. But I'm not promising anything.

MONK: Understood.

The two shake hands again.

CUT TO:

INT. '64 FORD GALAXIE – DAY

Monk and Kagen drive away and Kagen's cell phone RINGS.

KAGAN (clicking on phone): Hello? (he listens, then:) Thanks, Mina. We'll swing by there to see him.
He clicks off the phone, and over this says to Monk:

KAGEN: That was my assistant. She's got a friend over at Cedars. Alan is awake and lucid, and the cops don't know it yet.

EXT. '64 FORD GALAXIE

The car picks up speed along the city streets.

INT. BURN WARD, CEDARS SINAI HOSPITAL – DAY

Alan Ross is propped up in his hospital bed in the burn ward populated by several other patients, visitors, and hospital staff. His upper body is bandaged as is part of his face and head.

Numerous flower arrangements are spread out on the night stand and floor near his bed. Monk and Kagen stand on either side of his bed.

MONK: That's it?

ROSS (soft-voiced): 'Fraid so. He was young, about twenty-two or so, dressed in normal clothes (beat) you know, jeans and a sweatshirt.

MONK: Any logo on the sweat shirt?

ROSS: No, no it was plain.

KAGEN: And this kid was Arab?

Ross hesitates.

ROSS: He didn't have an accent but he was, well, brown-skinned and dark-haired.

KAGEN (to Monk): All the more reason to get to Odeh.

MONK: But he called you traitor?

ROSS: That's right.

MONK: Are you of Arab extraction?

ROSS: No, nor am I Jewish.

Monk says nothing, mulling over the information.

DISSOLVE TO:

INT. KODAMA AND MONK'S HOUSE, STUDY – NIGHT

In the comfortable and book-lined study, Kodama is sketching with a charcoal pencil on a freshly stretched and guached canvas on a easel. Monk sits and sips on scotch from a tumbler. His face is a barometer of his intense concentration.

KODAMA: Even if the attacker was Arab, that doesn't mean he was operating on anybody's orders. There's plenty of people inflamed on all sides of this who are more than willing to act alone.

MONK: Sure, but the reality is I've got to talk to Odeh to satisfy myself.

KODAMA: What if he ducks you?

MONK: Then how would you interpret that?

KODAMA: It doesn't mean he's guilty. It might mean despite Jabari vouching for you, he doesn't want to in any way further jeopardize his organization. He's doesn't know you to be the big, sweet, voodoo daddy I love.

She laughs and he grins.

KODAMA (cont'd): But you're right, you will have to have some face time with him.

She continues working.

Monk
– is sullen then brightens.

MONK: You got a sharp Number 2 pencil, baby?

KODAMA (stops sketching): What?

MONK (standing): Grab one and your sketch pad. We got a patient to see.

KODAMA (hand on hip): I am not your secretary.

Monk has crossed to her, his arm around her waist.

MONK: You're a renaissance woman, you know that?

He points at the canvas.

MONK (cont'd): And bring your glasses, baby. I want those lines crisp in this next drawing.

KODAMA: Kiss my ass.

INT. BURN WARD, CEDARS SINAI HOSPITAL – NIGHT

Kodama, wearing her glasses, sits next to Ross' bed, doing a sketch of the man who threw a Molotov at him. She stops and holds it up for the vp of development to see.

KODAMA: How's this?

ROSS: A little more shallowness in the cheeks and the eyes wider.
Kodama resumes working on the drawing.

ROSS (cont'd; to Monk): This is the second time I've done this. I described this guy to the police sketch artist the detectives who interviewed me sent this afternoon. (beat) They've got a head start on you, Ivan. I heard the younger one tell the older one they were going to check the drawing against the Homeland Security database. And canvas several Arab hangouts in the San Gabriel Valley a sheriff's friend was hooking him up with.

MONK: When you hesitated this afternoon in describing

this cat, that just wasn't about guessing at his ethnicity was it?

Kodama stops sketching to look at Monk.

ROSS
– chews his lower lip.

ROSS: It's just an impression.

MONK: Come on, share.

ROSS: As you know, I come into contact with a lot of actors. Not so much across my desk but at the hot spots, the watering holes that come and go on the A list one must frequent to keep up appearances.

MONK: And a starlet or two you might stumble over.

ROSS: Sure, there's that.

KODAMA
– makes a face.

MONK: Are you saying you've seen this guy at one of those places?

ROSS: No, like I said, it's only a feeling. (Beat) The way he . . . handled himself reminded me, well, like he was auditioning, you know?

Monk and Kodama exchange a look.

INT. TAYLOR'S STEAKHOUSE – NIGHT – CONTINUOUS

The steakhouse is an old school beef and booze joint with a dark interior and decor that hasn't been updated since the LBJ Administration. Under the din of the patrons, a basketball game plays on the TV at the end of the bar.

Monk and Kagen sit in a booth in the upstairs area, enjoying their heavy caloric intake.

MONK
– finishes chewing and swallows. He has a drink of water, then reaches over to extract a folded photograph out of his jacket's inner pocket hanging on a hook. He unfolds the photograph and places it on the table.

CU
– of the photograph, an actor's headshot. His hair is longer in the shot, but it's the young man who tossed the Molotov at Ross. On the credit line of the photo it reads: ALEX TUCCO

WIDEN
– Kagen shows no reaction as he samples more of his whiskey.

KAGEN: Good kid, he's got a kind of De Niro-Pacino thing going for him.

MONK: And I bet he's scared shitless, Walsh, wherever you got him stashed. I suppose your lawyer will argue in court that he never meant to set Ross afire. That like the other one you hired to chuck a Molotov at you, Tucco was supposed to miss. But Ross charged him when he was about to throw the Molotov, and it shook him.

Kagen calmly cuts a piece of his steak.

KAGEN: That's good, I'll have to remember that.

He eats.

MONK: You like to gamble, Walsh, you once got a two-picture deal in a poker game against a producer with a hand of trip kings.

KAGEN: I play the odds, Ivan.

MONK: Fake the attacks to build up interest in the property, and hire me to show you're still a player. But how the hell did you think engineering all this bullshit was going to get you a deal, Walsh? Nearly killing someone is a hell of a way to entice future prospects.

Kagen has another piece of his steak and cleans his palate with another swig of whiskey. He then clears his throat.

KAGEN: Nobody was ever going to make "Bring Me the Head of Osama bin Laden," Ivan.

MONK (pointing): But the attacks and the aftermath would generate coverage. You'd be the controversial writer-director on people's lips like you once were when you did "One Deadly Night."

KAGEN (misty-eyed): How many times have you seen it, Ivan?

MONK: At least four. The scene where Hackford has been beaten by the guards and pieces of glass ground into his face and he just grins and tells them, "The thieves and junkies will always be on my side." (shakes his head) Yeah, Walsh, you had it, man.
(beat) Of course you've guessed when I got up to use the bathroom earlier, I placed a call to the cops.

Walsh finishes his drink and dabs his mouth with his cloth napkin.

MONK (cont'd): It wasn't the potential money you could make, was it, Walsh?

KAGEN; The magic, Ivan, I missed the magic.

Kagen places the napkin gently on the table.

KAGEN (cont'd): Let's have some dessert and coffee. The carrot cake's great here.

FADE OUT.

THE END

To Live, Only to Die

Ivan Monk banked his '64 Galaxie hard to the left and skidded to a stop on the blacktop of the flour mill. Scarred .45 in hand, he tumbled out of the passenger's side as a burst of semi-auto fire dug into the cobalt blue finish of the car's hood. Over his rapid breathing, he heard his windshield explode and felt chunks of asphalt erupt around his ankles as he ran to relative safety across a corner of the lot. He dove beside a maintenance shack as another round tore through the air's purple twilight—the bullets like alloyed hornets tearing into the sides of the structure.

Down on his stomach, the private detective eased forward and hazarded a look around the corner of the shed. He peered into the gathering gloom among the flour silos on the far side, but could see no movement. Ruefully, he recalled the words of his sister, Odessa.

"Come on, Ivan, I know there's no money in this, but you'd be doing me a big favor."

Night was coming on full and the silos, elevators, and skeletal catwalks of the facility were becoming silhouettes as the light failed. He lizard-crawled back into hiding, trying to figure out his next moves.

"Ivan, I know you're not particularly fond of doing bounty hunting work anymore, but I know the mother from school, she's a cafeteria worker, she's really nice. Come on, don't give me that look. All right, here's the deal. Lin Nol has a son, Sar Gatt Nol, who goes by Gat, like, a gun, right? He's in this gang of other Cambodian immigrant kids called the Boat Boys. They operate out of Little Phnom Penh in Long Beach but do their crime over the border in Orange County."

Lying on the ground in the dark, his heart thudding, Monk could only laugh recalling his sister's words. He holstered his gun and jogged off in the opposite direction from the shed and the silos. Someday his family would be the absolute death of him. He just didn't want it to be today.

There was a chain link fence and beyond that a cluster of elevated cooling units. He got a foothold and climbed over, dropping onto the concrete riser. Feeling his way through the bulks of machinery, he imagined these somewhat indistinct forms were giant heads that had been rejected for an Easter Island pageant.

Progressing forward, he stopped, sure that he'd heard a faint footfall overhead. He pulled in tight against a cylindrically built unit, its humming motor sending vibrations through his spine. Even though the three Boat Boys he'd followed here had superior firepower, he had to hope that the invading darkness evened out the odds—at least somewhat. Oh yeah, his sister had assured him, he could do the job with his eyes closed.

"It'll be a cake walk," she'd said. "Gat skipped bail on an assault charge after his mother put her car up for collateral. I don't have to tell you that she can ill afford to lose that means of getting to work. And needless to say, mother and son haven't been getting along for some time. But she put herself out there for him, and he needs to make good on his bond.

"That's why she talked to me to talk to you. She's not naïve, Ivan. She's worried that even though he's young, he may be lost to her. But like any mother, she'd like to believe he still has a chance. He's only 21."

Old enough to kill, Monk knew. Cold and smooth against the fabric of his sport coat, Monk followed the contours of the cooling unit's shell. He rounded to the internal area between the machines and could hear more than see someone pad across a catwalk to his right. He put his gun back in his hand, crouching down and waiting.

A rip of gunfire exploded from the figure overhead. Bullets pinged and ricocheted off the pipes and metal. The young man was shooting blind, attempting to lay down a blanket of fire to hit Monk. Something hot zinged by him and Monk got his pulse under control, fear powering his resolve. He extended his gun overhead in a two o'clock direction toward the catwalk. He sucked in his breath and lit off three in the center of the arc of the flashing barrel.

There was a metallic clatter and then the lights came on. Blinking, Monk saw on the catwalk a retreating figure with a drunken sailor's gait. It was the gang member he'd wounded. The young man disappeared between some coruscating pipe works. On the riser lay the TEC assault weapon the lad had been wielding. Monk remained still.

He'd picked up Gat's trail in Long Beach's Cambodian community off east Anaheim Boulevard on a residential street called Atlas Way. The Boat Boys maintained a crash pad in the rear apartment of an open air courtyard layout. This was information the young man's mother had told Monk. And his check of public real estate business tax records revealed an owner with a Cambodian surname. He'd asked the mother if she knew this person but she didn't.

Since everyone in the neighborhood knew the place was the Boat Boys' crib, there was little effort at security, because no one would be stupid enough to fuck with the "B" Boys.

The evening Monk had slipped into the apartment, the taste of salt was heavy in the wind of the harbor town, and the gang members were out on some foray or other.

Prowling around with the aid of a flashlight, Monk discovered that the youngsters might be ruthless, but neat. Various types of mismatched furniture were arranged and recently dusted. Dishes had been washed and left to dry in the kitchen, and there was toilet paper in the bathroom. In one of two bedrooms, there was a Polaroid of Gat taped to the wall, his arms around a dark-haired teenager of indeterminable ethnicity too well-developed for a girl her age. His hair was longer in this picture than the one his mother had given him, but the same inviting intelligence glittered in those eyes.

Going over the room, he paused for a moment to examine a scarred thrift store desk and its top. Monk then found cassette tapes of various rap artists including Ice-T and that new group NWA, condoms, a few car magazines, and some porno in English and Khmer. There was also a mattress in a corner covered with a silk cloth with a muted design that Monk recalled was done in what was termed houl. When he was in the Merchants, he'd been in port in Cambodia once.

Holding each magazine by its spine, he'd shaken them, and out of one of the car magazines a few index cards had fluttered. Reading the compact block lettering, it seemed the organized Boat Boys were planning a series of ATM robberies. The idea seemed to be they were starting in the nearby upscale Seal Beach area,*- then working their way into Belmont Shores and further south into Newport Beach, across the border.

More probing turned up some of their firepower—handguns and assault rifles, and several shoeboxes containing bundles of cash in twenties and tens. He quit the house, taking the cards with him. He alerted his friend, the newly promoted

Detective Lieutenant Marasco Seguin of the LAPD to drop a dime with the Long Beach cops to be on the lookout for the Boat Boys knocking people upside the head at ready tellers.

"Ivan, what have you done?" his sister had yelled at him. Lin had come to work all upset. There'd been a shootout at an ATM, and two of the Boat Boys were wounded. The cops had staked it out, but Gat and some others had gotten away in a second car. "She's about to have a natural fit."

Monk backtracked to the maintenance building, replaying the last two days in his head. He'd returned to Long Beach to keep watch on the Boat Boys' pad after their robbery attempt gone wrong. Seguin had gone out of town on police business and Monk didn't know anyone on the Long Beach PD. And, even if he did, if he wanted to keep his license and not burn up a lot of lawyer money staying out of jail, there was no way he was going to admit illegally breaking into the apartment to obtain tainted evidence.

This afternoon, Sunday, after lying low elsewhere, Gat and a couple of his posse chanced a return to their place. He guessed they'd have to come back because that's where their traveling money was, and the scratch would be needed to make a getaway. And given the insular nature of the Cambodian community, the police hadn't yet learned of the apartment's existence.

Not wishing to risk a shootout where, if he lived, the residents would sue him for sure, Monk had tailed the trio across town through Wilmington into an unincorporated section of boat repair and auto dismantler yards. There they'd spotted him and had crashed through the gate of the flour mill.

Monk blasted the lock to the maintenance building and entered. Inside, it was evident it was a control room. There was an operating board, and apparently the lights were on an automated system, programmed to come on at a set time each evening. There had been no security guards and as far as he could tell, no alarm. Odd, but then, who'd steal processed flour?

It was part of the county that on a warm evening like tonight, the men who worked these yards were home drinking a beer and dreading the start of another week on the endless slog to oblivion. Or maybe they were reading a bedtime story to their kids and dreaming of Middle East peace. At any rate, it was desolate around here, and the detective wasn't too hopeful about the quick arrival of the sheriff's brown-and-whites.

Monk placed the TEC 22 on top of the control panel. Keeping an eye on the outside through the window, he quickly experimented with dials and toggles until he got the right pattern of light and dark he wanted. He heard sounds and hurriedly ducked down.

A volley leaped from a portion of the mill Monk had enveloped in gloom. Aiming high, the gunman blistered the thin walls of the control shed. Glass blossomed into shards of snowflakes as diamond-sized holes were punctured everywhere. Monk, on one knee beside the control panel, got all the lights back on.

The startled Boat Boy swore as Monk, having flung his body prone through the open doorway, grouped two in the young man's torso. He'd been bent low next to a flour tank, a straight line from the shed across the lot. The young thug went over backwards, spraying bullets helter-skelter. The slugs tore into the silo and steady streams of billowing white descended over the dead man—the mists of the afterlife greeting the departing soul.

Monk controlled his flopping stomach and bolted as fast as he could, having tripped the lights to go out again. His deceased father's .45 in one hand, he had a flashlight from the shed in the other. Gat was still around, and what about the one he'd wounded? Was he still a threat, too?

Added to that, if he shot Gat, despite his certainty of self-defense, there would be emotional repercussions with his sister and the mother. But what else could he do? The knucklehead had a better chance with him than with the law. Time to focus.

He maneuvered around various apparatuses of the mill using the flashlight sparingly. At some point, Gat was going to have to bust a move for freedom.

"Yo, man, hey, private cop," one of them yelled from somewhere.

Monk said nothing, ready and still.

"Yeah," the voice said again. He was convinced it was Gat. "I know you must be some kind of private eye like Rockford or some shit. 'Cause no McNab drives a cherry '64 Ford Galaxie like the one you got."

Monk tried to pinpoint the direction the voice was coming from, but the echo effect of all the metal made it hard.

"I also know my moms must have put you up to this." He paused and Monk stopped, wanting the young man's voice to cover his movement. "That was smart," he began again, "messing with the lights and what not. Taking out Xao like that." There was another pause, then. "Look, man, me and my homie just want to make it away clean, what's wrong with that? I'll pay you five-thousand to be cool."

It occurred to Monk that Gat was also moving about as he talked. Up high, a three-quarter moon gave the mill's tanks an unhealthy sheen.

"Hey, man," Gat yelled angrily. "You best be lettin' me and my man get to our short or I'm gonna have to hurt you, blood."

Monk was heading toward the entrance, where the cars were. He was positive that's where Gat was heading, too.

Another salvo rang out and he went low. Gat and the other

one had to be hot-footing it to their car, shooting to cover their escape. There was the opening and slamming of doors and a thunderous sound as their four-barrel carb Chevy Caprice coughed to life. The vehicle screeched a donut, its high beams seeking the concealed Monk. The car straightened out and lurched away at a terrific speed.

Monk dashed to his Galaxie and threw his coat over the broken glass on the seat. To his relief, the engine caught on the second crank and he, too, left.

• • •

Half of Gat's lanky frame was dipping into his emerald Suzuki Samurai with the 12-spoke rims and the lowered chassis when Monk pressed the cold muzzle of his gun against the young man's ribs. He reached across and withdrew the Beretta the younger man had on a belt clip.

"Shit," Gat exclaimed, turning toward the PI. "How did you find me?" Then he made a knowing nod. "Yeah, Sherry and me in that photo."

Prior to the shootout at the flour mill, Monk had his sister make inquiries in the school system about the young lady in the picture, Sherry Hernandez. Her name was carved in that particular graffiti style the kids did on the desk Monk had noticed in that bedroom. She was pissed at him, but he convinced her that at this stage of things, he was Gat's last best hope. Odessa turned up at the continuation high school she attended in East Long Beach. Her story about Gat's bad influence produced Sherry's address from the concerned administration. She'd been absent several days as it was.

"That's what I get for being gushy and stopping by to say goodbye," Gat lamented. He looked at Monk imploringly as the early morning light broke. "I suppose my mom won't be too happy either, huh? Bud I did drop Sandath, the one you

266

wounded, off last night at the hospital. That ought to be worth something in court, right?"

Monk didn't respond.

Gat glared at the ground and said, "What does it matter? I'm living just to die anyway."

Monk considered the young man and wondered about too many others like Gat. Kids who assumed life was a series of highs and no lows. Youngsters who lived for the moment and who threw away their futures because they came of age in an America that voted for David Duke and let savings and loan swindlers walk away with a wink and a nod. It was a country that preached bootstrapism and offered them jobs in the low end of the service sector.

Yeah, his mother and he had survived the Killing Fields, but found out they traded them in for the slow death of urban neglect.

A new sun was rising over the palm fronds and the street where Hernandez's house faced the Pacific. Monk cuffed the Boat Boy and put him in the front, passenger side of his car. He didn't think Gat would give him any trouble. And he told himself it was only the sharpness of dawn and his lack of sleep that made his eyes tear as he drove to police headquarters.

The King Alfred Plan

T *hat's right, Lisa. There's still a Sig Alert on the 5 due to a big* *rig that jack-knifed in the pre-dawn hours. It's spread across* *the three and four lanes with the Highway Patrol allowing only one* *lane open heading east out of downtown. Late morning commuters* *should use alternative routes. This is Chopper Dave signing off and* *I'll be back in forty-five."*

The traffic report on the radio went to a commercial about the versatility of avocados as Monk continued his attempt at programming the multi-functioning cell phone his girlfriend, the right honorable Judge Jill Kodama, had given him as a gift. She insisted that a man who drove a car with a carburetor, and who was known to search methodically for '30s-era flat caps, should make the effort to plant a foot squarely in the 21st century. And so here he was punching in the phone numbers of his significant other, his mother, his sister, nephew and those whose occupations dovetailed with his—beat reporters, morgue attendants, motel maids, liquor store clerks, and even a couple of lawyers.

Depressing two buttons with his thumb rather than the one he'd intended, Monk was annoyed that as technology compressed functions more and more, your fingers couldn't be bigger than those of a six-year-old. As he re-entered a series of digits, the phone chimed. He pressed one button, sure that was how to answer, but nothing happened. On his second try it bleeped, and holding it to his ear he heard a hoarse, "Hello, hello?" and then the line evaporated into white noise.

"Hello, hello," he repeated. Glowering at the cell phone, Monk made sounds in his throat as he sought vainly to use the redial. He tracked up and down and back again in the menu selections. Suddenly a picture appeared in the phone's window.

The frozen image was of a woman in a dark skirt and matching coat. She was rearing back, a hand latched onto her arm. It was a man's hand, he guessed, and it went off screen. He could also tell this took place in an office setting. Her body language and expression added up to one displeased individual.

"Dammit," he bellowed, uncertain of what to do to save the shot. "Delilah," he pleaded, shouting.

"What?" Delilah Carnes appeared in the doorway of his office. "You're muttering in here like Bernie Mac left in charge of a kindergarten class."

"Come here, would you?" He waved the cell like shaking a bottle of settled orange juice. He was already up from behind his desk and moving toward the office manager. "Can you save this picture?"

"Sure," she said, taking the phone and deftly pecking her nailed finger across its surface. "Want to download it to your computer?"

"Yes, please." Monk moved aside for her.

Carnes said upon studying the picture, "What is this? I mean, what's going on here?"

"Don't know, that's why I need your help with this."

She sat in his chair and extracted a wire from the side drawer where he kept the phone's charger and other accessories. She plugged the wire into the phone and the other end into the external Zip drive atop his computer tower. "Got a disk?" she asked. "I'll save it to that and on your hard drive."

Monk found a Zip disk with 'Big Bill Broonzy' scribbled on the label lying on a shelf. He handed it over and soon Carnes had downloaded the image so that it appeared on his monitor.

"Do you know her?" Carnes asked, pointing a lavender nail at the screen. The resolution was far from LCD quality, but the details were clear.

"No," Monk said slowly. "But she doesn't look scared, does she?"

"More like she's pissed at whoever it is that has a hold of her," Carnes observed.

Monk became absorbed by something else in the picture besides the obvious. "See that bobble-head of Shaq on the desk? That looks familiar."

Carnes looked closer. "A lot of people have that toy." Shaq referred to Shaquille O'Neal, the all-star center of the Lakers' basketball team.

"But I bought one for Parren, and that's where he kept his, on the left-hand front of his desk, not pointed outward, but toward where you'd sit behind the desk. He liked to bop the big fella's head now and then during the day."

She glared at him.

"What do I know?" he shrugged. "It relaxed him, he said."

She touched the monitor's glass. "You should call him or the cops."

"She's not being stabbed, Delilah. This could be just some kind of argument. Could even be a lover's squabble."

"Then find out."

"Okay." But his hesitation was all too evident. Yet the more he studied the picture, noting the color of the curtains framing the big window behind the woman, the more he was convinced that this was an office he'd been in many times.

"Don't like getting in your boy's business, I understand. But you have to find out, Ivan."

Monk grunted and phoned his lawyer and friend. "Is Parren in?" he asked after the receptionist answered. It was a voice he didn't recognize.

"Who shall I say is calling?"

He gave her his name.

"Does he know what this is regarding?"

"I've done work for Parren. He knows who I am."

"Very well," she said, "Just a moment."

Monk leaned back in his chair as Carnes sat opposite. That morning he'd put in a new garbage disposal at home and had come to the office in his cuffed khakis and work boots.

Momentarily, the receptionist returned. "I'm sorry, Mr. Monk, I was mistaken, Mr. Teague is unavailable right now." She provided nothing more.

"Give me his voice mail, would you?"

"Well, you see, he's out of town."

"Really?"

"Yes, uh-huh. He had to leave suddenly, a family emergency, and we're not sure when he's coming back. But I will definitely tell him you called when I hear from him."

"Thanks." He hung up and recounted to Carnes what he'd been told. "I'll call his cell phone."

"Sounds good," she said, fooling with Monk's cell. "You somehow erased the redial memory so I can't tell who sent you the photo."

Eschewing a defensive comment, he located Teague's numbers in his old-school manual Rolodex with its weathered card stock. He reached the attorney's voice mail and left a message for him to return his call sooner rather than later. He then tried the man's home and also got a recording.

Fleetingly, he considered calling both of Teague's ex-wives, but decided to leave that alone for now.

Carnes stood, smoothing her skirt over her *Maxim* covergirl hips. "Now what?"

"Get on my horse. I can't wait around here counting paper clips for Parren to call."

"'Cause you don't think he will. Or can't."

Monk was up and heading out. "You've been working around here too long, D; you're seeing bodies in the road when all it is are speed bumps."

"Take this." She handed him his cell phone.

As if it were dipped in anthrax, he gingerly accepted the device.

Carnes said, "It's charged, it's on, and if it rings, all you do is press the green phone symbol. When the call is done, it clicks off automatically. And to make a call, you dial in the area code, then number, and again press the green symbol."

"Got it. I'll check in later." He pocketed the instrument. "And D, would you call around to the courthouse clerks you know? See if Parren or any of the lawyers in his office have been seen around there today or yesterday. Don't know if that will tell us anything, but—"

"It damn sure can't hurt," she finished.

"Exactly." He left and once he got to Teague's mid-Wilshire office building, he walked through the parking structure. Scanning the stalls, he saw that the lawyer's late model Mercedes was parked in its assigned space. Peering inside, the red alarm light winked on and off at him on the dash console. He took the elevator up.

"Yes?" The receptionist asked as he entered through the glossy double doors. She was one that Monk hadn't seen before, but was sure she was the woman he'd talked to earlier.

He said as much to her, and added, "It's very important that Parren and I talk. Today. Where'd he go?"

She gave him a 'don't-fuck-with-me' glare but could tell it wasn't going to make him go away. "Sir, I've already informed you that Mr. Teague is not here for personal reasons. That's all I can tell you."

"What about Dennis or Elena, is one of them around?"

"Who?" But before he could speak she amended, "I'm afraid they aren't available either."

"Neither of his partners?"

"Yes."

"Bullshit." Monk headed around her. The young woman wheeled about in her chair and reached for him.

"You were asked to leave." The command of her tone and her solid grip on his forearm set off signals in Monk's head. Rather than ignore her he spun toward the woman. She blasted him with pepper spray.

"Fuck," he bellowed, his eyes burning and tearing as he flailed for her.

"Now you'll listen," and the point of her shoe sank deep into his groin, sending Monk sidelong into the hallway wall. She followed that with a looping right destined to dazzle the space inside his head. Realizing that he was dealing with a pro got him acting on automatic, and he managed to block most of the blow with his arm. Launching himself from his crumpled position, Monk collided with the woman, driving her back.

But he faltered and her kick caught him high on his biceps. He shifted his upper body, anticipating her next attack. Monk pressed close, fighting through the pain. He crowded her in the hallway and connected with a fist to her hard mid-section.

"Fucker," she wheezed, and answered with a chop of her hand against his shoulder blade.

273

White pinwheels flared between his temples and he fell against one of the art pieces Teague liked to have around. His vision blurry and indistinct, Monk dully registered the painting was a Ruscha while he yanked it loose and swung it. The edge of the heavy frame gouged the woman's throat.

She gagged and coughed, and, guided more by the sound than sight, Monk put a fist into her face. She went down, and he wasn't standing still to see if she was out or merely dazed. He stumbled toward Teague's office. Whatever reserve he was operating on was quickly dissipating, and he wanted badly to curl up on the floor and go to sleep.

But he couldn't stop. Crawling on his hands and knees, he got to Teague's door and put his hand on the latch. He was pleasantly surprised to find it unlocked and dropped inside. Monk struggled to stand and locked the door. The office, as always, was neat, with its papers, chairs, and pens all in place and just so. There were no overturned lamps, no spray of crimson across the carpet.

Using the desk as a brace, he leaned over to let his tears clear his sight. It ached in the lower part of his stomach and each step was an effort, but, squinting and grimacing, he searched the office—fingers before him like an insect's feelers. He had to find something that would help him figure out what was going on, and what had happened to his friend.

Three minutes had elapsed and he knew he couldn't have too much time left. He kept at it. Beyond the door he was sure there were whispers. The presence on the other side of the door got more pronounced and he got more anxious as he searched. On the floor just where the curtain broke above the carpet something gleamed.

"Police," the cops announced, and put their shoulders to the door. It buckled in the frame but didn't give.

On his knees, Monk went prone, plucked the small object

off the floor and put it into his pocket. The door gave in after the second heave and three uniforms rushed inside, Berettas bristling.

"Let me see your motherfuckin' hands," one of them barked.

His face down on the rug, one of the cops put a foot in Monk's back and a muzzle to his ear as he was cuffed and patted down and hauled away.

Four hours later the two detectives who'd been tag teaming him asked him to tell yet again how he came to be in the law offices of Parren Teague looking like he'd been on the wrong end of a match with the Rock.

"Ask the chick who whupped on me," he said, or a version thereof, for the umpteenth time.

"Let me remind you, Monk," the older one, McCandless, started. "There was no woman, nor anyone else, in any of the suites in Teague's office when the uniforms arrived." He held up a hand. "And again, it's none of your goddamn concern how it was the officers arrived on the scene in the first place."

"Then I'm still at a loss to see how the fuck you're holding me," Monk blared. "I didn't break and enter, and it's on record that not only is Parren Teague my attorney, I've worked cases for him."

"He wasn't there, either," the partner, Atkinson, said.

"My point exactly," Monk summed up. "The longer you keep me on this humbug, the better chance I've got to sue you."

McCandless yawned. "You said you don't know where your lawyer is."

"Now I know you don't think that's the only lawyer I know."

"And who else would that be, homey?" Atkinson taunted.

"Judge Kodama."

McCandless asked, "You know her? That ball buster? The

one that flayed the undercover narc the other week about the shooting at Park La Brea?"

"The light of my life."

The two shared a moment, then continued with their hammering until there was a knock at the door, and Atkinson went out to talk with whoever was there. Shortly he stuck his head back in and motioned for McCandless, who also left.

Monk was sore, his left eye was swollen, and he desperately wanted to pee. Some fifteen minutes ticked by and the older one, McCandless, re-entered.

"Bounce," he said, and left again.

Monk sighed and walked out. He retrieved the items they'd confiscated, including the key-chain ornament he'd found in Teague's office. Outside he was very happy to find a shadowy spot to relieve himself in a dark alley not too far from Parker Center where he'd been questioned.

There was something to be said for a Skid Row that bordered the downtown courts, city and county administrations, and Little Tokyo. Not that the area's proximity meant that the concerns of the homeless were a top priority to the insiders inhabiting those other sectors. In the race to convert industrial buildings to high-end lofts, and to further Manhattanize L.A.'s central core, it seemed the power brokers wished that the unfortunates would simply vanish into oblivion. That, rather than have to actually devise programs to alleviate the chronic situation.

And so the cops would conduct more bogus sweeps, arresting and harassing the Row's economically and psychologically precarious inhabitants. The goal wasn't permanent incarceration, but to make it untenable for them so that they would move somewhere else; anywhere but here.

Through the ink of the alley, Monk heard a shopping cart approach, the bottles and other paraphernalia in it rattling.

"Are you the Moon Man?" the stooped cart-pusher asked. The individual was swaddled in wrappings of filthy cloth, complete with a shawl covering the lower portions of its face. Neither the voice nor the shape gave away its gender.

"Just a traveler like yourself." Monk headed for the street.

"Oh, I know you have to be undercover," the person with the cart added. "I know you're here to show us the way, Moon Man, to beam your harsh light of justice on the devilish ones, the stadium builders and their ass-wipers."

"We'll see." Monk pressed a few dollars into a crusty hand and stepped into a low gust stirring around him and the others camped out on their cardboard futons along Towne Avenue. He dialed his sweetie on his cell phone.

"Where have you been?" Kodama asked sharply.

"Long goddamn story that we'll get into. Can you pick me up? I'm without my hoopty." A fog-gray Cadillac Deville without plates rolled past him on the street.

"What's going on?"

"I'll tell you, baby, but if you could put your fine self behind the wheel of your chariot—"

"I'm a Superior Court judge, fool. Who you talking to like that?"

They both laughed and Jill Kodama, lately of Courtroom 132 of the Foltz Criminal Courts, came to pick up her tired and bruised paramour. She took him to his Ford parked at Teague's building and from there they both wound their way to their house overlooking the Silverlake Reservoir.

"They wanted me to know they searched my car." Monk patted Kodama's outstretched knee and sat beside her on the couch in the study.

"The cops?"

"The ones that kung fu receptionist works for." He dangled the object he found on the floor in the lawyer's office.

277

"A key chain fob from the politically incorrect Redskins," she observed.

"Parren is a Tampa Bay Bucs fan."

"So a client of his likes Washington's football team."

"Could be," he mused. "Or it could belong to the woman in the picture. I picked it off the floor where it might have dropped in the struggle."

Kodama put a finger in the air. "Let's review what we know; then we can extrapolate and explore conjecture."

"Okay," Monk began again, starting with the photo that appeared on his cell phone and ending up with when he called her.

"Why'd the cops kick me loose?" he wondered.

"They had nothing to hold you on," Kodama said, picking up her glass of sauvignon from the coffee table. "Evidently none of the partners said you were trespassing."

Monk regarded her. "I don't think those two cops talked to anyone from Parren's office."

"But they kept asking you where Parren was."

"Right. And it wasn't like 'let's get him down here to corroborate what you're saying' or even the usual, which would be to lie to me that they talked to Parren and he didn't want to have anything to do with me."

"So they really wanted to know where he was."

"Yeah. And I'm guessing that's what the battling receptionist wanted to know, too."

"Call the partners."

Monk did so. Elena Glenn, who lived in the Mount Washington area, wasn't home, and Monk left her a message. He didn't have a cell number for her. He next called Dennis Litt, who lived in Westchester. His ten-year-old answered.

"Hey, is this Julie? Julie, it's Ivan Monk, remember me? I'm a friend of your father's."

"Hi."

"Hi. Can I speak to your dad?"

"Sure, hold on." She let the phone down with a bang and he could hear her sneakered feet skip across the floor. He heard her talking and distinctly heard her say 'daddy.' There was a mumbled response and Monk was sure it was a man's voice. The line was picked up momentarily.

"Ivan?" a woman asked.

"This Lisa?"

"Uh-huh," Litt's wife said. "I'm afraid Dennis isn't here right now. But I'll have him call you as soon as he's in. Okay? And, uh, say hi to Jill for me." She ended the connection without waiting for his reply.

Monk said to Kodama, "He was there and Lisa pretended he wasn't. Whatever the hell is going on means that Elena being out, or at least not answering her phone, is on purpose."

Monk started pacing. "And the cops are doing the bidding of whoever it is that's got Dennis and Elena muzzled. And it all gets back to Parren."

Kodama put the wine aside. "You're talking about somebody with pull, somebody with power. A gangster he might have defended?"

"How about the biggest gangster there is, the government?"

"Tofu lovin' commie" she retorted. "What about the IRS?"

Monk touched his bruised face. "I don't think they have those kind of debt collectors on the payroll."

"Then what?"

"That's what I have to find Parren for and ask him."

She pointed. "Maybe that's why they let you go, Ivan. Could be they figure you'll lead them right where they want to be."

"You might be right, honey. But what else can I do?"

"Let it alone."

A long drag from him.

"Being hard-headed about this is not conducive to a rational plan of action."

"They, whoever 'they' is, can't find Parren through normal means. Let's assume they've staked out his house and his time-share in Riviera Beach. And talked to his two exes."

"But the crafty Ivan Monk, the proletarian bloodhound, will outwit them all."

"I would expect a bit more faith, my sweet."

"Blind faith. Look, this is some serious shit. You don't know why they want Parren. He may have done something wrong."

"Come on, Jill, you know him."

"I know lawyers get tempted or get in arrears. And some abscond with clients' money, their trust shares or settlements in cases every week. You read the *Daily Journal.*"

"Sometimes with glee," he admitted. "But he's my friend. And he needs someone in his corner."

"You like to think that he does."

They were nose-to-nose. "What've you got against Parren?"

She didn't break contact. "He's a kid from South Central like you who made good, Ivan. And as he's older than you, he had that much more in the way of overt racism and the odds to overcome. He's talented and smart and ruthless and a hell of an advocate. But, since you asked, I've always had the impression that his playing the angles, his playing it too close to the bone would get him in deep one day. And that day may very well have arrived."

Monk let that simmer. "You think this could be over some case, a particular client?"

"Are you listening to me?"

"It doesn't change what I said."

She made an exasperated sound and picked up her wine glass. "Then what's your next move, slugger?"

"Put myself in Parren's shoes. Whatever went down, went down today, this morning.'

"When you got the photo over your cell."

"Right. My man comes to the office and the pricks in black are waiting for him. No," he corrected, "they came in a little after ten." He recalled that it was about fifteen minutes after that hour when the photo had appeared on his phone. "Better to catch him off-guard. A little chatting, hey, we just want to have a word with you about this matter."

Kodama picked up the thread. "But he knows something's up. Parren balks. The questioning gets heated. Maybe he tries to walk out."

"Or more likely make a call," Monk amended.

"Okay," Kodama agreed. "Could be the woman and probably her male partner try to stop him and that's when they get into their scuffle."

Monk frowned.

"What?"

"If it was you, wouldn't you be calling your lawyer?'

She nodded. "Parren was trying to call Blair Norris."

"And he got me by mistake. The next name in alpha order on his speed dial."

Kodama sat down again and had more wine. "Think our mystery crew know that?"

"They must know about Blair, but are they watching him and tapping his phone? His office?"

"You know his home number?'

"No. And now you've made me paranoid about using our own phone anyway."

"I know someone who might know Norris' number. But I'm not too crazy about calling them this late."

"The pursuit of justice, my dear colleague, knows no hours."

"I got your justice," she said, getting up, putting her shoes

281

on, and getting her coat. Soon they were in her convertible Saab 9-3, top up, tooling down to Glendale Boulevard.

"There," he pointed at the all-night gas station where Glendale and Alvarado intersected.

Kodama pulled in and they both went to the pay phone.

"Amazingly it's working," she commented, as she consulted her Palm Pilot and dialed a number.

Monk scanned their surroundings, realizing that a sophisticated surveillance wouldn't be detected, but it satisfied his growing unease.

Kodama said into the handset. "I really do apologize for bothering you at home at this late hour, Sabrina. And without so much as a how are you, I need a home number for Blair Norris." She paused, listening and put in a couple of "uh-huhs."

"I realize, yes," she added, giving Monk the bug eyes. There was more back and forth but soon she was writing the number on her Pilot's screen with the stylus. "I will, I'll tell you all about it. Thanks."

"Here." She handed him the Pilot. "He lives in Santa Clarita."

"How did you know your girl Sabrina would have the number for Norris?"

She crossed her arms. "Why are you so damned nosy?"

"I can't help it. Especially as she's also a judge."

"You are too lascivious for your own good health."

He wagged his tongue at her. "Ain't I though?" The call was answered and he spoke: "Blair, this is Ivan Monk. We've met a time or two, and–"

"I'm glad you called me, Ivan," the other man said evenly. "I was quite concerned they had gotten to you, too."

Excited, Monk grabbed Kodama's upper arm.

"Hey," she reacted.

"Who are they, Blair. Who's after Parren?"

"I'd prefer if you could come out here. Just you. It's safe here so we can talk."

"Give me your address . . . okay, right. I know how to get out there." Monk wrote it down and promised to be there within the hour.

"So what do you think?" Kodama asked him as they returned to their house.

"I don't know. He sounded calm."

"Like maybe somebody's there, listening in, making him say the right words," Kodama hedged.

"Only one answer."

She shifted gears coming off a curve. "This is getting creepy."

They went along in silence, streetlights and night clouds reflected in the Saab's windshield. "Maybe you should take your gun when we go out there."

"I ride alone, kemo sabe." He patted her thigh.

"Fuck that."

"Come on, you've got way too much on the line for us to be playing the dinner theater version of Nick and Nora." He let that sink in, then said, "We don't know what this is about."

"All the more reason you should have back-up."

"That's why you're my heart. But what if this is some sort of criminal shenanigans? What if it's this dude who got a dime dropped on him and figures now that he's out, Parren owes him for losing his case."

Her profile clenched. "You've been working on that theory for a while, haven't you?"

"Yeah. And I think it's pretty sound."

"You've got a candidate in mind."

"One or two, yeah. And if it comes to some shaky shit breaking out, your black robes better be elsewhere. As it is, the outcome of whatever's going on still might taint you, Jill.

We know the backwash of some of my cases have been the subject of whispering in the all-too political hothouse of the court system."

She came around the bend of Silver Lake Boulevard. "My career is not the only thing, and not the first thing that counts in my life."

Monk didn't respond, but let his fingers stroke the soft of her neck behind her ear. At the house, they kissed and held each other in the driveway. Thereafter, Monk drove to Blair Norris' place. He promised to call when he got there.

"Mr. Monk," the handsome, silver-haired attorney said upon opening the door some forty-three minutes later. "Please come in." He had a passing resemblance to the late James Coburn.

Monk shook the offered hand and stepped across the threshold of the Tudor-style two-story in a grove of large houses.

"Have a seat," Norris said, indicating a chair in the living room. There was a piano and a glass with ice and liquid sat on a coaster atop it. "Something to drink?"

"What's going on, Blair?" Monk was dialing Kodama.

Norris sat at the piano, noodling with some tune that Monk could only identify as classical. "We need to find our friend, Monk. For his benefit, and more, I need to talk to him, I need to bring him in."

"To who?" Monk wiped a hand against his forehead. He was starting to sweat and he felt queasy. The phone dropped from his suddenly listless fingers. "Ivan? Ivan?" Kodama repeated over the line.

It was if a super-charged flu had instantly swamped him. "And what's Parren supposed to have done?" He should pick up the phone, talk to Jill, but he couldn't summon the strength.

Kodama's shouted over the phone. "Ivan, what's happening?"

Norris played part of a fugue. "One piece of information, that's all they want, Ivan. And you can help." Norris reached for his glass, the temblor evident in his hand.

Monk regretted not packing his piece. "What the fuck's going on?"

"I'm sorry, really. But they gave me little choice."

Monk jerked Norris off his seat but the effort drained him. Heavy gauze had descended in front of his face and a fever raced through him. His knees gave out and he dropped to the floor, a tremendous weight bearing down on him. He clawed for the cell, trying to speak. "Jill," he said hoarsely. "Help."

"I'm calling the police, honey," Kodama promised.

A blurry Blair stood over him. "It's okay, Monk. It'll be okay." He peeled off a thin membrane from his hand and picked up the phone.

"Like hell," was the last thing he remembered muttering until he awoke later. Birds were happily chirping and tweeting, and sunshine warmed his face.

Monk got off the couch he was on and assessed his surroundings. The room was pleasantly decorated with plush chairs and the matching couch. There was a bricked up fireplace, innocuous prints adorning walls and three other nooks—a kitchenette, a bed and a toilet—off the larger area where he was. The whole of it was a main circular area and smaller nodules of off that. He crossed to the window and looked out onto a scene of any town suburbia U.S.A.

Trying the door, he wasn't surprised to find that it was locked. Monk was looking in a kitchen drawer for something to bust out one of the windows when there was a chime. It took him a moment to understand that it was the phone, a cordless L-shaped handset that looked like '60s-era futuristic design.

There was no punch pad on it nor, as far as he could tell, any method for dialing out.

"Yes," he said when he lifted the instrument.

"I hope you're rested," the comforting female voice said.

"Where am I?"

"The Hamlet."

"Strategic Hamlet?"

She had a throaty laugh. "A student of history, I see. No, Mr. Monk, this is not a rehash of Vietnam nor is this a pacification program. Not exactly anyway."

"What do you want?"

"Come and see me. The house at the end of the block, with the metal mansard roof." She clicked off.

Monk boiled but there was little else he could do but follow the subtle orders. As he stepped to the door, it swung open. He walked out and the door hummed closed.

His abode was part of a parallel row of duplicate concrete dome-like structures facing each other with postage stamp-sized lawns and no cars in sight. The end of the street was sealed with the only sign of alternate architecture, a three-story Victorian with the aforementioned roof.

Walking along, he spotted men and women in gray trousers and matching tunics, topped with black canvas caps, zipping back and forth on motorized scooters. That they were guards was evident by their heavily outfitted utility belts including alloyed batons.

On one of the lawns, a man with knotty knees sticking out of some plaid shorts sat on a lounge chair reading a newspaper.

Monk said upon nearing him. "How are you?"

"Just fine, citizen, how are you?" He kept reading his newspaper. It was called, naturally, the *Hamlet Clarion* and seemed to be chock full of news like who'd baked the prize-winning pie and the schedule for the next sprinkler inspection. At least that's what Monk got from perusing the front page.

"How long have you been here?" he asked.

"How long have you?"

"I just arrived. Hoping to get acclimated."

The man removed his reading glasses and, sucking on the end of a stem, gazed at the newcomer. "You play chess?"

The gentleman reminded Monk of someone, but he couldn't place him at the moment. "Not very well. Dominoes is more my game."

"When you get back from seeing her, let's have a go, shall we?" His lips worried that stem.

"Be happy to."

"That's the spirit. You'll do fine here, wonderfully fine."

"Be seeing you."

"Look forward to it, old son." And he returned to his news, the gray guards whistling by on their electric scooters.

Monk got to the house. It was the only structure with an address. A brass number six was tacked to the heavy door that swung open silently. The interior furniture was pseudo-Edwardian. Unaccompanied, Monk trod a green runner along a narrow hall that led to a metal door. As he got close, this door slid back, and Monk stepped into what could only be termed a control room.

There was a wall of monitors where the screens alternated from one big scene to individual displays. On a raised dais sat the woman who'd summoned him. She was forty something, white, with a severe haircut and a marathoner's rangy form.

She too was dressed in gray tones of slacks and long coat as she sat behind a modern desk empty save for the L-shaped communication handset, an inlaid touch pad, and a tea tray.

A lone chair rested before her desk. This was the woman in the picture on his cell phone.

"You like it with half and half only."

"Yes." There it was, that seemingly off-handed way of letting him know they knew all about him. But evidently they needed to know more—they needed to know where Parren Teague was.

"Have a seat."

Monk did so. She pushed one of the cups and saucers toward him, the coffee having already been poured and readied. It didn't concern him too much not to have a sip. For no matter how many drugs they pumped into him, what could he tell them?

"Do you believe in anarchy?"

"Do you have a name? Or shall I call you Number Two?"

Her face clouded then she laughed. "Very good. A sense of humor to mask your anxiety."

Monk let that ride. "You mean in the political sense as, say, Simone de Beauvoir meant?"

Agitation colored her voice. "I mean do you believe in destruction for destruction's sake." She stirred her tea.

"That's not anarchism."

"This is not a debate club."

"What is this?"

"Your new home."

"Fuck that."

"How manly of you."

"Lord knows I try."

"Really now, you know why you're here. You're not as dense as you let on."

"That a compliment?"

"Take it as you will." She lifted the cup to her lips, and he got a scent of crushed orange peels. "You can refer to me as Prefect if it comforts you."

"Titles matter."

"Part of our identities."

"But this place, this Hamlet, is about isolating undesirables, about making them conform. Or is this a variation of the King Alfred Plan?"

"I'm afraid I don't know that one."

Monk said, "When I was coming up, the King Alfred Plan was a rumor in the ghetto as the ultimate plan the Man had for us. The final solution for black folks if you dig what I'm saying. Everybody knew somebody who'd seen the secret Executive Order."

"And you believe that?"

"I'm here ain't I?"

She puckered her lips distastefully. "You are here because this is about you doing what's right."

"What's right for whom?"

"The body, the whole. That's something you'd agree with, isn't it?"

"Am I now or have I ever been?"

"Where is your friend? Where would he get himself to?"

"You're spying on his house, probably have taped the two ex-wives' phones, and no doubt know about his time share."

She regarded him evenly.

"Why should I tell you anything? What do you think I know?"

"You are a detective. You are a collector of data."

"What do you want him for?"

"That's our concern."

"Us being what branch of the government?"

"Tell me something."

"I don't know jack."

"Oh don't be so modest. You were at his office, looking around on Parren's behalf."

Monk let that ride, too. Better to let them believe he wasn't as clueless as he truly was. "What's in it for me to tell you anything?" The monitors switched from the street scene to an interior shot of one of the domed domiciles. For all he knew, it could be the one he'd come to in a few minutes ago.

"We have our methods."

"The iron fist in the velvet glove?"

She stood. "You are a colorful man. But know this. If you don't cooperate, matters might and probably will get to be unpleasant for you." The cup was noisily put in place.

"In a physical way?"

"In several ways. You do like your life, don't you? That house on the hill, the view . . . all that goes with it. Imagine how stressful it would be to have that disrupted?"

"Like the FBI on my ass? Or better yet, go after Jill? That's the level you people would go to, isn't it?

"We'll talk again. Soon."

"I can hardly wait."

"I'm sure."

Leaving, Monk wondered how long he could keep fronting. They, whoever they were, had him by the short and curlies and set the pace. So how to throw off their rhythm?

The balance of his day confirmed that he was in a closed set. Behind the housing units was a twenty-foot high sound wall and behind that, who knew? For each time he cut to a backyard, at least two guards would come zipping up telling him to move along.

"Respect private property," one of them scolded.

"This isn't a collective farm, Ho Chi Minh," another one said.

Added to that, there were several signs proclaiming homilies placed at various points around the so-called Hamlet. "Thy body is all vice, and thy mind all virtue," one said. And another read, "Labor to keep alive in your breast that little spark of celestial fire called conscience." And so on. He returned to his quarters.

"Where the fuck am I?" Monk railed and swatted a toaster onto the floor and kicked it viciously against the wall, breaking it. He looked up toward the ceiling with a resigned look, and then picked up his handiwork. He put the broken appliance back on the counter.

His stomach gurgled. There were canned goods and frozen entrees. The food might be loaded with dope, the untainted coffee merely a device to have him drop his guard. But he was hungry as a mother.

Monk prepared some penne pasta and meat sauce, and perused his meager bookshelf. The offerings ranged from commercial techno thrillers, including one by some guy named Joel C. Rosenberg, to biographies covering the likes of Ronald Reagan to Newt Gingrich—so much for subtle brainwashing, he concluded.

Chowing down, he was self-consciously aware he was being watched. He used his napkin more and was careful to chew his meal thoroughly—no sense having his captors comment on his lack of proper home training. Monk evaluated his situation. Rather, he ran through possible escape plans but all of them involved procuring an equalizer, a deadly weapon of some sort, and that was as likely as Paris Hilton forsaking the fast life to live and aid the poor in Appalachia. Not that, he added to himself while washing his plate and spoon in the sink, the fine and self-absorbed Ms. Hilton wasn't a good person.

Restless, he stalked about his room. At nine-twenty, the front door was locked via remote control. Twenty minutes after that a soothing voice came over hidden speakers and told the citizens of the Hamlet they had until ten and then it was lights out.

Taking the Reagan biography in hand, he lay on the bed and started reading. Precisely at five to ten a voice in the most pleasant of intonations announced how much time was left. He brushed his teeth and lay on the bed, fully clothed. He didn't know what would happen once it went dark, and wanted to be as prepared as possible. Despite or probably because he was keyed up, Monk was dozing some forty minutes later.

That lasted another fifteen minutes; then his room was flooded in brightness and screeching heavy metal music.

"Phase two," Monk growled, pulling the blanket over his head. He'd read about such conditioning inflicted on the suspected *al Qaeda* members held indefinitely at Guantanamo. The idea being that constant sensory overload broke down your resistance. Monk had no delusions about being stoic to the point of stone and thus immune to such treatment. But in his case, his ignorance was armor. He couldn't tell them anything about Parren's whereabouts, but that wouldn't preclude them from driving him to the brink.

At some point the music stopped and the lights went off. Sunrise wasn't too far away, so maybe they were into energy conservation, he groggily joked to himself. Red-eyed and a steady thrum making a vein in his head pulse, he got out of bed and used the bathroom a little after six. By now, he hoped, Jill and Seguin had talked, and his cop friend was sweating that mealy-mouthed fuck Norris. Though he knew what that drill would be, unfortunately.

Blair would claim that Monk never made it to his house, despite the insistence of his old lady. The Galaxie would not be in evidence, and what would Seguin have to go on? Sure, there was the earlier incident in Parren's office, but that would lead nowhere.

Seguin would question those two Fulbright scholars, Atkinson and McCandless, but to what good—if they were in on it, they'd keep hush. And if they weren't, they didn't know from nothing anyway. It would stink, him being gone, but there were too many obstacles to find out what the source of the rotting was.

Jill would stay on the cops to continue searching, but Monk knew this was not amateur hour. At some point the hunt would get quashed or sidetracked. The latter being the more likely strategy given Jill had resources she'd employ. It would seem there was progress, say a sighting of him in Arizona or a possible lead in Ohio. All this to build her hopes up, pretend there were leads, but it would all be a ruse. He was their prisoner, and it was going to be up to him to get himself free.

The morning consisted of Monk attempting to sleep, but music from White Snake to the yodeling of Slim Whitman rattling his windows prevented that. Outside, he prayed for a nook to crawl into to lay his head down, but that was not to be had either due to the omnipresent gray guards.

"Nice day, huh?" he goofed to a pair of them scooting by as he wandered about later, up one side of the street, then down the next in the afternoon haze. They didn't even bother to grunt at him. He trudged along, yawning and weary from being on his feet. Aside from his potential chess partner, who he hadn't seen again, there didn't seem to be any other inhabitant of the Hamlet. Were they told to hide or was he only the first rat in the maze?

Once again back inside, he flopped onto the bed, and Wayne Newton's "Danke Schoen" pervaded the room. The tune built in intensity, Newton's voice like a tear gas that couldn't be abated, seeping under his skin and into his cells. The song repeated, louder, but Monk wasn't going to give in. Fuck 'em, they couldn't shake him, he vowed, clenching his fists and grinding his teeth.

After that it was more electronic feedback assailing his nerves. But he wouldn't move, he wouldn't let the bastards win. Not this goddamn easy. With the blanket wrapped around his ears he remained curled on the bed, eyes clamped shut. Eventually he achieved a purgatory between sleep and wakefulness wherein he started to imagine he was elsewhere.

Jimi Hendrix was holding out his hand, a bandana tied around his billowing 'fro. He helped Monk onto the deck of the Misty Blue schooner piloted by Dolly Dagger. The view beyond the horizon was gorgeous as the purple haze lifted.

"Wake up, this isn't a bed and breakfast." A big guard, blonde with bushy eyebrows, kneaded his nightstick into Monk's side. "Come on, get on your feet, the Prefect wants to see you." He had to shout over the boom of Marvin Hamlish's theme from "The Sting." The song ceased.

Monk didn't react. Underneath his covers, he recited a series of numbers and letters very quietly.

"Playing cute," another one, a female, said. "Let's show him what we do with assholes who try to show us up."

"Exactly," a third voice, male, said eagerly.

They grabbed his legs and pulled him off the bed. Monk went to the ground and as hands reached for him he lashed out and connected flush with a jaw. On his feet, shoulder down, arms spread, he barreled forward and took two with him to the floor. The third drummed his baton on his back, Monk was busy throwing lefts and rights.

"Fuckin' numb nuts."

"Teach him."

"Watch it."

"Stay down, you fuck, stay down."

Using his forearm for blocking, Monk got to a knee and took a hold of bushy brows' shirt. He yanked and the man tipped over for Monk to use as a shield. He then pushed upward, making the other two back off several steps.

"Let go, motherfucker," the guard he held onto swore.

Monk stood and using his upper body he twisted and heaved like one of those backyard yahoos emulating their favorite pro wrestler. He brought the big guard up and over, body slamming him onto the kitchen table, which collapsed from impact.

He kicked the dazed man on the side of the head as the woman tore into him with vicious swipes of her T-handle—twenty-six inches of composition alloy turning his kidneys into paste. Monk's stomach flopped as he fought passing out and he caught her with a straight right to the bridge of her nose. Blood covered his knuckles but she wasn't through.

"Bring him down, bring his ass down," she wailed. The other guard leapt on Monk, taking him back down. Monk got in a few more licks but by now other guards had swarmed into the room. One of them pointed a piece that looked like a shotgun only its barrel was bigger.

Monk knew what the weapon was and was attempting to get behind the female guard but she was hipped to that. She spun away from him and a hard rubber projectile, the size of a D battery, punched him flush in his forehead. His vision went fuzzy and his legs became unhinged. They were on him like wolves on an antelope as he huddled on the floor, doing what he could to protect his head from permanent damage.

"That's enough. He's subdued." The voice of the Prefect was the last thing he remembered until he sank beneath the surface of consciousness.

• • •

Rumblings coursing through his lower back brought him around, at least to the extent that he could recognize sounds. He was in a moving vehicle.

A man said, "Fuck she talking about that we overreacted? This asshole's the one that started it." He guessed this was the one with the bushy brows.

"I know, but we've got to be more together when a situation like this happens. I see this as a learning experience," a female said. He was certain it was the other guard from the fight.

"Yeah," the man snorted, "you learned to swing like A-Rod and he learned that his head could swell up like a pumpkin." His laugh was short and harsh.

Monk resisted rolling onto his side to breathe easier. There was a cramp in his right leg and he wanted badly to stretch it but didn't do that either. Surprisingly his head didn't hurt, but maybe that was because the pain bursting like land mines over the rest of his body eclipsed any hurt above his neck.

"Can't believe there wasn't an infirmary already online," the man groused.

"Beta testing," the woman said. "The opportunity to use the Hamlet came up with this Teague matter, so you know the pencil dicks wanted to see how the project would work."

"But now they'll strap him down and shoot him full of joy juice to get this fucker to talk." There were sounds of the high-way, then, "I'd sure like to finish what me and him started."

His female companion said, "Better take it easy on that. This isn't Abu Gharib. They want this one broken down psychologically. He's their test subject. They want to be able to flush their heads of their warped concepts about religion and what they think their cause is and remake them as, well, I guess, docile if not true believers."

Monk imagined the man giving her the 'what-the-fuck' glare

due to the long silence. "You hoping for a cluster on your collar or what? Could you be more gosh gee surfer girl fuckin' wow?"

"Hey, I read the manual," she protested. "I stayed awake in the orientations."

"This stiff prick is just your typical junior grade American gristle-headed dickwad. He's no Koran-quoting, rag head shoe bomber. They put the snatch on him 'cause he knows something about the real dude they want." The guard banged the toe of his boot against the gurney. "But I'd eat my shit-stained skivvies if this clown was some kind of mastermind." That laugh again.

"I'm just saying," the woman responded.

"Fine," he said. "At least once we get Buster Douglas here settled in, then we get some down time."

Fleetingly he weighed his chances of trying to make a break. But he was too weak from his beating, and slight tugs informed him that each of his arms were handcuffed to the gurney's side rails. Too bad he didn't have a plan, but at least he was being taken to a different location. That still meant levels of scrutiny, yet it might also mean a few steps closer to contact with the outside world.

Still feigning being in the land of nod, he peeked through eyelid slits as they unloaded him from the van. It was an overcast day and he shivered in the damp air. He saw the tan camouflage of soldier's legs and heard the crisp retort of answers and responses. It was a base or at least a military compound. He was wheeled across blacktop and into a nondescript corridor with dingy acoustic overhead tile.

"He's awake," a soldier said. "His head moved."

"Shit." A gun barrel dug its way into Monk's armpit.

Monk moaned, and it didn't take much acting on his part to feel the pain.

"What's he going to do, sue? He's got to find his lawyer first," Bushy Brows chortled.

"We gotta get him into the room." The gurney was hurried along until the small caravan arrived at a closed door and a keypad was tapped. He was bumped into a room fresh with the smell of antiseptic compounds.

"Come on," one of them ordered, rushing. The cuffs were clicked off his wrists and scraped against his skin as they pulled them free. The prisoner was roughly dumped onto a bed, a sheet listlessly draped over him. Their footsteps retreated and the door was once again secured. He was still in his work clothes. And he'd been in them for . . . what? Three days was it now?

Monk stirred, attempting to sit upright, but the best he could do was prop himself on an elbow. His hospital room was spare, as if designed by B. F. Skinner—devoid of any niceties save functionality. There was his adjustable bed, a bed pan hanging on the side, a baseboard nightstand, no phone, no windows, one chair, and subdued lighting. The room had all the warmth of an android's womb.

"Are you comfortable?" The immediate quality of the Prefect's voice was as if she were right next to him.

"Smashing," he creaked.

"You are something. I know why you started the fight."

He lay back.

"But there's no more chance of you getting out of here than there was in the Hamlet. Not," she added with the proper pause, "until you give me what I want."

He started to speak, choked down loose phlegm, then started again. "What is it you need to know?" he asked haltingly.

"One thing only."

"What about his property in Oklahoma? Little town called Taft."

There was the briefest crackle in the hidden speaker. "What is this you say?"

"There's an old house, belonged to his grandfather, Jacob I think."

"We know of the grandfather, but this house you talk about. There's no tax record of such. No building permit."

"Not in his name. And this is a little town, this house was built back in a time when in that part of the county they used to issue a driver's license 'cause you were big enough to reach the pedals. Permits were for city folk."

"Why suddenly so cooperative?"

"When I heal, back to the Hamlet?"

"Depends."

"That's why."

"Where is this house?"

"Don't know the street, just know he mentioned that it was down there. A place he paid a local to take care of, clean up the trash, repair the crawl space screen when the possums got in, that sort of thing."

"Bullshit."

"Okay."

"How would you verify this?"

"That's your job."

She didn't respond. He called out but the transmission was over. In a short while the door to the outer hall opened and one of the gray guards entered. It was the one with the bushy brows. He was built like a white Lawrence Taylor in his prime, and he accompanied a woman with a syringe. He aimed his assault rifle at Monk's head, and wordlessly the woman injected him.

A warm pleasant sensation flowed through him, and this lifted him toward a silvery sky. He hoped he'd catch up to where Jimi the Rainbow Bridge paratrooper was captaining the Misty Blue.

"Now, let's have a chat, you and I." The Prefect stood next to his bed, hands clasped before her.

Monk found it enjoyable that the colors behind his pupils were starting to run, and the sharp angles kept getting lost in infinity.

"Hellified shit," he muttered pleasurably.

"Relax," she said.

"Free your mind and your ass will follow," he giggled.

"About this house."

"What house?"

"In Taft."

"Oh yeah. When's the boat gonna get here?"

"Soon, I promise."

"E Ticket. 'Member when that was the one to have at Disneyland when you were a kid? That's what this shit is that you shot into me. Damn, I see why junkies like junk."

"About the house. Where Parren might be."

"Like I said, don't know much except it's down there, in that pissant town in Oklahoma."

"But because it's off the books, so to speak, he might hide out there?"

"Yeah. I'm trying to help here."

The Prefect leaned closer, holding Monk's jaw between strong fingers. "We've checked every possible place where Teague could be hiding. Besides his house in Los Feliz, we have both his ex-wives under surveillance and that cabin of his in Florida." She paused, looking intently at the prisoner's face. Her other hand was bloodless due to her tight grip on the railing. "And yet, something's not right."

"Why you say that, chief?"

"You gave in too easy."

"I got my ass handed to me, twice."

"I know about you. You've taken worse."

"I was younger, stupider. I got the message."

She released her grip and studied him in his narcotized state. "You get some sleep. I'll have some food brought in. We'll talk again after I've checked this out."

"Long as you bring this same bomb-ass party favor."

The Prefect took a last look at him before the door opened and she left.

The effects of the psychotropic wore off gradually, like floating back to earth on giant feathery wings. He attacked his meat loaf and home fries like a starving bear. Afterward, longing for a cigar, he loped about the room, working aches out of his muscles from his two beat-downs. He could turn the lights on or off via a switch, and they'd brought in a few magazines for him to read—of the *Source* and *Tongue* variety, nothing too meaty like *Time* or *Newsweek*. It was okay to see pictures of pretty women in their underwear and read about the laid cribs of Snoop and Jay-Z, but not about current events or thorny issues like welfare reform or banning the Confederate flag at public buildings. No, his captors knew the correct opiates to administer to effect his reeducation. The way to constructing the compliant prisoner was by way of reinforcing his baser desires for booty and bling bling. For surely the next step after your mind rinse was to lust for brand names.

At some point, as night and day were unknown to him, he sat on the side of the bed, took off his shoes, and lay down and went to sleep. When the lights snapped on accompanied by techno music, he came awake gradually.

"You're playing games with us?" The Prefect strode in with the big guard by her side. She held another syringe.

Meekly, he said, "I don't know what you mean."

301

"The house story was bullshit." She advanced as the guard sighted down his barrel, the muzzle of his weapon steady on Monk's skull.

"I did what you asked me." There was a quaver in his voice.

"You will with this dose." She signaled for the guard to come closer and he did, a wide grin splitting his face. With the barrel of the Ingram M-11 pushed close to his head, Monk didn't resist while the Prefect held his arm and inserted the needle in his vein. The two then stepped back to judge the results.

"Why did you lie?" she asked. A watery sheen opaqued Monk's irises, and his body went flaccid.

"If I tell you, will you make me a sergeant?" He pulled the blanket up to his neck and snuggled his arms under the covers as well.

"He's off his nut," the guard cackled.

The Prefect chastised him with a look. "What are you talking about, Monk?

"If I tell you what you want to know, will you make me a sergeant?"

"That's what you want?"

"Right, like my father."

The Prefect arched an eyebrow. "Your father?"

"Yeah," he slurred, "don't tell me you ain't read my file thoroughly."

"What is this about? What does this have to do with what I need to know?"

Monk clucked. "It's always about you, isn't it?"

The Prefect shook him. "Stop playing games."

"How come he's not more responsive?" the guard asked.

The Prefect didn't have an answer. "You want to be like your father, that it?"

Monk laughed again, a strained, high-pitched utterance that grated on the other two. "I want you to make me a sergeant and charge the booze." He began to bounce in the bed and convulse and twitch his body as if covered in fire ants.

"You must have given him too much," the guard said. "You've fried his mind."

"I know how to do my job." The Prefect put hands on Monk's shoulders. "You have to be calm, Ivan. Soon this will be all over and you will be home again. You want to go home, don't you?"

Monk stopped his contorting and turned toward the wall, pulling into a fetal position. "You aren't going to let me go home," he pouted. "You said."

"No, no, that's not so," she said. "All I want is the whereabouts of your friend."

"Parren?"

"Yes. Tell me where he is."

His body stiffened. "I don't know where he is."

"How can that be?"

"Think about it," Monk challenged, turning his face toward her. "If I was in on this, why the hell would I have come to his office? Knowing you'd be watching it after he escaped from you the first time?"

She pointed at him, anger tightening her voice. "Since you know that, you must know where he is."

"I know many things."

"Tell me." She kicked the side of the bed. "You can't deny me."

Monk cried out in pain.

"I told you," the guard warned, "you gave him too much. He's O.D.'ing or something."

The Prefect stomped about the room. "You will tell me where Parren is," she shouted.

"I can't tell you if I don't know, genius," he yelled back.

She stopped pacing. "That can't be."

"Why, 'cause you don't have any other lead? That's hardly my problem, is it?"

She returned to his bedside and pulled back one of his eyelids to check the pupil–which was suitably dilated.

"Maybe he's telling the truth," an unattached male voice said.

"Shit," the Prefect said. "I can't believe that." She didn't get a reply.

"What do you want me to do?" the guard asked.

"Do?" Monk cut in. "Why make me a sergeant and charge the fuckin' boo-oooze," he crooned, bouncing up and down on his back under the covers. He stopped, rose up, and pointed at the guard. "Anyway, you can't make me a sergeant. You can't do shit." And then he lay down again and returned to his caterwauling.

The guard eagerly advanced toward the bed. "Let me shut him up."

The Prefect held up a hand. "Forget it. Let's leave Nat King Cole here to his rehearsal."

"Make me a sergeant and charge the booze," Monk repeated as the two left. He continued this for several minutes, then went mum like some rundown wind-up toy. He lay still, breathing rapidly. Beneath the blanket, he undid the lace from his boots that he'd wrapped around his penis and balls, and that he'd pulled on repeatedly during the interrogation.

He hadn't done this for an S&M kick, but as a way to cause pain to cut through the effects of the psychoactive drugs she'd pumped into him. He felt woozy like a drunk walking home– he knew the way but was having difficulty getting there. He laid staring at the blank wall and mumbling a series of numbers and letters to himself.

"You think you're hot shit, don't you?" Busy Brows had returned.

Monk scratched his whiskered face. "I know I can put you down like I did before, be-yatch."

"You have an answer for everything, don't you?" He came closer.

"Just about." Monk remained folded up. "But really, I don't have to work up too much of a sweat for your simple self."

"I haven't forgotten about what happened at the Hamlet."

Monk didn't speak, didn't move.

"Oh, did I mention I've turned off the monitors? It's just you and me now, sweetheart." The squeak of the baton sliding back and forth across his leather glove filled the room. "What's a matter, scared, fuckhead? Got nothing to say now?"

He sprang toward the bed and Monk whipped his leg around and uncoiled his foot. The guard was tagged precisely on the point of his jaw. The man was rocked, and Monk was on him. He couldn't give the larger man an opening or he was done. And that meant fair fighting was not a particular concern.

The guard hit him in the side with his baton but Monk worked combinations on the man's mid-section. This got the guard hesitating, and he leveled a fist straight into Bushy Brow's face. The guard's grip slipped on his nightstick, and Monk latched onto it with both hands and yanked the stick free.

The guard stormed forward and Monk struck him with the club.

"Shit," the guard wheezed, reaching for his opponent.

A sideswipe of the T-handle across the larger man's face got him blinking stars and Monk followed up with a short chop alongside his head. The guard staggered and Monk brutally hit him in the groin with the head of the baton.

Bushy Brows buckled and Monk rained blows on the man who could only impotently get his hands on Monk's legs. Mercilessly he hammered at Bushy Brows till he shrunk prone to the floor, his head a mass of swelling lumps and purple bruises.

"I give, trooper." The man rolled onto his back, his eyelids fluttering.

Monk smiled wickedly at the damage he'd caused and tossed the baton away. He then stripped the unconscious guard of his clothes and put them on—the gray shirt over his own but opting to take off his pants for the guard's own. Monk's boots weren't as polished as the other man's, but he hoped no one would look that closely. Without another glance at the injured man, he exited.

Condensing cold air escaped his mouth. Monk proceeded around a corner of the infirmary and saw other squat buildings in the near distance. There were lights on inside them. As this was a military base, that meant an entrance gate with guards on duty. But would his gray uniform allow him egress was a question there was only one way to answer. Getting his bowels and nerves under control, he strode along a concrete walkway toward the lights.

Two soldiers, PFCs, in regular Army garb passed him and he nodded. The two retuned the gesture and kept walking. The way Monk figured it, the gray uniforms were no doubt designated to the rest of the base as hands-off. And given what he understood about need to know, that meant unless he ran into the Prefect or whoever the hell talked to her in his room, he'd be good. But he also knew time was against him, that the guard was going to be found sooner than later.

Closer to the buildings, he changed his mind. The gate would be useless. He didn't hope to successfully bluff his way past the soldiers who'd be stationed there. If he had a vehicle, that might be different. By now he was near a set of buildings and could hear voices in one of them off to his right. This he assumed to be a mess hall of some sort, and that meant a pay phone should be around too.

He found an unused phone among a row of them. The others were commandeered by male and female enlistees grousing about the grub, their assignments, or how much they missed the person they were talking to over the line. In the guard's pocket he found some change, and utilizing his phone card number, which he'd memorized, he made three calls. Stepping from the booth, he wasn't all that surprised as an alarm whooped and it was announced over the PA that the base was on lockdown.

Soldiers hustled past him and Monk calmly entered the canteen. He was pleased to find a couple of stale hamburgers under an array of hot lights. Using the last of his change, he got a root beer from a soda machine, and together with a bag of chips, he completed his meal. He was grubbing on his second burger, when the Prefect entered with a cortege of her fusiliers.

"You are getting to be one very large pain in the ass." She sat opposite him, hands clasped on the bench's tabletop where Monk sat.

"I got news for you, Red Rider. I intend to be an even bigger obstruction."

"What the hell are you saying?"

He told her about his phone calls.

"You're lying."

"Check."

She did and by the time she returned she was ashen. "What have you done?"

"Fuck with you like you did me."

"What we did was for a greater good."

"So you say. Let's let the public judge."

"Don't play naïve; it isn't *you*, darling," she said acidly. "And you'll probably be facing criminal charges."

"One of those secret tribunals, Prefect? Not hardly. And you won't be able to railroad me in regular court—*that* I can assure you. Those like you seek to cast the net of Homeland Security far and wide. But you can't have carte blanche to kidnap American citizens and subject them to physical and psychological torture all in the name of fighting the evil doers."

"The guard you attacked will require hospitalization."

"Again, let's get the facts straight. He attacked me and I defended myself."

Monk rose, tossing a balled-up napkin aside. "Now either take me back to town or, if you insist on acting the fool, Prefect, send me to some other base or back to the Hamlet." He squared his shoulders. "Bring it on.

"But you sure as shit know the reporters I called will stay on this like flies on bad meat until they get some answers. Bury me, and you dig your own hole deeper."

The Prefect folded her arms, frowning.

At oh-three-hundred hours military time, Monk was deposited in the City of Commerce with his wallet, keys, and watch returned to him. Once he found a phone booth in an all-night truck stop, he immediately called the reporters he'd previously contacted. He reached one of them, Kelly Drier, who was en route to the base that held him. The 760 area code and phone number had been printed on the phone box at the base. And Drier, who'd been an anchorman in local news but who now had a show on MSNBC, was able to use his outlet's resources to backtrack and find out what address that number was billed to.

Together with a camerawoman, Monk was picked up at the café. The three drove back out to the edge of Death Valley in the desert where he'd been kept at Fort Markstein. They were able to get some shots – including a prime one of a disgruntled Perfect leaving the base in a chauffeured vehicle with a government plate.

Of course they were denied access and of course no one in any official capacity would come out to talk to them. Though a jeep load of soldiers under the command of a master sergeant arrived at the gate and chased them away.

"I might get a Peabody for this, Ivan," Drier spun on their way back to L.A. "Government abuse, patriotic zealots, this shit is great. I'll fuckin' grill Ashcroft, get the network to give me a special hour–hell, an hour and a half for that stuck-up prick." He lapsed into visions of awards and accolades and no doubt a big book contract at the end of his personal rainbow of ratings.

Monk had no such happy ever-after movie playing for him, but no sense cooling the other man's roll. At least between the TV reporter and the *Newsweek* writer Monk had called, after first calling Jill Kodama who supplied the respective numbers, there was going to be some noise and some shaking up. But he didn't believe that the head of the office of Homeland Security Tom Ridge, Attorney General John Ashcroft, let alone the Prefect, if she could be ID'd, would ever be drilled by the media on this matter.

Tired, he dozed until Drier dropped him off at his house in Silverlake.

"Incredible," Kodama said, after they'd made love a second time.

"Why, thank you."

She bit his shoulder. "That too, sweetheart."

He pulled her close, his arm tight around her waist.

"I'm glad you made it back," Kodama said.

"You're telling me."

"Ivan?"

"Yeah?"

"Is Parren safe?"

"Should be."

"You going to see him?"

He snuggled against her. "Let's not worry about that now. Let's get some sleep. I need it."

They held each other close in the bed. Because both of them were too aware they were possibly being surveilled, they'd left the house and obtained a room at the Hotel Figueroa downtown near the Staples Center.

The next morning Monk finished his fourth TV interview and had just gotten off the phone to a fact checker at *Newsweek*. It had happened so fast, events seemed to be running together for him. He rubbed his hands over his worn face.

"You should get away, get some rest." Delilah advised.

"I will. But I've got one more thing to take care of."

"What?"

He didn't answer and left his office. He drove a rental, in case his Ford was bugged, to where he guessed Parren Teague had gone to ground. When he gave the Prefect the story about the house in Oklahoma, that was not entirely invented. There was such a house that had belonged to a relative on Monk's father's side of the family. Using that, and given the less powerful dosage they'd pumped into him the first time, Monk had been able to stick to the fiction he'd created. But he knew once they found out that was bogus, he'd have to use more drastic measures to counteract the effects of a more potent dose.

But he hadn't put it together where Parren might be until the guard attacked him.

The house he arrived at was a modest frame job on a street on the border of Maywood, a humble municipality east of the 110 Freeway. Around back was a set of four small second-

310

floor apartments and he knocked on apartment B. There was no answer, as he expected. He wrote a note and slipped it under the front door. Presently the door was opened and Parren Teague, clean-shaven and in pressed jeans, let him in.

"You've been all over the news. I was preparing to come see you." Behind him on a coffee table there were several yellow pads of papers and legal case law books. Jimmy McGriff's "The Worm" played on a CD unit.

"You held out." He hugged him. "I knew you would."

Monk said, "Just my natural thick-headedness. He gazed about the shuttered room. I haven't been back here in a long time."

"Still, I know they worked on you hard."

"I couldn't give them the satisfaction, now could I?"

"Damn straight."

Both men shared a brief laugh.

"Come on, I was just making some tea."

Monk followed him to the kitchenette and leaned against the counter. "Grace around?"

"Uh, no, no, she's not around right now," Teague stammered. He prepared two cups with tea bags and removed a pot of boiling water from the stove. "So it's been that long. I mean, since you were here." He poured the water.

"Had to have been '84 or '85." Monk seemed genuinely perplexed. "I can't be that old."

Teague chuckled. "You were a mere lad, then." He handed him his tea. It smelled of crushed orange rinds.

"Weren't we all?" Monk blew on the concoction, steam rising and settling on the hairs of his goatee, some of which were turning gray.

Back then, he didn't have a goatee. Back then, he hadn't been shaving that long, had he? But that wasn't really how it was. He was past the legal drinking age—though he'd been downing Buds and Jack at after-parties since being first string linebacker on his Fremont High varsity football team. And he damn sure was into his thing as a bounty hunter, making some long money and being all American Giggolo'd when he made the clubs in the Marina. Or maybe he'd follow through on this notion of his and spark it up again with Tina Chalmers, his high school steady, who was now working in the Tom Bradley administration in City Hall.

But right now he had to be on his 'J' as he pulled up closer to the address, Prince's "Head" unwinding on his car's cassette deck. It was a neat frame house not far from Maywood, a part of town that once his father, a mechanic, had to come to to get a friend's stalled old DeSoto going. And where both men, being colored, as was the term before Cassius became Ali, had to snatch up heavy crescent wrenches to stare down a gathering crowd of white men at the Western Auto Parts store where they'd gone to get an accelerator spring for the friend's carburetor.

Sometimes, when Monk was a kid, and his father talked about that incident, he chuckled, and other times he got real quiet.

Even now as he crossed the street after locking his Sebring Satellite with the gold metal flake finish, black faces were scarce this side of the Southern Pacific Railroad tracks. The sun was almost set, but the streetlights weren't on yet to cut the descending gloom. That was fine by him. Passing along the walkway, he could hear that goddamn "We Are the World" playing from inside the house. Monk resisted the impulse to put a bullet through the window to silence the stereo.

On the stairs to the apartments in back, Monk proceeded cautiously, one foot carefully laid above the other on the ascending steps. The object of his ten percent return ticket was Ernest Franklin, who was called Cuda by the gents and the ladies. A nickname shortened from Barracuda, earned from his days amid the swamps on recon in Vietnam. This and a few other pieces of history LaSalle, a bail bondsman Monk did frequent search and retrieves for, had imparted to him.

Which made Cuda older than your average do-rag-wearing bail-jumping felon, more experienced, and thus more dangerous.

Monk was on the landing, getting it together. He'd been on the prowl for Cuda nearly four days and had finally picked up his trail this afternoon after leaving a kill and dress poultry market on Alondra in Athens Gardens. The proprietor of the store was Selma Rawls, an acquaintance of Monk's mother Nona. Rawls was a big-boned specimen with half of her little finger on the right hand missing.

"You goddamn right I wants that cock's mother found," she seethed and brought her clever down, severing the neck of a plucked chicken. "Owes me plenty for that dry cleaning business of his he charmed me into investing in. Talking about how it was gonna be me and him living easy, and me not havin' to strangle another bird 'cept for Christmas dinner. Shit."

Her blunt fingers expertly separated the pinkish flesh of the chicken, and she chopped off a wing. "Can't say for sure where he is," she went on, smearing muck on her apron, "but I know he's holed up before, like when he got back from overseas, at this auntie on his mama's side's place. It's down there near where the Spook Hunters used to run. Them white boys that used to fight with the brothers, the Slausons and the Del Vikings? She's one quarter white herself if I recall correctly." She neatly cleaved the breast in two.

Monk thanked her with a twenty after she'd given him more precise directions. He started to leave and she mentioned,

"The reason I ain't gone down there to get my money is 'cause Cuda kept that M-16 of his from the war. And he damned sure knows how to use it."

Breathing shallowly through his mouth, standing to the side of the door to Cuda's apartment, he could hear the set on inside. The newscaster was going on about Washington gossip; that there could be congressional hearings into disclosures of illegal arms shipments to the contras in Nicaragua. An operation purported to be run out of the basement of the Reagan White House. Good to know that the Cuda liked to keep up on current events, Monk noted. He lit the cherry bomb he'd brought with him. Hopefully that meant his quarry was relaxed and would be caught off-guard as he planned.

He braced, his handcuffs out. The big firecracker went off at the door's jamb causing a loud bang, blistering the cheap pine. As expected, Cuda rushed to throw open the door, but he was cradling his rifle and jabbed it in Monk's gut as he tried to jump him.

Cuda then brought the barrel tight to the bounty hunter's nose. Monk's .45, the one that had belonged to his Korean War vet father, filled his hand.

"What's it gonna be, blood?" There was East Texas in Cuda's slow and steady voice. From within the darkened apartment came the fragrance of marijuana and the sound of a commercial for lemon-scented Pledge.

"You missed your court date."

"So?" That M-16 didn't move, didn't waver.

"You let down friends and relatives that put that collateral up, man."

"That psychology? You trying to make me feel guilty? Like I'm going to start ballin' and snifflin' and shit and then you grab my axe and slap me in the head with it?"

"Look, man—"

"Ernest, put that damned thing down 'fore you scatter what little brains this fool's got all over my new paint job." The woman who spoke from below was thin with large eyelashes and emerald earrings balanced from her ears. Standing next to her was a tight-lipped dude in a charcoal Pierre Cardin number.

"Earnest, listen to your Aunt Grace, please," the sharp-dressed cat said.

Cuda drawled, "Who the fuck is you?"

"My name is Parren Teague. I'm a lawyer and your aunt has asked me to help you with your situation."

"Situation," he repeated, like the word was dipped in vinegar. "I know how to handle my situation," he enunciated.

"That's one way, yes," Teague replied, indicating the rifle. "But I think my method will offer a solution that won't involve bloodshed."

"I'm for that," Monk stated.

"How you know my aunt?" Cuda inquired. The M-16 hadn't moved.

"I do the books for his office," his aunt answered. "Just started last week, but I told you I was working on something. You've got to relax."

"That true?" It wasn't clear who Cuda was asking for verification.

"Why would she be jeffin'?" Monk asked plaintively.

"Let's all talk this over. But we first have to start by putting away the guns, okay?" Teague started up the stairs.

"That sounds right to me." Monk holstered his automatic.

Cuda's suspicious orbs, floating in his reddened whites, moved from Monk to the man coming up the stairs, then back again. "Got your word you won't try nothin' till I gets to speak?"

"Yes."

315

"You just saying that 'cause you got that steel-jacketed slug aimed at your skull."

"Fuckin' right. But I'll mean it when you take the gun down, too," Monk said.

Cuda acquiesced and lowered the rifle. "Okay, trooper, you win."

• • •

"Funny how people meet," Teague reminisced. He held up the teapot. "More?"

"I'm fine," Monk replied. "I heard Cuda wound up in Belize after that beef."

"Yes, I heard that too, but I don't know what happened to him down there."

Monk nodded, putting his cup down. Teague had represented Grace Ivie in a few other matters over the years. And as she didn't have pocketfuls of ready cash, she'd made a handshake deal with the lawyer that he could use her property—a property he helped her save once from an IRS seizure due to back taxes. And Teague had had to hide more than one client or witness in one of these apartments over the years.

His friend sipped reflectively. "Say, Ivan, this might sound funny, but don't you think you should let Delilah know where you are?"

"What does that matter?"

"Just to make sure that somebody knows where we are in case they try to snatch you again or both of us." He put down the cup. "We should cover all the bases."

He hunched a shoulder. "Okay." Picking up the phone, he started to dial, then stopped. "You didn't tell me how all this got started, Parren."

"Barat Minghia. He's linked to some questionable activity

the authorities want to know about. He works as a baggage handler at John Wayne Airport."

"So he was being hassled by his bosses. I gather somebody dropped a dime on him."

"He's come under scrutiny."

Monk considered this. "You make it sound like you figure he's guilty."

"Just saying, is all. There's some reason he was signaled out."

"And you've seen proof of," Monk waved his hand, "whatever it is he's suspected of doing."

"Yeah, well," Teague began, "apparently he sticks to the all-American story. Born and raised in Cerritos, star on his high school baseball team, blah blah. Says it was the jealous ex of the girl he's dating, but who knows?"

Monk registered that and asked, "How'd he come to you?"

Teague put a finger to his ear, then said, "Not sure. But he's disappeared. Make that call, will you?"

Monk picked up the handset again and asked, "How'd you know I didn't tell Delilah?"

"I—" he began. "I know you, man, I'm sure you haven't told anybody."

"Why are you nervous, Parren?"

A thin smile. "You know what we're up against. I'm jumpy as hell like you are. Go on, make the call."

There was sweat on Monk's forehead and he could feel his heart rate skip in tempo. A warning kept creeping at the edge of his consciousness. "What's going on here, Parren?"

"You know."

The handset felt like it was fifty pounds in his hand. "No I don't. And I don't know why you sound more like a prosecutor than a defense attorney."

Teague was looking beyond him. "That's not it, Ivan."

317

"Then what is it?" He was sweating more. Like dancing forms seen intermittently under a flashing strobe, images pulsed in his brain. He was being led away from the mess hall, docile as if a sleepwalker. Now he was in a hotel room but he could see the end of the walls as if it were a movie set. There was glass behind that.

"They want Minghia for crimes his associates have committed."

"And you're gonna help them? You and the Prefect bosom buddies now? Then why'd you call me? Why am I in this mess?" His anger made him perspire more and the images got sharper.

"Relax, Ivan." His friend reached out for him. "Come on, make the call."

Monk stared at the handset and at his friend. "What the fuck did I go through, why'd you go on the run only to punk up now?"

"Look, just make the fucking call, Ivan."

"Sure." He cracked it against his own skull.

"Stop him," the Prefect yelled.

Teague was wrestling with Monk, but he managed to hit himself two more times in the head. Dazed, the walls of the apartment dissolved. Monk leaned against a console. He was in a glass walled room encased in a motion capture body suit. The suit and his head had all manner of wires and tubes connected to various beeping and blinking machines.

In a corner of the room was a bed. Near that was a copy of the desk and chair from his office in front of a green screen used for projection. There was also a bench seat and steering wheel attached to a dash that looked like the interior of his Ford Galaxie.

"Fuck you," Monk threw the phone at the glass where the

Prefect and some others, in civvies and uniforms, stood on the other side. They scattered as the pane burst.

He ripped at the wiring and wiped at the blood dripping from his forehead. "When you'd put me back under? The mess hall, right? Pumped some shit into the air ducts I bet. But I made my goddamn calls. I know I did." That was all he had, it had to be real.

The Prefect said nothing. A claxon sounded and the group trotted out, including a man who Monk could now distinctly see was made up to look like Parren Teague.

Weak and scared, he gritted his teeth and fought to keep awake. Unconsciousness meant they might invade his dreams and steal pieces of his life and make it a mockery. And that he couldn't allow again.

The alarm continued bleating. From the rooms beyond there was the rushed approach of footfalls. Be they rescuers or tormentors he couldn't say. On his back now, eyes fluttering and desperate to stay alert, Monk heard Jill's voice call his name. But he didn't have the strength to answer, and darkness was suddenly all around him.

KELLY EVERAERT